# Sins of the Mother

## Chris Stenson

Moorhead Friends Writing Group

Cover Art by Gina DelVecchio

Cover Design & Wrap by Tiffany Fier

Edited by Scott Dyson

# Dedication

No words can express my thanks and gratitude for those who've helped me along my writing journey.
To my wife and daughter, without your support and love this book wouldn't have been possible.
To my father, the man who taught me the love of words and books, I hope I made you proud.
To the Moorhead Friends Writing Group, thank you for always being there.

# Prologue

The boy leaned against the streetlamp, book in hand, violin case by his side. The instrument was special, given to him by someone even more special. He stared at the house across the street. The girl and her mother would be arriving soon. He'd been sitting here all summer, watching and waiting, as he'd been instructed.

The windows of his own apartment were dark. Opal, the woman playing the role of his foster mother this year, was asleep after a night of entertaining. Since the Dark Ones killed his birth parents, he had been assigned multiple 'mothers' and Opal was the worst. Some of his foster parents were simply indifferent; to most, he was nothing more than a paycheck. Opal was different. She found inhumane ways to be cruel, just for shits and giggles.

He hoped the girl, Isabelle, could be his friend. He needed friends. If he succeeded in winning her over, he'd then have to make a tough decision and finally pick a side: should he protect her–or kill her.

Neither choice would be easy.

# Chapter 1

S omeone pounding on the door woke Isabelle from her slumber.

She rolled over, swatted at her alarm clock, and mumbled.

Bang. Bang.

"Mom. Someone's at the door."

Bang. Bang. Bang.

Isabelle opened her eyes. Tall, green grass swayed against the far wall. A floral scent, wildflowers, and honeysuckle wafted from the corner. The stars above her bed disappeared. The birdsong ceased. For an instant, her subconscious flickered between her dreamscape and the reality of her room. A tight fist of nervousness clutched her stomach. The remnants of the dream slipped away.

"Mom."

Isabelle closed her eyes in hopes of recapturing the lost threads, the glimmer of light on a fading path. She needed to get back there; yearned for the boundless feet on bare earth experience.

She dreamed of horses, a man with a wicked scar, and a vague warning.

Bang. Bang. Bang.

Muffled voices accompanied the pounding this time.

She glanced at the clock. What the hell?  "Okay, okay, I'm coming."

Isabelle slipped on a pair of sweatpants and stepped into the hallway. She passed by her mother's bedroom. Had the door been closed earlier?

Her heart pounded as she walked into the living room. What scared her the most? It wasn't the occasional drug dealer who hung around on weekend nights, the creepers who prowled the street daily, or their landlord, Bob, the king of creepers. What scared her the most?

The thought of her mother dying and being all alone.

With sweaty palms, she grabbed a knife from the kitchen drawer, just to be on the safe side and braced herself against the front door. "Who's there?"

"Sheriff Erickson and Officer Ellis."

Isabelle yelled down the hall. "Mom. Wake up. The police are at the front door. Mom...."

"Open the door. Your mother's with us."

How could that be? Isabelle would have heard her leave. Not convinced the police waited outside, she pushed open the door to her mother's room and flicked on the light. "Mom, the police...."

An unmade bed, but no Sharon. The curtains fluttered. For a moment she imagined a face in the window. She took a tentative step. "Mom?"

Isabelle hurried to the open window, stepping through the screen leaning against the wall. "Goddamnit."

A shadow darted, then disappeared behind a small grove of trees. Vertigo struck. Her legs rubbery, Isabelle grabbed the windowsill with both hands. They had one tree in their backyard, not a small grove.

A door appeared.

Her flesh prickled; someone was watching her from the shadows. A horse neighed, its hoof beats echoing in the distance. The animal's musty smell lingered. She closed her eyes, took a couple of deep cleansing breaths, and opened her eyes. Is this just a dream?

The pounding on the door resumed.

She glanced at the clock. 12:10 a.m. Happy sweet sixteenth birthday to me.

Back in the living room, she peeked out the window. A police cruiser sat in the driveway. Mom, what did you do? She fastened the chain and opened the door a crack, the knife clutched in her hand. Two police officers held her mother upright.

Her mother smiled. "Is...a...belle."

Even with makeup smeared, her dark hair matted on one side, her clothes askew, and too drunk to stand on her own, her mother still managed an air of haunting beauty.

"Is this your mother?" Sheriff Erickson asked.

"Yes," Isabelle said, "What did she do this time?"

"Will you let us in?" Officer Ellis said.

Isabelle unhooked the chain.

Stopping in the doorway, the Sheriff pointed at her hand. "Isabelle, you need to put the weapon down."

"Oh right, sorry," Isabelle said, setting the knife down on an end table. "Mother, what did you do?"

The officers sat Sharon on the couch and gave Isabelle an inquisitive look.

Sharon tottered and fell forward. She could not answer with her face squished against the arm of the couch.

Before Isabelle could shut the door, a flash of light caught her attention. A curtain fluttered in one of the second-floor windows of the apartment across the street.

"Officer, is she being charged?"

"No, we hadn't planned to. Just wanted to make sure your mother got home safe."

"I'm not a prostitute," Sharon said, slurring her words as she tried to sit up.

"We found her... in a compromising position." Officer Ellis said.

"I was giving that man a blow-job of my own free will."

Isabelle blushed. Oh God, Mother, not again.

"Do you need any help with her?" Sheriff Erickson asked.

"No, I can get her to bed myself. I've had practice."

The sheriff extracted a business card from his jacket. "If you have any more problems with your mother, give me a call."

***

Fifteen agonizing minutes passed before the anticipated knock echoed in the living room.

"What took you so long?" Isabelle asked Carson, her neighbor and her best friend–maybe her only friend. Earlier that summer, the day she moved in, Carson had walked across the street, grabbed a box of packed books from the moving van, and carried it into the house. While helping her to organize her bookshelf, he had said, "We're going to be great friends."

"Opal just went to bed," Carson said. "Why were the police here?"

"They brought Mom home from the bar."

"What did she do?"

"Just being drunk and stupid again." Isabelle handed him one of the flashlights. "Follow me."

His eyebrows rose.

With her mother tucked into bed, Isabelle eased the front door closed. No need to take chances. As they rounded the house, she flicked on her flashlight. She stepped into the knee-high grass of the backyard and painted the ground with her light. The dark shadow and grove of trees she'd seen earlier disappeared but the perception of being watched persisted. Lurkers watched from the outer limits of her vision. She sensed them.

"What are you looking for?"

"Horse shit."

"Horse shit?"

"Yes, you know, horse turds."

"Horses in your backyard? Are you nuts?"

She might be. Tonight, the backyard felt different. Bigger, darker, and the smells more intense. They reached the edge of the yard, and she pointed her light between the houses. What had she hoped to find?

"Isabelle," Carson said. He gestured behind them.

She glanced back at the house. Her mother's legs dangled from the bedroom window.

"Mother, what are you doing? Get back inside."

By the time they crossed the yard, Sharon lay in a drunken heap on the ground. Her nightgown was bunched and twisted around her neck. A flush crept across Isabelle's cheeks as she quickly straightened her mother's clothes and covered her nakedness.

They grabbed Sharon under her arms and lifted her to her feet. As the pair reached the corner of the house, Sharon mumbled, "I need to find the man."

"Mom, what man?"

A horse whinnied.

"Carson, did you hear that?"

"I didn't hear anything."

Isabelle glanced at him in confusion. "You didn't?"

"No."

His eyes gave him away. Why was Carson lying to her?

They tucked her mother into bed, locked the window, and put the damaged screen back in place. Isabelle followed Carson to the front of the house. Wordlessly, he crossed the street and entered his building.

Isabelle rested her head against the door before locking it, then checked every window and door, making sure her mother could not escape again tonight. As she crawled into bed, she searched for some meaning behind Carson's actions. Unable to find answers, Isabelle fell into a restless sleep.

Her alarm clock woke her far too soon. She stumbled into the kitchen where her mother nibbled on a piece of toast. "Good morning, Mom."

"I'm sorry about last night."

Isabelle shrugged.

"I mean it. That won't happen again."

"What won't happen again.? You won't get drunk? Act stupid?"

Her mother threw her toast on the counter. "I'm late for work."

Isabelle did not put much faith in her mother's words. Sharon had relapsed too many times. This was not the first time she promised change. Could she win her battle over alcohol? Suppress the demons? Isabelle crossed her fingers. The credo of Alcoholics Anonymous and the Twelve Step Program: Don't expect any more than one day at a time. Every day sober brought her mother closer to overcoming her addiction.

Isabelle had woken with a headache. Her mother leaving hadn't improved things. She gagged down a couple aspirins, preparing herself for her babysitting job. The pay wasn't good, but seven-year-old Trish behaved well. Isabelle trudged the few blocks to her job and collapsed onto their couch.

As the morning turned into afternoon, her headache progressed into a fist of pain, like an ice pick jammed into her right eye. The severity surprised her. She hadn't experienced a migraine since they moved to Moorhead.

Since the age of thirteen, after her first period, headaches had dominated her life. Along with the headaches, strange voices began manifesting out of thin air, memories, and thoughts that were not hers.

The feeling that she was two different people, in different places at the same time, was ever-present.

She kept those symptoms to herself. Isabelle's doctor recommended birth control pills; her mother recommended they leave his office. No daughter of hers would be on the pill. End of story.

If she could close her eyes for an hour, the pain might go away. She sent Trish to her room so she could relax.

***

A man's voice pierced the silence. "Rise and shine, sleepyhead. Isabelle, we have a surprise for you."

Isabelle's eyes snapped open, her nerves at full stretch. She held her breath and listened. The voice didn't belong to anybody who should be in the apartment.

"Are you sure Trish is in her room? The boogeyman, the man with the dark eyes, is coming soon. He wants her."

Isabelle sat, but immediately jumped on top of the cushions, the hair on her arms standing on end. The afternoon light had faded and undulating shadows filled the corners. In the dim, half-light, feral children, their yellow eyes gleamed and their small fangs glistened, encircled the couch. Holding hands they danced around Isabelle chanting a messed up nursery rhyme. "Ring around the rosie, a pocket full of posies, ashes, ashes, Trish falls dead."

Isabelle covered her face with a pillow and screamed. "You're not real. I'm dreaming. Please," she begged, "go away."

The wild-eyed children's giggles echoed off the walls.

"No. No. No." Isabelle squeezed her eyes shut

Without warning, the chanting stopped. The room grew too quiet. She dropped the pillow and bounded to her feet, heart thumping against her ribcage. "Trish...Trish!"

Halfway down the hall, a door opened. Trish stepped out. "Yes, Isabelle."

Isabelle exhaled hard, relieved to see her unhurt. "Can I get a hug?"

Trish wrapped her arms around Isabelle and pulled the loose strands of hair away from her face. "Are you better?" she asked. "You don't look better."

Colors swirled behind Isabelle's eyes. The urge to lay down overwhelmed her. "Give me fifteen more minutes. I'll be good as new."

She made her way to the couch on shaky legs. As she closed her eyes, laughter filled her head.

***

"Isabelle, wake up," Trish said, "Mom will be home soon."

"Okay." Isabelle rubbed her eyes and jumped to her feet. "Oh, my God. What time is it?"

"Almost 5:30."

"Don't tell your mom I slept all afternoon."

"I won't. I'm good at keeping secrets."

Isabelle ruffled Trish's hair.

She wasn't as good as new, but she felt better. Some effects lingered. She hoped they would go away before her birthday supper that night.

Five minutes later, Trish's mother Brenda walked through the door. The young girl ran to her room and came back with a card and a present.

Brenda smiled. "I'm surprised she waited all day."

Isabelle unwrapped the present. Inside were two black and white composition books, a set of nice pens, and five dollars. "Thank you. How did you know I needed more?"

She picked Trish off the floor and gave her a big hug.

"Be careful," Trish whispered.

Isabelle's heart raced; unknown dread percolated through her veins. She swallowed her mounting fear, set Trish back on the floor, and forced her best smile. "I should be going. Mom's taking me out for supper with some of my friends."

Trish squeezed her hand.

"Happy birthday," Brenda said.

"Thanks."

"Where are you going for supper?"

"Italian Moon. They have the best pizza."

"A big party?"

"No, just a couple of friends."

"Have fun." Brenda draped an arm over her daughter's shoulder. "Goodbye, Isabelle."

Isabelle hurried from the apartment, trying to untangle the meaning of Trish's warning.

*** 

As she stepped out into the fading late afternoon sun, Brenda's last words replayed in her mind. Before she could comprehend their finality, she recognized the dark green car parked at the end of the street. Shadows partially obscured the front seat, but Bob's wise little eyes, bright and bemused, studied her, a greasy smile splayed across his face. He seemed to spend a lot of time in her neighborhood. More than necessary. Such a vile man. Her skin crawled all the way home.

Later, Sharon took Isabelle out for her birthday meal. Disappointed that Carson never showed, Isabelle nevertheless enjoyed a nice evening with her mother. They even stopped for ice cream.

When they arrived home, Carson wasn't at his regular post, in front of her house, sitting under the streetlight with a book in hand. Instead, she found a beautifully wrapped box. She sat and unwrapped the present. Inside she found a pair of the softest fingerless gloves she had ever worn. Embroidered on each glove was a fancy key. She opened the note and read. "A Birthday Gift for you. Use them wisely." She scrunched up her face and kept reading. "You have been given the rare ability to absorb other people's thoughts, feelings, and memories by touching them with the palm of your hand. With great talents comes great responsibility."

"Isabelle, why don't you come in? You have presents to open."

She kicked the ground. It was so unlike Carson to break a promise, but with foster parents like his, she had to give him some leeway. "Okay."

"I'm sure he has a good excuse."

Too many presents awaited Isabelle inside the house. Sharon had gone out of her way to make up for the morning's police visit. Worn out from her long day, Isabelle headed to bed as soon as she had opened the last gift.

Her mother kissed her cheek and whispered, "This will be a year to remember."

# Chapter 2

The stifling air clung to Isabelle's skin like a warm blanket. Beads of perspiration dotted her forehead. She brushed the sweaty strands of hair from her face and groaned. The remnants of a headache lingered. Every time she drifted close to sleep, the pointy end of a thought jabbed into her brain. Behind closed eyes, her imagination played tricks.

Earlier that afternoon while babysitting, unknown voices had threatened. Someone had been trying to steal Trish. Isabelle had been certain that she would wake from her headache-fueled nap, and the girl would be gone. How could she imagine something which seemed so real? And the finality of Brenda's goodbye seemed permanent.

When she dared to open her eyes, the evil thoughts that circulated inside her head transformed into strangely-shaped shadows that slid along the walls. Malaise and the unknown lurked in the corners of her room. She gripped the sheets, curled into a ball, and slipped into a thin sleep. Somewhere in the murky depths of her mind, she dreamed.

"No!" Isabelle screamed. "Let go of me."

The bedding clung to her legs like a death shroud. She kicked at the twisted, sweaty sheets until they came off the end of the bed. Once freed, she rolled over and waited for her heartbeat to slow. Her eyes opened to the familiar shadows of her room. "Thank God."

She pressed her palms to her eyes and let out a huge breath. Trish and the strange children were only a dream. The unknown voices weren't real either, but still, the heavy weight of fear pressed down on her from all sides.

***

Tired of her overactive imagination and sweaty sheets plastered to her like a second skin, Isabelle threw up her arms in resignation. "You win. I couldn't sleep anyway."

She turned on the bedside lamp. Read or write? A tough decision.

A pebble tinged off her window.

"Isabelle," Carson said, "Are you awake?"

She crept to the window. "Not so loud. Mom might be awake."

"Sorry I missed your party," Carson whispered.

"It wasn't much of one."

"John's home," he said, his voice brimming with distaste.

Isabelle understood all about the troubles with fathers, even temporary ones. Hers hadn't even called to wish her happy birthday. Since he remarried, the visits became more infrequent, but he had never before missed wishing her a happy birthday. It had to be her fault.

The two times Carson's foster parent John visited, he brought trouble. Carson told her he was a drifter and drug dealer, coming and going as he pleased. A man of the shadows, an urban nomad. Isabelle pulled on her favorite pair of sweatpants, pushed open the window screen, and joined Carson under the streetlight in front of her house. They sat on the curb across the street from Carson's apartment building, shoulder to shoulder. Above their heads, moths thumped against the weak light of the street lamp. Tears rolled down Carson's cheeks.

"What happened this time?" Isabelle asked.

He shrugged, pointing at his building. "Just listen."

John and Opal's argument sounded like a bar brawl. Objects smashing against walls punctuated each word and Isabelle's stomach churned at each sound. Carson needed a friend, but his parents' fight reminded her of events she wished to forget.

"Mom was 'entertaining' when John showed up," Carson explained, making air quotes with his fingers. "He wasn't supposed to be released until after the New Year."

The front door of the apartment building burst open from the weight of John and a naked man locked in a struggle. They lost their balance, spilled onto the front steps, and continued their wrestling match on the ground for several minutes. Once John got the upper hand, he punched the naked man in the face until the man slumped unconscious to the ground. John grabbed him by the hair and dragged him to the end of the sidewalk into the gutter. "Get the fuck out of here."

Opal had followed the men out the open front door. She tossed the naked man's clothes into the yard. Isabelle cringed; Opal was dressed in a negligee not meant for a woman of her girth.

John rummaged through the man's wallet and extracted a handful of bills. "Don't ever come back, or I'll kick your ass again, motherfucker," He tossed the wallet at the man, turned, and pushed Opal towards the door. "Get your fat ass inside. I'm not done with you."

Carson's foster parents' fight continued. Isabelle wrapped her arm around Carson. "Should I call the police?"

Carson shook his head and leaned against her shoulder. She held him close as fresh tears trickled down his face. The noises from within the house eventually subsided, but not soon enough. Isabelle needed to find a way to distract Carson, to pull him out of this funk, and put a smile back on his face.

"Are you ready for school to start?"

"Yes, school's great, especially science. I have Adam – I mean Mr. Harris this fall." Carson wiped his eyes. "Did you know alchemy was one of the first sciences? Mr. Harris started a Medieval Science club this summer."

The front door of the apartment building opened, and John strode out. As he approached the pair, Isabelle pulled her arm from Carson's shoulder. "Is she your girlfriend?" John asked.

Carson wiped his face with his sleeve. "No."

"What are you crying about, boy?" John shook his head and muttered something under his breath. He pulled a couple of five-dollar bills from his pocket and tossed them at Carson. "Find someplace else to stay tonight." He patted his pocket and smiled. "Opal and I are going to have some fun."

John turned, pulled up his pants, and swaggered away, exaggerating a right-legged limp.

Isabelle asked, "Aren't they divorced?"

"Technically, they are. Every time John needs money or a place to crash for a few days, he comes here. I'm sure he brought home fun in a needle. It's the only reason Opal would let him stay."

"Fun in a needle?"

"Smack. Heroin."

"Oh." Isabelle shoved her hands in her pockets and stared at the ground. "I'm sorry, I didn't know."

"It's okay."

"Where will you stay tonight?" He could sleep on her bedroom floor, but if her mother found him there in the morning, she would be livid. Sharon liked him, but that wouldn't stop her from going postal.

"I'm not sure. Maybe the park."

The naked man groaned and pushed himself to his knees. He spat a glob of blood-tinged phlegm and grimaced. Rising to his feet, he stumbled over the curb and onto the dried lawn. He fetched his clothes. He pulled on his pants and slid his shirt over his head, struggling to get it through an armhole. He picked up his wallet and staggered in their direction.

Carson blocked his progress. "Back off." The drunken man swayed on his feet. Carson, his brown eyes filled with anger, pushed him away from Isabelle. "Leave her alone."

The man looked past Carson and inspected Isabelle. "Sorry, my lady, if I have offended thee."

He smelled of alcohol, seemed disoriented and anxious, but his gaze appeared clear and crisp. Isabelle ran her fingers through her hair, bewildered why any sober man would sleep with Opal.

She recognized the man. A memory she could not bring into focus. His face, disfigured by a red, jagged scar that ran from mouth to ear? A scar one couldn't forget. She shook her head; nothing made sense. Why couldn't she remember who he was?

"Have you seen my horseless carriage?" the man stammered. Bob's dark green sedan screeched to a stop at the end of the block. The man bowed. "Sorry to have bothered you. My ride is here."

She frowned as the man entered Bob's car. How do they know one another? She wiped Carson's tears. As her fingers brushed his cheeks and her palm touched his skin, a raw fierce burning started in her lower spine and spread throughout her back. The air shimmered and a kaleidoscope of colors and lights flashed in front of her eyes. Her head filled with pictures and sounds of his life. The show ended, her eyes opened, and she broke into a cold sweat. Carson no longer sat next to her.

She jumped to her feet; her heart thudded in her ears. Where did Carson go? She spun around, spotting him at the end of the street, but he wasn't alone. A dark figure followed.

Dread swirled like flies on a bloated carcass. Whatever followed Carson meant him harm. She swallowed her fear and crept closer to the pair. As they neared the park, she touched the creature.

Her knees buckled, a cold, white mist swirled all around. She shivered and wrapped her arms around herself. When the fog cleared, she stood on the ice, no longer in the park. Darkness pressed down on her from all sides.

"Doesn't he have beautiful eyes?" a young voice asked.

An adolescent girl, mirror brilliant and ice cold, stepped out of the shadows in front of Isabelle. Her dark eyes, a vicious glint in the moonlight. A scream crawled up the back of Isabelle's throat.

The girl held Carson's severed head in her hand. "He likes beautiful boys."

"What did you do?" Isabelle groaned.

The girl moved so fast, she appeared to float rather than run. In an instant, she crossed the space between them. A finger pressed against Isabelle's temple. Blackness swirled, the cold world faded.

Isabelle found herself back in the park, her breath a cloud of ice crystals. Bewilderment and nausea surged from her core. She rose to her feet and stumbled back down the street toward her house. Behind her, the street lights flickered. One by one they burst, sending sparks of electricity into the night sky.

Isabelle crawled back through her bedroom window, her soul filled with sorrow. She curled into a ball and let the images and pain of Carson's life play out in her mind. Agony pierced her heart. Tears flowed non-stop. Even if she could have stopped them, she wouldn't have. Carson needed somebody to care.

She did.

But many of his memories eluded her, devoured by an unseen presence. What dark secrets did Carson hide?

# Chapter 3

The floor creaked, and the little girl opened her eyes. Someone stood outside her door. She peeked under her arm, her favorite blanket clutched in her fists. A thin stream of light sliced across the room. Hoping it was only her mother, she rolled over, curled into a ball, and shut her eyes. On several occasions, she had fooled her mother by pretending to be asleep. It was way past her bedtime. If her mother knew she was awake, she wouldn't be happy, might even yell.

The door swung open, and a shadow danced on the wall. The little girl held the covers tight under her chin. She watched through squinted eyes as the shadow grew larger. Footsteps whispered across the floor, inching closer and closer to her bed. The little girl froze

"Are you asleep?" the shadow asked. The voice was not her mother's.

With her heart thumping wildly in her chest, the little girl squeezed her eyes shut. Could the man hear how scared she was? Her heart beat so loud.

"Do you want to be a big girl like your mommy?"

Isabelle gasped, a scream caught in her throat. She slumped against the shower wall and let the hot water cascade down her back. Her body shuddered from her revulsion, from the vile image etched in her memory. With the water turned off, she stood until goosebumps formed and then eased herself out of the tub. She wrapped a towel around her torso and headed to her room. She needed to leave in thirty minutes for her babysitting job at Trish's.

The two black and white composition books Trish had given her sat in a neat pile on her desk. Maybe she should sit down and capture the last few dreams or memories. Perhaps Isabelle could write about the dreamscape of nightmares or the horror sliding through her veins. She remembered the tang of misery that had coated the back of her throat. She shivered and kicked her damp towel aside.

Now dressed in a t-shirt and faded shorts, Isabelle stood in front of the bathroom mirror brushing her hair. The fan hummed overhead. Condensation beaded and slid down the glass. In the harsh bathroom light, her face appeared too pale. Her light blue eyes, accentuated by dark, bruise-like bags, were those of a haunted creature she didn't recognize.

Her stomach gurgled, reminding her how long it had been since she'd eaten last. She flicked the light off and walked to the kitchen. Nothing in the fridge appealed, but a glass of milk might settle her stomach. The clock above the stove told her she had enough time to write a few sentences.

She took a seat at her desk and grabbed the top composition book. A jolt of apprehension stopped her. Somewhere in the corner of her mind, disquiet and dread ripened. Her hand trembled as she flipped to the first page and read the words Trish wrote.

Mom's new boyfriend is a bad man.

Isabelle stared at the words. She bit her lip and turned the page.

He told them where to find us.

You can't even trust mommies.

Her heart pounded. She ran her fingers through her hair. "Trish. What are...."

The page flipped over on its own volition.

Keep the Watcher Man safe.

They want him next.

Isabelle rocked in her chair. Cold fingers of fear caressed her skin. "No. No. No."

She dropped the book and raced from the house.

Jumping off the top step, she stumbled and ran across the street in search of Carson. She pushed open the door to the building, making a beeline for the stairs to his second-floor apartment. If she ran into trouble at Trish's, she could not think of anyone she'd rather have by her side than her best friend.

She pounded on the door.

Seconds turned into a minute. Where the hell was Carson? He never woke before nine. Her internal alarm sounded. She couldn't wait any longer.

She took the stairs two at a time, her pulse racing. She forgot something important, something unpleasant from her earlier dream. Trish's words resonated. "Isabelle, it's too late. They found us."

Who found them?

After one block, a stitch in her side forced her to slow the pace. She walked into the park, panting. Past the green space, the basketball court, and the softball diamond just beyond the neighborhood pool, she spotted the apartment where Trish and her mother lived.

Children filled the park with excitement. Boys shot hoops, girls fielded ground balls, and the pool overflowed with youngsters taking swimming lessons. Mothers watched from the benches. Isabelle gripped the chain link in her fingers, resting her head against the fence.

Sharon had tried being a mother one summer.

The memory made Isabelle smile. Her mother brought her to swimming lessons and took her on picnics. As a family, they spent weekends camping and swimming at the lake. Hugs and kisses had been abundant until the drinking and fighting started. She pushed against the evil thoughts until a wary happiness returned.

Early morning sunshine caressed her skin, the oppressive heat hours away. The joyful voices of children playing calmed her. Her mind slowed as she re-evaluated the craziness. She had overreacted to the dream and the writing in the notebook. How could something so nefarious as the vision of Carson's death happen so close to a park that brings joy to so many?

A car door slammed.

A thin sheen of cold sweat beaded on her forehead.

Tires squealed.

All her instincts told her to run, but she needed to stay calm and think without emotion. No need to hurry. When she reached the pool parking lot, she immediately saw Brenda's little blue car parked in front of their building.

The air around the car shimmered unnaturally, drawing her attention away from the building. Isabelle hesitated, taking slow and measured steps towards the vehicle, wary of any impending danger. She peered inside. Trish's favorite blanket and stuffed animal lay on the car seat.

A cold gut punch of terror slid through Isabelle's veins when her hand grasped the car door handle. Trish was in trouble.

Like an invisible path, glimmering footsteps led straight to the front door. Most days upon Isabelle's arrival she would be buzzed in, or Trish raced down the stairs, and they would walk up together. Today, the doors were propped open.

Each step brought a sense of uncertainty. At the top, Isabelle hurried down the hallway. The door swung open before she had a chance to knock.

"Hello?"

No one answered.

"Trish?"

Isabelle stepped inside. Stagnant air filled her nostrils. Particles drifted in the morning light, a thin layer of dust covered all the surfaces. Not a single item of furniture remained except for the faded words written on the dust-covered wall.

Suffer the children

A different writing style than the one penned in the composition book. Behind the stale air, Isabelle caught a whiff of Trish and her mother. She followed the scent down the hallway. Inside Trish's bedroom, her head filled with whispers. Some of the voices tasted like poison.

Trish's room was empty and covered in dust. Isabelle didn't understand. How could any of this be possible? Isabelle turned in a full circle, stopping in front of the closet doors. Whispered words filled her mind

"Momma, what did you do?"

Isabelle whimpered and gripped her head.

"Mommy, where are they taking me?"

"Trish, I'm sorry."

She needed the voices to be silent. Without hesitation, she stepped forward and yanked open the closet doors. Inside, a door drawn with thick black lines.

Driven by a compulsion she could not control, she reached for the handle. Her fingers clutched the cold metal. The cacophony of voices in her head fell silent. She stared down at her empty hands.

An aura of sadness enveloped Isabelle and weighed heavy on her heart. She rubbed the haziness out of her eyes. Her mind raced, searching for answers. All summer she babysat Trish in this apartment. How could a family pack and move so quickly? Where had Brenda and Trish gone?

Carson rushed into the room. "Isabelle, you need to leave. Bob's on his way."

"What? Why are you here?"

He reached for her arm. "We need to go."

"Trish's gone."

"I know."

Isabelle pointed towards the closet. "They took her through the door."

Carson's eyes grew wide. "What door?"

She turned. The door in the closet was no longer there. A headache bloomed, tendrils of pain reaching into the deepest crevices of her mind. "No. It was just there."

He tugged on her arm. "Let's go."

Carson hurried Isabelle out of the apartment. They ducked around the corner and hid in the bushes.

Bob's sedan bounced against the curb and came to a stop. He exited the car, chomping on an unlit cigar stub. The heels of his snake-skin cowboy boots struck the sidewalk like gunshots. He flung open the door to the apartment and disappeared inside.

Isabelle whispered, "Where—"

Carson's hand covered her mouth.

Several minutes later the apartment door flew open. Bob, his face now flushed a deeper red, clutched his cowboy hat and stomped down the sidewalk. At the curb, he hitched up his polyester pants. Sunlight sparkled off a hint of a belt buckle, the remainder hidden underneath the girth of his stomach. Glancing around as if he knew someone watched, he spat on the ground and climbed back into his beat-up car. The tires squealed as he sped away.

Could he be Trish's mom's new boyfriend, the bad man? Bob did remind her of a used car salesman or a creeper, but could he make children disappear through imaginary doors?

Isabelle sprang from their hiding place, dashed up the stairs with Carson on her heels, and into the entryway. The security door was locked. She pushed all the intercoms, but no one answered. She pounded on the glass. The pain in her head spiked and her legs grew weak. "Ohhh...."

Carson caught her before she fell. "I'll help you home."

They walked in silence. The children had left the park and took with them the energy of youth. Isabelle studied her friend's face. He was lost in his own private thoughts. When they arrived at her house, Isabelle sat and patted the steps next to her.

"Where were you this morning?"

Carson didn't shift his gaze from the ground. "I was at the library, taking a test."

"A test?"

"Yes, a test. If I want to join Adam's Medieval Chemistry group, I need to pass his test."

They sat in silence as the heat of the day pressed down on them.

"Are you the Watcher Man?" Isabelle asked.

# Chapter 4

Carson stared at a single spot on the sidewalk. He raised his head and looked at Isabelle. "I don't know what you're talking about."

Isabelle studied her friend. He had improved his lying. This time his eyes did not betray him.

"Am I going crazy?" Isabelle asked.

"Forget about Trish."

"Why?" Isabelle cupped his chin in her hands and gazed into his brown eyes. "What are you hiding from me?"

Carson sighed. "Fretting about Trish won't do you any good."

"I'm scared. Tell me she's real."

He ran his fingers through his hair and walked down the steps. Halfway to the street, he turned. "How's your mom?"

Isabelle sighed. "Drinking again."

Carson sat on the bottom step. "At least she doesn't do drugs like John and Opal."

"Don't change the subject."

"Memories fade and crumble like leaves in the fall," he said. "I'm begging you, let it be."

"Carson, what's going on? Tell me the truth."

He shook his head. "I can't."

"Can't or won't?"

"Someday."

Isabelle reached out to hug him but stopped short. The coppery smell of blood filled her nostrils. Blood dripped onto the step next to her. The image of the girl holding Carson's severed head appeared. Isabelle recoiled, a scream lodged in her throat.

"He likes beautiful boys," the girl said.

Isabelle buried her face in her hands.

Carson would die soon. She didn't know why or how, but she knew. The worst part? She couldn't stop it. The knowledge bore down on her heart like a millstone. Tears scolded her cheeks.

"Isabelle, what's wrong?"

With a quick peek into the compartment in her mind where she stored his memories, she gleaned the truth. He already knew as well. "I'll protect you," Isabelle promised.

"I know you'll try," Carson said.

"You're my only friend. I can't lose you." She leaned in and kissed his cheek.

Carson jumped to his feet, his eyes feverish and bright, and ran a few paces. He stopped, curled his hands over his head, and sprinted until he reached the middle of the street. "I'm just a friend who thinks you're special beyond measure."

***

Teary-eyed and trembling, Isabelle went inside. She sat on the couch, but anxiety paced the halls of her mind. She couldn't rest, so she rose and walked to her room, but dizziness and a churning stomach plagued her. After several minutes staring out the window, she decided to try to write, to lose herself in a world more compassionate than the one in which she lived. But after several false starts, she slammed the cover. Trish refused to leave her mind.

"I'll find you."

Isabelle flung open the closet doors. While studying the space, she rubbed the back of her neck. How to start? She grabbed a handful of hangers and tossed them onto the bed. In a flurry of pent-up frustration, she emptied her closet, tossing the contents on the bed. Her foot tapped on the floor. Where were they?

She yanked open each desk drawer until she found a large black permanent marker. She closed her eyes and imagined the door in Trish's closet. Inside her own empty space, with a few pen strokes, she duplicated the drawing.

Isabelle placed her hand on the center of the door and closed her eyes. Her fingers followed the grooves, the tiny slits and valleys of the wood. An earthy, rotting soil smell filled the closet. She brought her fingers to her nose. A hint of smoke lingered. She grabbed the pitted metal of the door handle. When she pulled, the door rattled but would not open. She opened her eyes; the lines were there, but the actual door she'd pictured in her mind was gone. Overwhelmed, she sat on the floor and waited.

***

The darkness approached faster than the Keepers of the Key had hoped. Carson closed his book. His studies would have to wait. Everyone had a role to play, and his changed daily. Tonight, he needed to protect Isabelle from herself.

He eased his bedroom door open, tiptoed down the hallway, and sneaked past his wasted foster parents. Thanks to the two empty syringes on the coffee table, the whole neighborhood could have stomped through the apartment and they would not have noticed. Some days they played their roles too well.

Carson stepped outside. Bob's green sedan rolled down the street. The man with the scar sat in the passenger seat. The car slowed and stopped in front of Isabelle's house. Carson ducked back inside.

Bob stunk. Carson smelled him from here. The fetid odor of rotten meat wasn't caused by bad hygiene but from the unnatural cloying stench clinging to him like a second skin. Those who employed Bob survived on sorrow and anger. The fragrance of death lingered wherever his employers went.

Carson shook his head. Maybe the smell of death didn't bother Bob anymore. A phrase he read somewhere came to mind.

"...they bathed in the blood of the innocent."

To Isabelle, Bob was just a Creeper, a two-bit hustler. Carson knew he was much more. Not only was he the eyes and ears of the Dark Ones, but he also collected children for them. He used his connection within Social Services and the Foster Program to find those lost souls that fell through the cracks and wouldn't be missed. He sent those he found to a realm called Otherworld where the children were drained of their blood and souls. When a soul was ripped from an innocent child, something was always left behind. Feral children, little monsters with sharp teeth.

At this time, the man with the scar was of greater concern. For him to make an appearance meant the timetable had changed. Cold sweat beaded on Carson's forehead. Seconds felt like minutes. Minutes felt like hours. Perspiration soaked his underarms. At last, the car pulled away from the curb.

He needed to be careful. The Others would be coming soon. More doors would open. All the windows in the neighborhood would sprout eyes. Someone would always be watching. Men like Bob would make sure of that.

Carson looked both ways before he crossed the street.

He rang the doorbell.

No one answered.

He knocked, waited a few seconds, and opened the door.

"Isabelle?"

Muffled sounds came from her room. He walked down the short hall and stopped in the doorway. Isabelle sat cross-legged on the floor, staring into the closet. Her lips moved, sounds gurgled forth in a continuous loop of words. "I need to open the door. I need to open the door. I need to open the door."

"Isabelle, is everything alright?"

She gazed up at him, her eyes glistening. "What am I?"

"Oh, Isabelle."

Her eyes pleaded with him. "What am I? Every day, chunks of time keep disappearing. One moment I'm here, and the next moment I'm somewhere else. Never knowing. Never remembering who I am."

"You're the light in the darkness."

"What?"

"You're tired."

"You might be right."

Carson knelt beside her and placed his hand on her forehead. "Oh, Great Mother, hear my call. Heal Isabelle of all illnesses. Rebuild her mind, body, and spirit." He gently closed her eyes. "Isabelle, sleep away the pain, numb away the pain. When you awaken, your mind will be refreshed. In the name of the Father, the Son, and the Holy Spirit."

Isabelle mumbled and crawled into bed. Carson tucked the covers under her chin. He kissed her cheek. "Sleep well." He opened his violin case, took out his instrument, and ran the bow across the strings. He played Isabelle, a soothing, restful piece. When he finished, she was at peace.

At the door, Carson turned towards his sleeping friend. "It was too soon. You were not ready."

Soft, cushioned footsteps approached. A shadow fell by Carson's side, and a hand clutched his. Help from the Guardians had arrived, but for how long? "A stubborn girl."

Carson nodded. "Her mind's strong. Her memory will be fuzzy, but she won't forget." He faced the girl with sky-blue eyes and stared at her for several minutes. " The Guardians and the Keepers of the Keys need to tell Isabelle the truth about what's going on. You need to tell her about the approaching darkness and what her role will be in closing the doors. She's alone and lost."

"Yes, I know, but if she doesn't get lost, she can't be found."

# Chapter 5

Bob slammed the car door, slid in, and pounded his hands against the steering wheel. "Son-of-a bitch." The trap had been set perfectly. The little witch should be in the hands of The Friar and the Dark Ones. What the Hell happened? He would pay dearly for this mistake.

The door to his apartment was ajar. A warning. Bob knew the Dark Ones never entered through the front door. Father Abrams sat in his chair, his hands folded in prayer. "You have disappointed the Friar...tremendously."

Father Abrams's words sent a chill through Bob's marrow. "Someone other than the little Guardian must be protecting her with magic," Bob said.

The apartment filled with the scent of pine and murky water. The girl with the poison green eyes stepped out of the shadows of the hallway. "No shit," the girl said. "Father Abrams, are we ready? He's getting impatient.

Bob looked at the grim faces of the pair. He swallowed, but his fear grew into terror. He took a step towards the door.

"Children," Father Abrams said.

The door opened and closed without a sound. The gleaming eyes and glistening fangs of the feral children stood in Bob's way. His fight-or-flight instinct came too late to serve any purpose other than to make his heart flutter uncontrollably. He wiped his sweaty hands on his pants and waited for instructions. "It must be the boy."

Father Abrams glanced at them both. "Are you sure the boy has chosen?"

Bob nodded. He followed Father Abrams down the hall and into his room. The contents of his closet lay scattered everywhere. A pine-scented breeze wafted from his closet. The door to wherever they were taking him was open. He hesitated.

Father Abrams laughed. "You have Hell to pay for your poor planning."

He shuddered. The Dark Ones were going to fight magic with darker magic and that required blood, his blood.

***

Carson sat in his usual spot, leaning against the street lamp pole with a book in his hand. He read from the thin volume, but mostly he watched the house across the street. He had so many secrets he wanted to share with Isabelle, no...truths she needed to hear. Who he was, who she was, and her destiny. Isabelle was his Queen, the savior of worlds. He fingered the key that hung around his neck. Trish and the Guardians saved his life and he made promises.

His heart ached. It was more than the doors opening between worlds that frightened Carson. It was the approaching darkness, infinite and absolute, and the evil escaping from the shadows that terrified him. So many innocent souls would be lost if Isabelle didn't see who she was.

He was restless. He stood and paced, his mind in overdrive, his thoughts jumping from one topic to another, Bob was getting worrisome. But there were far worse individuals than him out there.

Carson didn't want another set of foster parents. He cradled his head in his hands and cried. How could he tell Isabelle about how he watched his parents die? He missed them so much. Could he tell her how Bob punished his first set of foster parents because Carson didn't follow orders? With each new set of caregivers, their cruelty increased tenfold. John and Opal were sadistic bastards. He wanted them dead. He wanted to run. But he loved Isabelle and made promises. Why were the worst monsters, humans?

# Chapter 6

Isabelle stared at the ceiling. Over the last couple of weeks, the tension in the house had increased tenfold. Most nights her mother arrived home late, her breath tinged with alcohol. Her mother's drinking caused rage to bubble inside. Would Sharon ever keep a promise?

Carson had passed his Medieval Chemistry test. He spent mornings buried in old books; afternoons he disappeared. Isabelle tried to pry and coerce the location out of him, but the harder she pushed, the more obstinate he became.

Thunder rumbled like a slow-moving freight train. An occasional streak of lightning flashed across the sky. Isabelle pushed back the covers and walked to the window. Carson sat under the lamp post with a book propped in his lap, a few strides from her window like he did every night.

She knocked on the window.

He glanced up and waved. Abruptly his gaze swiveled toward his right. Isabelle followed his sightline to the end of the block. Bob's green sedan rolled down the street.

Carson closed his book and stood; his hands were clenched by his sides. He didn't relax until the car disappeared.

A second set of headlights turned down their street and slowed. Sharon.

Her mother had made it home. While trying to park, she drove over the curb, onto the grass, and thumped back onto the street. The car shuddered and died. She stumbled as she exited, grabbing the fender for balance. She weaved as she walked towards the house.

Isabelle shook her head in disgust as a bolt of lightning ripped through the sky.

"One thousand one, one thousand two, one thousand three...." Like an awakening giant, Isabelle spun away from the window; her anger at her mother raged just below the surface. The door to her room opened.

The thunder boomed. Isabelle flinched. The storm inched closer.

Sharon stood in the doorway, partially hidden in the shadows, her face revealed in the intermediate flashes. "Isabelle, you're still up?"

Isabelle ignored the question. "Long day at work, Mother?"

"Yeah...big project."

"The overtime will be great, won't it, Mom? All that extra money."

Uncontrolled, dazzling white tongues of lightning licked at the sky, again illuminating the room in brilliant light. Anger rippled across her mother's face. Isabelle waited for one of her mother's snide replies, but instead, her mother asked, "Are you excited about starting a new school?"

Isabelle shrugged. "Just another new school." She counted each finger as she raised them. "Seven. I'm only a sophomore, and this is my seventh school. Are we shooting for an even ten before I graduate?"

Her mother's lips curled into a cruel smile. "Try and make a few friends this time."

Thunder echoed like cannon shots outside.

Isabelle's false smile matched her mother's. "Don't you think you should sleep this one off? You still have a job to go to tomorrow, right?"

Sharon took an unsteady step forward. "How dare you?"

Isabelle returned to the window. "Close the door when you leave."

"You can't speak to me like that."

"You're drunk. Go to bed."

Her mother slammed the door as she left.

Rain lanced the windows, Mother Nature unleashing her pent-up fury. Carson no longer stood guard outside. Isabelle assumed he had gone inside, but with John visiting for most of the summer, he could be anywhere. Isabelle and Carson still talked often and spent time together, but conversations about Trish and what happened the day she and her mother disappeared were off-limits. Isabelle wrestled with unresolved knots of emotion.

Nobody in the neighborhood mentioned Trish. It was as if the girl never existed. At times Isabelle's thoughts seemed disconnected, her memories of Trish disjointed and fuzzy. She picked up a few other babysitting jobs, but they were dull children who lacked imagination. None of the youngsters interested her like Trish had.

She sat at the edge of the bed listening to the rain thrum against the house. Her eyes grew heavy. Maybe if she just closed them for a moment....

"Isabelle, I miss you."

"I miss you too, Trish. Where are you?"

"It's getting dangerous."

"What is?"

Trish whispered. "Bad people everywhere. You need to find the magic inside of you, close the doors...."

Isabelle's eyes snapped open. Foggy remnants of a conversation remained. Wiping the drool from her chin, she searched the room. Was Trish just here?

The sky, full of gray scrud, crawled overhead. Droplets of water slid down the glass, but the rain no longer fell. Isabelle pushed open the window. Clean, fresh air filled the room, cleansing her soul of the anger and anxiety she experienced earlier. She inhaled deeply.

Refreshed, Isabelle sat at her desk and opened one of the composition books Trish had given as a present. She flipped through the pages until she found the right one. The words on the page blurred. She rubbed her eyes. Letter by letter, the ink faded.

"What the hell?"

She turned the dusty pages. A musty odor wafted from within. The paper crumbled in her fingers.

"No...no." An ice-cold dagger of fear pierced her heart. "Not Trish. Please, not Trish."

The edges of the paper turned brown. The corners curled. Tiny pieces of yellowed paper, the last remnants of Trish, sat in a pile. A breeze cut across the room, sweeping what was left of the pages off the desk.

A sharp giggle pierced the air. Is she finally dead now?

Tears dripped down Isabelle's cheeks. She crawled into bed, curled into a ball, and wrapped herself in a cocoon of blankets. The large void that Trish's loss created in her mind and heart was now filled with anguish and grief. She was getting tired of the cruel world they lived in. She closed her eyes tight, hoping to block out the world. When sleep approached, Isabelle didn't fight it.

She woke with an uneasy stomach, her eyes gritty. Had she only dreamed of Trish? Last night, she gazed into the frightened eyes of a lost child, a child with no way home. Was Trish gone?

She walked to the bathroom, pulled back the shower curtain, and adjusted the water temperature until satisfied. Standing under the scalding stream, her mind wandered in all directions.

Her mother offered one true statement last night: Isabelle needed to make a friend. Yes, Carson was her friend, but she needed girls that were friends.

She dressed in a hurry, flung her backpack over her shoulder, and trudged the few blocks to school.

The first day of school held many possibilities. A fresh start. Nobody knew her or her mother. She hoped, even imagined, this school would be different.

She skipped up the stairs. When she neared the top, the group of girls, who laughed and joked seconds earlier, stood silent.

"Hi, I'm Isabelle," she said, extending her hand.

In unison, the girls turned and headed into the building.

Isabelle almost cried. Nothing was different after all.

The rest of the morning improved. The teachers were helpful, some of her classes would challenge her, and a few of the nerdy kids smiled and said hi. A full lunchroom meant she didn't eat alone. The excited conversations characteristic of the first day of school bubbled all around. The afternoon provided more of the same.

Isabelle walked down the hall, her spirits buoyed by a decent first day, and found a group of girls gathered in front of her locker. A pretty blonde jabbed a well-manicured finger in her direction. "There she is, the girl I told you about."

Isabelle's stomach lurched. "And what did you tell them?"

"That your mother's a whore."

Isabelle stepped forward, her fists balled. "Say that again."

"You heard me. The cops found your mother in the backseat giving someone a blow job, didn't they?"

Isabelle listened with a vague sense of unreality. How did this stranger know what happened? The fact that her mother's dirty little secret wasn't a secret made Isabelle livid. The entire school would know by tomorrow.

The blonde laughed, then led her group of friends outside.

Nothing changed. This school would be like all the rest.

A locker banged shut beside her. "You do know her dad is the sheriff, don't you? Welcome to Sarah Erickson High School." Isabelle turned in time to see the random student walking away.

With her head down and her dignity dragging behind, Isabelle walked out of her new school like so many other first days.

# Chapter 7

Sharon's intercom buzzed.

"Can you come to my office?" her boss asked.

"I'll be right there, Mr. Hanson." Sharon swiveled in her chair. "Carrie, can you watch the phones until I get back?"

Carrie gave her an insincere smile and nodded.

Sharon pulled her purse from the bottom drawer of the desk and rummaged inside until she found what she needed. After she scrutinized her appearance, she touched up her lipstick. A last-second bra adjustment and she strutted to her boss's office, knocked and let herself in.

"Hi. What do you need?"

"Take a seat. I have a question for you. What makes this law firm successful?"

Is this a trick question? It couldn't be. Mr. Hanson wasn't smiling. He sat rigid in his expensive-looking suit, crisp white shirt, and his favorite red tie. His fingers drummed on the top of his desk.

Her heartbeat picked up speed as she struggled over the expected answer. "I would say honesty, dedication, and hard work."

"All of those are good answers, but you missed the most important quality. Integrity is the cornerstone, not only for this organization but for everyone. My father started this firm seventy years ago based on that.

Many in this firm thought I was crazy for hiring you. They said you lacked integrity. They asked me, does this firm want a single mother with a drinking problem and a questionable past to be part of the Hansen family. My reputation is at stake here. In the short time you've been employed, fortunately for all of us, you've done excellent work." He pulled a half-empty pint of vodka from his top drawer. "I assume this is yours?"

Sharon hoped her expression didn't betray her. She never expected anyone to find the bottle. In the past, the toilet tank provided an excellent hiding spot. What could she say? The bottle wasn't hers?

Didn't matter. If they wanted to get rid of her, to fix what they saw as a mistake, they'd find an excuse to do so. She couldn't accept responsibility and would deny any knowledge of the bottle.

Mr. Hansen's stare penetrated her calm demeanor. She shifted in her chair.

"You haven't been following the stipulations stated in your employee contract, have you?"

Sharon peered defiantly at him and tried to keep the emotion out of her voice. "I'm sure you think this bottle belongs to me; I swear it's not mine."

"I'm disappointed you think so little of my intellect. I had a drinking problem once, so don't bullshit a bullshitter. We know this bottle belongs to you. Stand up and own it. Show me you have integrity."

Her bottom lip quivered. Wiping her clammy hands on her pants, Sharon couldn't stop herself from lying. "If you could prove this bottle was mine, you would have fired me already. You didn't find it inside my desk, did you?"

"The janitor found this bottle in the toilet tank of the middle stall in the women's restroom."

She stood. "Are we finished?"

"Sit down," Mr. Hansen said, his eyes narrowed, his cheeks mottled red. "We're not finished."

Sharon sat. "Are you firing me?"

"Not today. You're right, I can't prove the bottle is yours; however, there's something else we need to discuss."

"And what is that?"

"This is never easy to say, so listen carefully and heed my warning. Stay away from Tom."

She found the situation funny. For once, it wasn't her having sex with a married co-worker. She'd heard the rumors but passed them off as office gossip. Sharon resisted Tom's charm, good looks, and the tales of his substantial personal assets.

Mr. Hanson's mouth fell open. "Are you smiling? I find your behavior very inappropriate."

"I'm sorry, it's just-"

Mr. Hansen pulled open his bottom desk drawer, extracted a piece of paper, and placed his reading glasses on his red, bulbous nose. Satisfied with the contents of the document, he set the memo in front of them. "Did you know that the Diocese of Duluth is one of Jennifer's clients?"

Sharon pulled at the collar of her blouse; her eyes darted towards the door. Oh, shit. What's on that letter? Did it happen to have anything to do with the Catholic Church? This wasn't good.

"Um… no, I didn't."

He smiled and patted the paper. "Insurance."

"Let's talk about another of my concerns." He leaned forward, resting his folded hands on the desk. "Tom has a weakness for women with low morals, easy targets for his charm and good looks. I'm sure you're aware of the rumor floating around the office about an affair with someone from this firm. My daughter is concerned. Like any good parent," Mr. Hanson paused, "when my daughter is concerned, I'm concerned."

"I understand." Only a couple of females work in this office; his daughter, his assistant, and the part-time high school student. "Jesus Christ! How stupid of me. You said it yourself, I'm a single mother with a checkered past. Your daughter thinks I'm the one her bastard husband is sleeping with."

"Do not use that tone with me."

"Are you for real?"

"You have the rest of the day to think about resigning. It would be best for both of us. A couple of local firms are hiring administrative assistants. You would get a good reference from the firm."

"Why would I quit? I haven't done anything wrong."

Mr. Hansen's lips curled with cruel confidence. "I have a friend who attends your AA meetings. He said you confessed that drinking and sex go hand-in-hand in your life. It's not hard to connect the dots from there."

Sharon stood. Another level of betrayal, this one in what she'd thought was a safe space. "That son of a bitch."

She stormed out of his office and slammed the door. Once out of his sight, her tears flowed, and she trembled. She stopped at her desk for her purse.

"Are you alright?" Carrie asked, her voice tinged with sarcasm.

Sharon wiped her eyes, gave Carrie a "Fuck you" smile, and left.

She searched her purse for her car keys. "Son of a bitch."

They still sat on her desk, but she couldn't go back inside.

As she contemplated what to do next, Tom's car pulled into the parking lot. She slammed her fist against the window.

Bastard.

How would she get home?

"Sharon, why are you crying?" Tom asked, walking around the back of her car. "What's going on?"

"Like you don't know. You can't keep your little boy in your pants."

"What did you say?"

"Don't play stupid with me. You know."

"I don't have a clue as to what you're talking about."

"Your father-in-law accused me of sleeping with you."

"He didn't."

"Yes, and so did your bitch wife." She jabbed her finger into his chest. "Now I'm being forced to quit because of you."

Tom raised his hands in mock surrender. "Hey, wait a minute. Can we talk about this?"

"Why the fuck should I listen to anything you have to say?"

"Give me a chance to explain." Tom gave her a disarming smile. "Over lunch?"

Sharon spun around, grabbed the door handle, and yanked. "Goddamnit."

He laid his hand on her shoulder. "Hey, I'm sorry."

Sharon stepped away from him.

"You do great work. We can't lose you."

She leaned her head against the window of her car. The wheels in her head spun. How could she get out of the giant hole she'd dug this time? Could she use Tom's weakness for easy women to her advantage? Maybe. She wiped her eyes.

"You think I do good work?"

"Yes, I do."

A plan was formed. Risky. Sharon might need to move again, but she might enjoy the rewards.

"Okay."

"Good. We need to find a way to resolve this."

Sharon chose a Mexican restaurant downtown because she wanted something spicy. As they waited for their food, Sharon asked. "Is your wife any different when she's away from the office?"

"You mean is she always a bitch?"

"I...."

"She works hard and plays hard. She doesn't like to lose. Neither do I."

"Does she know about your other women?"

"We ignore each other's deficiencies." Tom's eyes lit up. "She's not as big an asshole as her father."

"You're not fond of Mr. Hansen?"

"Hell no. Andrew likes me even less. But he puts up with me because I bill out a ton of hours and make him a shitload of money."

He exuded charm. His icy blue eyes ooze sexuality, and the rest of him melted Sharon's insides. Now she could understand why so many women took off their clothes for him. The man was exquisite. No other word could describe him. Sharon could sit all day drooling, but it was time to get to the issue at hand. "Who is it?"

Tom sat up straighter, his expression grew serious. "None of the women at work, if that's what you're asking."

"You're having an affair though. Correct?"

"Yes, nothing serious...yet."

Was it her imagination or did he just flirt? His eyes glinted with pure masculine interest. Sparks of unwanted excitement shot through her.

Oh, God.

This couldn't be happening, could it? Sharon approached dangerous territory. She only agreed to lunch so she could prove Mr. Hanson didn't control her. This complicated her chances of keeping her job. Her mind told her to run, but her body begged her to stay. She wanted to stop. No, she needed to stop her self-destructive behavior. But could she?

"Would you like to see what they have for dessert?" Tom asked, but his eyes suggested more.

What should she do? She liked the job at the law firm. Could Tom help her keep it? Maybe... with a little incentive. She uncrossed her legs and played along. "I heard the cheesecake is fabulous."

Sharon slipped off her shoe and ran her foot up his calf. Tom's eyebrows rose but he continued to talk about his new client. She feigned interest in his conversation as she fantasized about him. When dessert arrived, Tom slid closer to Sharon and fed her cheesecake. Licking the strawberry from her lips, Sharon rested her hand on his thigh.

Tom smiled. "Would you be interested in finding a motel?"

"Aren't you jumping to conclusions? I'm not that easy."

"What about a drink? Give me some time to change your mind?"

A drink would be grand, but she shouldn't. Maybe one drink to relax, no more. "A drink would be a pleasant ending to a wonderful lunch."

Even as she spoke the words, guilt hit her. She loved her daughter with all her heart, but she was tired of the responsibilities of motherhood. Sharon could only hope that one day Isabelle would understand and forgive her transgressions. She told herself that this was for both of them. She would convince Tom to save her job, and everything would work out fine. She would continue to attend her weekly AA meetings and follow all her steps. But she had needs. My God, look at him...

Tom and Sharon stopped for one drink at a college hangout they both knew. The alcohol loosened her grip on her responsibilities. Once again, the pattern of her life repeated. One drink turned into one too many, and her thoughts turned towards sex.

"Mom, he's married. Look at the ring on his finger," Isabelle shouted.

Sharon closed her eyes and tried to quiet the voice in her head. Damn her. How could Isabelle be right all the time? She shouldn't be doing this. Tom was married. Did she expect he would leave his wife and their white-picket fence for her? She took a couple of deep breaths and threw on the brakes to slow her descent into depravity. "Do you have any children?"

"No." Tom said, "You have a daughter, don't you?"

She pulled a picture from her purse. "This is my daughter Isabelle."

Tom's eyebrows rose. "Wow. She's gorgeous, like her mother."

Sharon blushed. "Thank you."

Tom finished off the last of his drink, leaned back in his seat. "How long have you been divorced?"

"Four years."

"You're originally from Northern Minnesota, aren't you?

Sharon almost spilled her drink. Did everyone know she'd been raised in Minnesota? "No, born and raised in Grand Forks."

"Oh really? Are you a college hockey fan?" He glanced at his watch. "Do you want another drink?"

Her mind blocked the advice of her conscience. "Vodka, neat."

Tom had glanced at his watch several times. Could she be missing her chance? He appeared ready to leave, with or without her. She couldn't lose another job. A gulp of vodka and she whispered, "Are you ready?"

Sharon led Tom into the parking lot by the hand. Someday Isabelle would understand the power of sex and the female body, the trump card women could play anytime.

From an early age, Sharon understood the weakness of men. A little cleavage, a twitch of her hip, soft lips, and a sexy voice procured all she wanted. No man could resist.

Isabelle's voice echoed in her head. "Do you really get what you want? How has that worked so far?"

Sharon ignored all reason. "Let's go someplace, anyplace, and get naked. Now."

# Chapter 8

"Isabelle, could you see me after class?" Ms. Dahl asked.

Sarah Erickson snickered. Isabelle's cheeks flushed. If she could slap Sarah across the face, it would bring a huge relief–maybe even a smile. Since that first day of school, the animosity between them had bubbled like lava. She'd gone out of her way to steer clear of Sarah and her friends.

Isabelle glanced at the clock. The bell would ring any moment. Her heart raced, and her hands grew slick with moisture. As the last seconds ticked away, she wiped her hands on her pants. What had she done wrong this time?

The bell chimed, announcing the end of class.

Isabelle closed her composition book and stood. Behind her, Sarah whispered something snide.

Isabelle pivoted and glared. "Leave my mother alone."

"I wasn't talking to you," Sarah said, her eyes cold, and pitiless. "If I were you, I would mind my own goddamn business."

Ms. Dahl stood at her desk, hands on her hips. "Sarah, Isabelle, do we have a problem?"

Isabelle counted to three and smiled. "No, Ms. Dahl. Sarah gave me advice on studying for tomorrow's test, that's all."

Sarah's smug expression revealed an air of conquest. "No problem here."

Isabelle neared the end of the row, her thoughts in a million places. Stepping wide of Sarah, she caught her foot on a desk and stumbled, her arms pin-wheeling in desperation. She put the brakes on, but momentum carried her forward into her teacher. They crashed, arms wrapped around each other. The instant their flesh touched; Isabelle cringed at the onslaught of information.

Noooooooo!

The scenes of Ms. Dahl's life rolled through Isabelle's mind. None of them came into focus; they moved past her eyes too fast and disappeared somewhere into the archives of her mind. Some memories settled in the dark recesses, but the pointy ends of others pushed at the edges of her conscience. Were they remembrances of the past or glimpses into Ms. Dahl's future? Isabelle wasn't sure. Her teacher's images acted differently. When Isabelle's mind reached out to grab some, the darker, scarier ones floated out of reach. As the reel of memories stopped, she could almost hear film flapping as it left the projector and see the black velvet curtains coming down onstage.

Isabelle stepped back, mortified by the experience.

A confused Ms. Dahl stared back at her. Isabelle smiled without conviction. Why had she grabbed her teacher without the protection of her gloves? Hadn't she learned her lesson with Carson? If she had pulled them out of her pocket, she could have avoided all of this.

Armed with a great deal of practice and patience, Isabelle pushed the memories into a corner. She could take her time and sort through them or ignore them. Sometimes the unwanted memories broke out and visited while she tried to fall asleep; they would pop in uninvited and nudge her until she woke. At first, it was exciting, like playing with a new toy. Over time the ability became a curse. Other people's lives depressed her.

Isabelle leaned over, hands on her knees, and trembled. She might be sick.

"Sarah, I saw what you did." Ms. Dahl said.

Sarah stopped at the door and flashed her best doe eyes. "I don't know what you mean, Ms. Dahl. What did I do? It's not my fault Isabelle's a klutz. She tripped."

"Ms. Dahl, it's my fault. I am a klutz. Sarah didn't trip me."

Before the day grew any worse, Isabelle needed to go home and disappear. "Ms. Dahl, what did you want to talk to me about?"

Sarah glared at Isabelle.

Ms. Dahl scowled, her face a mask of consternation, as Sarah left the room. With her back turned to Isabelle, Ms. Dahl sighed. "I'm so tired of that girl."

"Excuse me?"

"Hmm...Oh, right, Isabelle. Sorry, I'm distracted." Ms. Dahl opened a folder. "Are you ready for tomorrow's test?"

Isabelle gazed down at her feet. "I plan to study tonight."

Mrs. Dahl pointed to Isabelle's name on the printout. "If you would turn in these three assignments and get an A on tomorrow's test you would earn a B for the quarter." She closed the folder and clasped her hands. "Isabelle, you are not a C student; you're far from average. You're probably the most intelligent student in this class. I expected better."

Isabelle avoided eye contact. She'd let someone down yet again. She wished she cared more about school. She wished she cared about something. "Can I go?"

"Yes, you may go."

Isabelle hurried to her locker and left the building as soon as she could. She trudged home, her mind as heavy as her backpack.

Isabelle had good intentions that night. She finished the first assignment, even started the second, but her mind wandered. She worried about her mother. Would Sharon come home drunk or bring back another loser? Maybe both.

***

When stressed, Isabelle often escaped into a world of make-believe. She used her free time to write about a fairytale world of Kings, Queens, and Princesses, a land where good triumphs over evil. The previous night, absorbed in her writing, she had fallen asleep at her desk and awoke in the morning to a pool of drool and a stiff neck. She neither finished her assignments nor studied for any finals. Worst of all, the take-home portion of Ms. Dahl's history test sat untouched on her desk.

A knock on the door. "I'm leaving. Hurry up; I don't want another call at work."

Yes, Mom, everything's always about you, isn't it?

Isabelle waited until the front door closed before leaving her room. She stopped in front of the bathroom, pulled her hair back tight to her skull, and stared at her reflection. "Girl, you need to get your shit together."

She undressed and stepped into the shower, but the water brought no relief. Anxiety boiled over into frustration. She pounded on the wall. "Why...why...why?"

Isabelle had her own troubles. Why should she worry about her mother? Did her mother worry about her when she drank? The water turned cold and she stepped out.

Stress-induced short ragged breaths made Isabelle concentrate on relaxing. She tried to push away the images and thoughts in an attempt to get her feelings under control. Naked in front of the mirror, Isabelle spoke to her reflection. "Hello. My name is Isabelle and my mother is an alcoholic."

Her life revolved around that fact for as long as she could remember. Not only did her mother's alcoholism snuggle up to her at night, but it also walked like a shadow by her side every day. She couldn't deny its existence or run from it. Like a cat or dog, brother or sister, her mother's disease was part of the family. Their life resembled a roller coaster ride headed off its tracks.

"Is my mother sober today?" Isabelle asked her reflection.

Short of any answers, Isabelle left the bathroom and pushed the hangers around in her closet. An outline of the door she'd drawn remained from summer, a period of time she wished she remembered better. Trish became a tickle in the back of her mind every time she thought about her. Those thoughts quickly slipped away. A black veil moved painfully behind her eyes. She shook her head. Not today.

What kind of wrinkle could she toss into her wardrobe today? When it came to personal style, she tended to be a free spirit, not trendy like her mother. She didn't want to be pigeonholed into any of the traditional groups at school either. Isabelle wasn't a nerd or a jock, wasn't artsy (maybe artsy?), or in a band. She wanted to be her own group of one. She wasn't a loner, just enjoyed being alone.

As she dressed, a soft, sweet voice emerged from the chaos in her mind.

"Belle?"

"Trish, is that you?"

No, my lady, the Queen has partaken in too many spirits today. She's carrying a heavy burden.

"My Lady? The Queen?" Isabelle asked, puzzled by the voice. "Who are you and who is Belle?"

You do not know? The Queen understands your concerns and wishes you not to worry.

Isabelle caught a glimpse of a face in her dresser mirror, a face she should recognize. But the image disappeared before she could make sense of it.

"Did you leave me?" Isabelle asked. The specter tugged at her memory. As she laced up her black boots, she found the girl behind the voice, hidden in the corners of her mind.

# Chapter 9

Isabelle glanced at the clock. She could not spare any more time to identify the voice. Not on the last day of the quarter. If she didn't hurry, she would be late for the third time this grading period. Not only would she get detention, but the office would call her mom at work. Not a good idea—her mother had warned her in no simple terms. She grabbed her jacket and hurried out the door. Her mind raced with endless possibilities and the consequences of what she had experienced earlier.

The things the voice said left her confused, empty, and betrayed. Her mother would never change. Once a drunk, always a drunk. How could Sharon do this to her again so soon after she had relapsed? Isabelle shook her head. Did she have the strength to relive another nightmare? At sixteen, she was too young to be her mother's keeper. Tears of disappointment dripped down her reddened cheeks.

Her feet pounded the pavement, Isabelle reached the doors moments before the janitor locked them. Her fingers stung when she grabbed the cold metal door handle. She searched the pockets of her jacket and pants but found no gloves. Not good. Isabelle needed to be extra careful; she didn't want any more intrusions into her world. The janitor held the door open. "The bell's going to ring any second. Better hurry."

She slid around the first corner. After regaining traction, Isabelle sped down the hall. Laughter echoed all around the door to her homeroom.

She peered down both ends of the hallway. Not a soul in sight. She sat down at her desk just as the final bell rang.

Giggle.

The sound came from inside of her.

A torrent of voices, only some of them familiar, filled her mind to overflowing and pushed at the boundaries of her self-control. Many belonged to those she labeled as "the Others"; people who didn't understand how much their words hurt. The why or how of the Others left her confused. Their voices expressed dark, violent thoughts; the ones she feared the most. Ever since her sixteenth birthday, the mysterious utterances became more aggressive and more frequent visitors.

Your mother is drunk again!

Hehehehe, hehehehe!

Isabelle did not want to listen, but her mind acted like a radio; the stations tuned into other people's thoughts. The volume of the giggling, barbs, and taunts were never louder than a whisper. The harder she tried to ignore the sounds and words, the more pointed they became, like a hornet's nest inside her skull. Pressure built behind her eyes. The progression never changed, first the headache then the voices. What did it all mean? Insanity or something worse?

She tried to relax, to take measured breaths, but her body would not respond.

Relax, Isabelle, concentrate. Find your calm, quiet place.

All her tricks failed. The voices continued gnawing at the edges of her sanity, trying to break down her resolve.

You're a worthless piece of shit, just like your mother.

Her father loved words that stung.

Spread your legs, little girl.

One of her mom's drunken friends slurred vulgarities.

Isabelle twisted her fingers in her hair. Stop, please stop.

Slut, slut, slut...

The dark and violent voices wanted to send her into the abyss of utter chaos. They wanted her to give into the darkness that haunted her. Isabelle fought to stay in control, grabbing her head and covering her ears.

"No more!"

Isabelle searched for a calm pool; the soothing waters that helped filter the noises, her place to hide until the torment receded. A scream crawled up her throat. She was ready to admit defeat and give the voices what they wanted—her sanity. To let the blackness in her soul take over. They wanted her to be broken, just like her mother.

The bell rang, and the other students filed out. Isabelle sat up straighter and glanced around. Why was everyone leaving? Perhaps a fire drill? How could she have missed an entire class period?

Mr. Harris watched as she rose from her chair. "Are you alright?" he asked.

She managed a weak smile and pushed open the door. She only had five minutes to figure out what she would do next. The din of the hallway exploded inside her skull. She headed toward study hall, but instead of working on her take-home test for Ms. Neely, she would hide out in the quiet of the library; she would try to restore some sanity. She'd finish her test at lunch.

"Yes," Isabelle whispered when she walked into the library. Nobody sat at the front desk.

At the back of the library, a seldom-used small study room stood open. Isabelle made a bee-line to the door and slipped inside. Her pain reached ten, and she struggled to form rational thoughts. "Oh God, please help me." She placed her cheek on the cold table and closed her eyes.

"Freyja...Freyja.

Her mother's handmaiden scampered up the stairs to where Isabelle waited. The two of them were close in age, constant companions, and, most of all, friends. Belle stood in her mother's study, holding an empty wine glass in her hands.

"Yes, Belle."

Belle showed Freyja the wine glass. "Is my mother drinking again?"

"Yes, she is."

"Why?"

"Since the King has been gone, the Queen has many burdens placed upon her shoulders."

Belle paced the room. "She cannot be trusted when she's drinking."

"She understands your concerns."

"Does she really?" Belle glared at her friend. "Where is she?"

Freyja's downcast eyes told Belle all she needed to know.

Belle stormed out of the study and headed straight to the stables. She would find her mother and talk some sense into her. The King would be home soon, and he could not find out about the Queen's drinking.

"Fun time is over," one of the voices said.

***

Isabelle rubbed her eyes and lifted her head from the table, uncertain why she wasn't in the library anymore. The last of the students filed out of the lunchroom. Her food and her test sat untouched. Her head no longer threatened to explode, but a sense of lethargy wiped her out. If she could just lay her head down for a few more minutes, everything would be better.

***

The loud ringing bell pulled Isabelle back from her trance. She blinked several times, trying to refocus on the now. The surroundings let her know this was her seventh-period history class, and that ringing bell had been the last of the day. Had she sleep-walked her way through the afternoon? Her uncompleted final test sitting on her desk seemed to mock her.

"Oh shit," Isabelle muttered.

"Pencils down and pass your tests forward," Ms. Dahl said.

The class groaned in unison. Sweat sprang from Isabelle's pores. She met her teacher's gaze and cringed as she passed the test to Sarah. Isabelle hoped Sarah would listen to her own advice and mind her own business.

Didn't Sarah have bad days? Isabelle did not think so. With beautiful hair, trendy clothes, and the most popular friends, Sarah and her life appeared flawless. Why did Sarah get spoon-fed the perfect life when hers sucked? Unable to find an answer, Isabelle grabbed her book bag and headed for the door.

"Have a great weekend," Ms. Dahl said.

Sarah looked at Isabelle's blank test and smirked. "Aced! How did you do? What's your excuse this time, Is-a-belle? Drinking with your mother again? I know, you spent the night in the backseat, with your legs spread. Rent is due, isn't it?"

The students remaining in the room all laughed.

"Hit the bitch, smash her in the face!" the voices said in unison.

Isabelle didn't want to give them the satisfaction of seeing her cry, but angry tears fell anyway. She pictured her fingers wrapped in Sarah's hair, pounding her face against the desk until no longer perfect. Smashed again and again until pools of blood and gray matter splattered the floor.

"Please shut up. Please leave my mom alone."

"Are you talking to me?" Sarah said.

"Do it now, I know you want to," the violent voice teased.

"What...what have I done to you?" Isabelle's mind misfired, tiny explosions behind her eyes, like Black Cat firecrackers on a 4th of July evening.

Isabelle, you chicken shit. You better run or Sarah will kick your ass.

A sheen of sweat covered Isabelle's forehead. Her eyes pleaded with Sarah to stop. She stumbled and grabbed Sarah's bare shoulder for support. Before she pushed her way past, Isabelle leaned close to Sarah's ear and whispered, "I know everything."

"How dare you push me, you freak. Ms. Dahl?"

"Sarah, enough already. I warned you yesterday about your behavior." Ms. Dahl picked up the phone and spoke into the receiver.

Sarah regarded Ms. Dahl with a look of disbelief before glaring at Isabelle. But typical Sarah, she managed a fake smile and said, "Sorry, no hard feelings."

"I called the office. I've had enough of you and your friends," Mrs. Dahl said, giving Sarah her best knock-this-shit-off look. "Isabelle, are you alright?"

Isabelle's eyes never left her shoes. "It's been another craptastic day."

She left the room, scanned the lockers, and headed towards one of the side doors.

"Way to fuck with her," one of the dark voices said, then burst into hysterical laughter.

Isabelle shrugged. Why couldn't she keep her big mouth shut? She usually avoids confrontations at all costs. Another encounter with Sarah and her friends would be unfortunate. She slipped outside—unnoticed, she hoped—only to be greeted by the foul mood of Mother Nature.

Gray clouds, heavy with precipitation, raced overhead. A biting fall Minnesota wind met her head on. The cold, stinging gusts made her eyes water and her nostrils stick together. She tried to piece together everything that had happened. Before she could take her second step, someone behind her pushed her down the last two steps. She fell on her right wrist; a spark of pain shot up her arm. Sarah stood above, her mouth curled with hatred.

"Did you think I didn't hear you?" Sarah's hands balled into fists. "What did you mean when you said, 'I know everything?'"

A voice in Isabelle's head answered for her. "You like fucking your uncle."

Isabelle shook her head in disbelief, a look of bewilderment plastered across her face. She pushed herself to her knees, grabbed the bike rack with two hands, and winced from the pain in her wrist. Her stomach clenched tight like a fist and she dry-heaved onto the sidewalk, staggering upright. Pressure built in her head as a headache moved from behind her eyes to attain a vise-like grip on her temples. Her knees buckled and she stumbled forward. Her foot caught on the bike rack and she fell to her knees. She scraped her palms on the rough cement, tearing a new hole in her jeans.

"Did you have a nice trip?" someone in the crowd yelled.

Isabelle groaned. "Sarah, why are you doing this? I didn't say anything!"

Who does your mom have in her bed today?

"You lying bitch," Sarah said, a little braver with a crowd behind her. "I'm the one person in this school you do not want to fuck with." Her eyes gleaming with vengeance, she drew back her leg to kick Isabelle. When Isabelle flinched, Sarah laughed.

"If you knew everything, you would be scared shitless. You're a welfare brat, and your mom is a drunken whore." Sarah turned towards the crowd that had gathered to watch the fight and chuckled. "By the appearance of your clothes, your mom can't be much of a whore."

Isabelle ignored her jeering peers, stood, and brushed herself off. She closed her eyes and took a few slow, deep breaths to steady her nerves.

Time to leave. She tried to zip up her jacket—a thrift store special—but the zipper caught.

She has a bottle of vodka on the table, and it's almost gone.

Isabelle would show the voices they were wrong. Her mother wouldn't be home.

Isabelle moved down the sidewalk, one small step at a time, balancing her head carefully upon her shoulders. If she walked too fast, her head would explode. The heavy rain turned into a November sleet and rain mixture. She stuck her hands deeper into her pockets and plodded home.

Step after step, block after block, an inexplicable, unnamed uneasiness returned. Her pace increased, her adrenaline level rose, and fear of the unknown writhed in her stomach. Isabelle crossed the railroad tracks, then jogged.

"Mom, I'm coming."

A fog enveloped her, twisting and swirling inside her head. She ran faster in an attempt to escape. The faster she ran, the thicker the cloud became, until it caught her, and she fell into the darkness.

# Chapter 10

An Excerpt from Isabelle's Composition Books

Princess Belle sprinted from the castle. She mounted her horse, Ghost, a dappled gray gelding, and raced through the meadows, heading south to search for her mother, the Queen.

What caused her mother to start drinking again? Her father warned his wife, the next time she became melancholy, he would send her back to the convent. The Queen would wither and die in such a sterile environment.

Belle pulled up on the reins. Ghost obeyed, but he pranced in a tight circle and fought her for control. On the open ground, he wanted to run. She patted his neck with assurance. "Soon," she whispered.

A lone rider approached, a growing speck on the horizon. One of her father's guards was sent to spy on her. Who else would be out here? She scanned the landscape. The perfect place to lose him would be in the forest. She turned Ghost's head westward and squeezed his side with her legs. She clicked her tongue. "Let's go."

Ghost plunged into the forest. The trees flew by; branches poked and scraped against her back, almost knocking her out of her saddle. Her eyes closed; exuberance bubbled to the surface. She couldn't contain her laughter. Her body became one with Ghost. She kept her head down and let Ghost pick his own path. Moments like this, she became invincible. They headed deeper into the western forest.

A quarter of an hour later, Belle slowed Ghost to a walk. She dropped to the ground and led him to a small stream where they both quenched their thirst. With the guard left behind, her attention turned back to thoughts of her mother. The Queen hadn't ridden south; she used that as a ploy to lose the guard. Her mother went north of the Keep. Like her mother, Princess Belle didn't follow orders well either.

Her father, the King, warned Belle against riding north of the castle. Evil lived in the dark and foreboding woods, he said. She also needed to stay away from the coast with its churning waters and huge, unpredictable waves.

Was the north a place of evil? Outlandish tales of trolls and dragons filtered into the village, but who could trust the drunken fools spouting such gibberish? Beware the north wind, the priests warned; it carried evil to all points of the compass. She didn't believe any of that nonsense. Other than the King and his men, travelers seldom ventured farther north than the Forks. Nobody knew for sure what lay hidden in the frozen northlands. Isabelle wasn't scared by the tales, and she wished her father wouldn't worry. Trained by his best horseman, Belle could out-ride most men.

Ghost's ears flickered, and he nudged Isabelle. She touched the hilt of her sword as she scanned the trees. Nothing appeared out of place. Could it be the King's guard that Ghost sensed? Maybe they didn't lose him? He wouldn't be the first guard she bamboozled. Belle and Ghost could disappear into thin air. Belle closed her eyes and wished her father would stop punishing those she eluded. Even a couple lashes from his whip were too many. He could be cruel.

Belle fed Ghost a handful of oats from her saddlebag. She adjusted his blanket and cinched the saddle tighter. Now rested, they needed to move on before the guard picked up her trail.

Belle continued her sojourn north in search of her mother. She and Ghost picked their way around bogs and deadfalls. The farther north they progressed, the slower their pace. At the edge of the forest, she dismounted and led Ghost out. The air was thick with the briny smell of the sea. The waves echoed as they crashed against the cliffs. How could they be so far off course? A picture of a dark fissure in the rocks flashed in her mind; a black mouth which swallowed her dreams. The same image burned into her brain over the past few weeks. An actual memory or a hallucination? She wasn't sure anymore and didn't care. She was close to finding what haunted her dreams. Pulled towards the coast by an invisible string, her mother's plight temporarily forgotten, she followed her instinct. She ran her fingers through Ghost's mane and smiled. "I think we've found it."

She dropped to the ground and hobbled Ghost. She wrapped her arms around her horse, ordering him to stay. As she walked away, he neighed, pawing at the ground. Belle's shadow, the young handmaiden, would be there waiting for her. Belle never once lost Freyja. She knew where Belle would be before Belle did and, as predicted, Freyja stood at the top of the cliff, at the edge of the forest, and watched.

Belle waved.

Zigzagging down a steep, moss-covered slope peppered with loose stones, Belle made her way to the dark cave below. If she lost her balance, she would fall to the sea; its icy waves crashed against the jagged rocks guarding the entrance. The trek to the cave below, though it hinted of danger, held profound implications. Why did an unseen force want her to find it?

A large swell broke against the rocks, sending a chilling spray over Belle and dampening her head and brown wool tunic. She shook the seawater from her hair. The air crackled with magic. The electricity of anticipation surged through her veins. As she stared at the rocks below, a massive wave crashed behind her. She turned too quickly to avoid the brunt of the swell and lost her footing. She grasped at the loose stones searching for a handhold, but her cold, wet fingers could not find any. Her heart raced as she slid to the edge. Rocks and pebbles rained down on the sea and her booted feet dangled in the air.

"I have you, my Lady," said Freyja, getting a firm hold of Belle's shoulders and stopping her descent.

Belle found leverage with her legs and, with Freyja's help, settled on solid ground. She knelt on the path, her arms and legs weak, her forehead pressed against the rocks. If Freyja hadn't been there, they never would have found her body.

"You need to be more careful, my Lady. The Queen would not be happy if you were swallowed by the sea."

"Thank you! How did you know I needed your help?"

"We need to hurry. The King is on his way back, and we need to warn your mother."

"My father is not supposed to be back for another week. How do you know he will be back so soon?"

Freyja only smiled and started the climb back up the path to where their horses waited. Isabelle's mind struggled with too many unanswered questions. She couldn't keep up with the sure-footed handmaiden. "Wait. Freyja, wait."

Out of breath, she caught Freyja at the top and grabbed her by the shoulder. "I command you. Stop."

"Yes, Princess Belle."

"I asked you a question. Why is the King on his way back?"

"He found what he was searching for," she said, then climbed on her horse and headed back into the forest.

Belle mounted Ghost with a quick leap. She snapped the reins, Ghost bolted, and the chase began. Freyja was more than her mother's handmaiden; she was an enigma. Someone who baffled Isabelle. Just when she caught sight of the entrance to the cave, the cave which filled her mind with so many questions, Freya kept her from it. Why? Urging Ghost on, they closed the gap. She wanted answers.

To the north, the sky darkened. Clouds gathered in a towering display of fury. Exiting the forest, Freyja stopped and gazed north. She sniffed the air, dismounted, and knelt on the forest floor, her hands buried in the dark, damp earth. She pressed her fist to her mouth, remounted, and kicked her horse forward. As they neared the village, Freyja broke the silence. "The King will be back before dark. Go find the Queen. Do not judge her tonight. She needs you, as her daughter."

Belle dismounted as Freyja rode away. A heavy sigh escaped. She snatched the reins and walked to the royal stables. Just like Ghost, her unanswered questions followed. As she stepped through the double doors of the stable, Freyja's words finally sunk in. "Do not judge her!"

"Mother, what have you done?"

Belle turned and ran blindly through the darkened village, following the worn paths. Her mind wrapped around Freyja's words, she didn't see the cat until she tripped over it and sprawled headfirst into an old woman. They crashed to the ground in a heap.

The old woman leered at Belle, her mouth full of rotten stumps and gums leaking green pus. Belle grimaced; the old woman's foul breath, smelling like decomposed fish, circled her head like a vulture and lingered on her skin even after they separated. The crone's gnarled, knobby fingers clawed at Belle's legs as she tried to stand. Belle stepped backward, suddenly afraid.

The crone muttered obscenities until she found her cane, then struggled to her feet. The amulet around Belle's neck seemed fair payment for the inconvenience. She grabbed the jewel and cackled. "Your mother's lust is uncontrollable. She ruts in bed like a common whore."

The old woman grabbed her bag. She held out her hand and the cat that Belle tripped over leaped into her arms. She pointed north where lightning riddled the dark, ragged clouds. "Do you smell it?"

Belle turned north. "Smell what?"

"Evil," she hissed. "It will be among us soon."

Familiar laughter filled the air. Belle turned toward the sound, trying to confirm its identity when two strong hands pushed her.

"Evil is already here," she thought as she sprawled headfirst in front of the oncoming wagon.

# Chapter 11

S lush sprayed Isabelle's face. The oncoming traffic ground to a halt. Tires squealed; horns bleated. A driver, the one who came within inches of ending her life, leaned out the window and shouted, "Are you crazy? Do you want to get yourself killed?"

Isabelle peered over her shoulder at the empty sidewalk. She recalled the hands on her back. Who pushed her? Someone should be standing right there or running away. She scrambled to her feet.

The driver stepped out of his car. "Are you alright?"

She gave him a sheepish smile and crossed the street amid the chorus of horns and catcalls. What the hell happened? How stupid could she be?

Isabelle's nerves calmed. With each step closer to home, she pushed the voices deeper inside. She sat down at the bus stop in front of Romke Park. Her home was around the corner– three minutes max. Did she really want to know? The more she thought about why her mother might be home, the heavier the sinking feeling in her stomach grew.

The sleet transformed into giant wet snowflakes and drifted down like fluffy cotton balls. Isabelle couldn't resist. She wasn't a child anymore, but she still caught one, only one, with her tongue.

But she wasn't an adult either. Life requires choices. Could Isabelle help her mother quit drinking, again? Running away and starting fresh would be easier, but where could she go? Would her father and his new wife welcome her, or would they send her home? It didn't matter. She lowered her head and waited for the next bus to somewhere, anyplace, away from this misery. Would her mother even notice her gone?

Darkness descended on the park. The snow now covered the brown fall grass with irregular spots of gray. The uneasiness of Isabelle's solitude scared her. No one played on the empty basketball courts. The basket's stanchions cast long dark shadows that appeared to be creeping closer. The leaves, which only days before had danced and skipped along the ground, were piled up like bodies, stuck harshly against the fence, collecting the newly fallen snow. The pool, bleak and stark against the winter sky, had closed months ago. Children's laughter no longer filled the air. The bones of the park had been picked clean of happiness.

"Quit it, Isabelle." She wiped her arm across her face. "No more tears."

Enough was enough. Isabelle sat up straighter. Judging the time to be close to four-thirty, she guessed the next bus would arrive soon. The traffic hypnotized her. The black wheels went around and around. The tires slipped and sliced through the wet snow, spraying the slush halfway onto the boulevard. A cloud of diesel fumes announced the arrival of the bus. This was it, her chance to escape.

***

Carson squirmed from his parents, edging closer to the window. Isabelle sat at the bus stop, her gaze far away. Bleakness radiated from her in waves. She planned to do something drastic, find a way to disappear. Or something worse. Give into the darkness.

Carson fogged the glass with his breath. As his fingers encircled the amulet he wore around his neck, he mouthed a silent prayer. In hushed tones, he recited the words and drew in the condensation, the runes he needed to stop Isabelle from leaving

"Boy, are you listening to me?" John's large hand swiped the glass clean. "Enough of this shit. Didn't you learn your lesson?"

Carson had skipped school so he could spend the day researching the next step in his project. The school contacted Opal, who tracked down John. They traveled to the public library and made a big scene. Since he had been assigned as Isabelle's Watcher, he was on his third set of foster parents, and he hated this pair the most. Horrible human beings.

The bus passengers stood, crammed in the aisles like cattle, reeking of loneliness and desperation. With a whoosh, the bus doors opened. Isabelle stood at the bottom of the steps, ready to board.

He was flanked by his foster monster, an obese, greasy-haired, disagreeable woman, and John, the biological father of two of Opal's five children. Carson's foster parents grabbed his shoulders. Knuckles white, clutching a handful of his jacket, they dragged him down the steps.

Carson allowed himself to be manhandled. He hoped Isabelle worried about his well-being instead of her own, forgetting the reason she wanted to flee: Sharon

Isabelle's eyes meet his. "Carson, what's going on? Hey, you're hurting him."

"Mind your own business, bitch!" John said.

Opal gave Isabelle a distressed look. "Stay away from Carson. You filled his head with enough garbage about books and magic. He needs to live in the real world."

John tightened his grip on Carson's arm. "Are you just stupid?"

Carson's eyes grew wide as he felt Isabelle's world begin to spin.

***

"Isabelle, your dad is at the door," Robin's mom said.

Isabelle gulped in a mouth full of air. "My dad is here?"

Robin nodded.

Isabelle squeezed her eyes shut and recited a short prayer. Her father leaned against the front door, his posture rigid, his eyes a vicious glint.

She forced a smile. "Robin, thank you for inviting me to play. I had a lot of fun."

"Come back soon."

"I will."

Isabelle and her father stepped outside and as the door closed behind them, he grabbed her and dragged her down the steps

"Are you just stupid?" he asked her.

He pushed her into the front seat and tossed her bike in the back. Isabelle rubbed her arm; the outline of his fingers glowed red. She cringed when he slammed the door. Robin and her mom stared out the window with pity-filled eyes. Would Isabelle ever get to go back and play? She didn't think so

On the ride home, her father remained silent. Not a good sign. The longer he brooded, the greater the explosion. What did she do wrong this time? She had written a note telling him where she had gone.

"Isabelle." Anger distorted his face. "How can you be so consistently stupid? How many times do I have to tell you to lock the house when you leave?" With each word, he slammed his fist on the steering wheel. "How...many...times...."

She flinched as each thump reverberated inside the cab, though venting his anger now would help.

"Somebody could have stolen my new stereo. If you keep being so fucking stupid, you'll never amount to anything."

Isabelle slumped against the seat. She was stupid, but not enough to let her dad see her cry. Tears would give him an excuse to take out the belt.

"Dad, I'm sorry for being so stupid."

"You'll get your ass into the house and spend the night in your room. No supper. No lights. No books."

She spent the night at her desk and wrote until the lines on the paper blurred. She kept asking herself how she could have forgotten to lock the door, but no answer would have mattered. Worn out and finally sleepy, she slid her journal under the mattress and crawled into bed.

A few hours later something woke Isabelle. A search of her room turned up nothing out of the ordinary. No strangers or ghosts lurking in the shadows. She listened to the creak of the house, the whisper of the wind against her window.

The grandfather clock chimed, and she whispered, "One, two, three. Three a.m."

The muffled sound of a car door interrupted. Was her mother finally home? The front door slammed. Her mother usually didn't make a sound when she came back from work. Couldn't be her.

Heavy footsteps resounded throughout the house. Someone slammed down the phone receiver. More heavy footsteps, each step angrier. Her father's shadow paused in her doorway. She pretended to be asleep. His presence dominated her room; his anger palpable, alive, and raw. He hovered at the edge of her bed. She bit her lip, a scream clutched in her throat. She pulled her legs in tight and willed her body to be still. The tension built. The entire house seemed to be holding its breath, waiting for her mother to get home.

It seemed like hours before her dad left her room. She sucked down a quick breath.

Oh God, she needed to pee.

Isabelle struggled to fall back asleep, but time slowed, and every sound in the house amplified. Each noise outside became a car door opening and every scraping sound a key in a lock. The seconds turned into minutes, and the grandfather clock kept ticking.

The clock struck four.

Her father no longer stomped around the house, but she could taste his venom and hear his muttering. He never liked Mom working, especially at night. Isabelle anticipated a huge fight, a battle more prominent than the last few. She didn't know if she could take any more shouting or the harsh words they flung at each other. If she had only remembered the rules, the ones she always forgot.

Relief surged through Isabelle when a key turned in the front door lock. This had to be her mother, but the commotion she made bumping into the walls several times was not a good sign. She was drunk, again. Isabelle could picture her father sitting on the couch, ready to pounce.

"Where have you been?" The calm tone of her father's voice worried Isabelle.

"Where have I been?"

"Yes! Where have you been? Do you know what time it is?"

"I'm not sure. We had a couple of drinks after we closed."

"The fuck you did."

"What do you mean?"

"I drove by the restaurant, and your car wasn't there! Where did you go?"

"We went to Deb's."

"Do not walk away from me when I'm talking to you," her father warned.

"Ouch! That hurts, let go of me."

"Who were you with?"

"Let go of me. I don't have to explain shit to you!"

"Were you with Brad?"

"No."

Isabelle covered her ears. Paralyzed with fear, her words of protest dribbled down her chin. She didn't know if she could hold her pee much longer. She squeezed her legs tighter together. A loud crash reverberated outside her room, and the door flew open. Her father held her mother by the throat, their faces pressed close together.

"You lying bitch!"

Her mother laughed. "Do you really want to know what I was doing?"

He slammed her into the wall. "Whore!"

He raised a fist to strike her, and she laughed louder.

He turned towards Isabelle. "Do you see what a drunken whore your mother is?"

Isabelle couldn't manage sound, just tears, and she didn't care if her dad saw them. If only she could disappear.

Her mother stepped in front of him. "Yes, I was with Brad. Is that what you want to know?"

"Shut up! Shut up!" Her father threw his wife on the floor in front of Isabelle's bed.

He drew back his arm again. Would he hit her this time?

Her mother twisted on the floor and moaned.

"Enough!" The effort it took to scream the word released Isabelle's bladder. No time for shame, she had to find a way to stop her father.

"Sharon? You okay?" He'd unclenched his fist. "I didn't mean to push you so hard."

To hell with the consequences, Isabelle jumped between them. Glaring at her father, eyes full of hate, she wrapped her arms around her mother.

She had chosen a side.

***

Isabelle sat with her head bowed. Carson craned his neck to keep her in sight, but his foster parents yanked him away. At the end of the block, they let go of his jacket and pushed him forward. They bickered the rest of the way home. Accusations of poor parenting spilled forth. Carson chuckled at the irony but ignored most of the conversation, concentrating on Isabelle's state of mind. He probed her thoughts and whispered words of encouragement into her subconscious.

Carson recognized Sharon's car in the street. The sight of a fancy sports car sent chills through his veins. He needed a closer look to explain his reaction. His skin prickled as he drew near. Then the smell hit him. The rotting stench of death knocked him backward. Sharon entertained one of the King's Black Cloaks, and Isabelle needed to be warned.

He began his sprint across the street.

"What the hell do you think you're doing?" John said, grabbing his arm. "Get your ass home."

Carson jerked to a stop and yanked his arm free. "Let go of me."

John blocked his path. "Are you deaf? I said, get your ass inside. I won't tell you again."

Carson had other ways to warn Isabelle. He hurried into their apartment and went straight to his room.

# Chapter 12

"Hey, are you getting on?" the bus driver asked.

Isabelle rubbed her eyes and glanced around. "Are you talking to me?"

He nodded.

The last thing she remembered was Carson's haunted eyes begging for assistance. She'd seen that frightened look before, not just in Carson and the children she babysat, but in her own mirror. The eyes of an unloved child whose family had disintegrated; the children who blamed themselves for their parents not loving them. They shouldered this burden alone. If parents really loved their children, why did so many put them through hell?

She searched her pocket for her bus pass and shrugged. Fate had intervened. She wasn't going anywhere but home. The bus driver closed the door, muttering something about wasting his time, and the bus pulled away from the stop.

Her mother needed her. Chin down and mind determined, she hurried the next few blocks. Every step closer, her mood darkened, her thoughts entertained violence.

In front of the house, two vehicles sat bumper to bumper—her mom's and an expensive black sports car.

"God damn you, Mom."

Her mother promised to get her life together. What excuse would she use this time? What would she buy Isabelle to smooth things over?  Another bribe to win her love? She stopped in front of the door. Do I really care anymore? She pushed the door open.

Kill them both; be rid of your mother once and for all!

"Get a knife and stab and stab!"

"Isabelle, be careful!" A different voice resonated in her head, but she didn't have time to think about it.

A half-empty vodka bottle sat on the kitchen counter mocking her. Reality flickered then popped like a burnt-out light bulb. The darkness gained entrance and took control of her body. Isabelle hid in the corner of her mind and waited for this to be over.

She scanned the kitchen, smiling when she spotted the right drawer. She yanked and tossed the drawer to the ground, rummaging until she found the biggest knife. Grabbing the whetstone, she ran the blade across its surface several times. She inspected the edge, satisfied with its sharpness. She squared her shoulders and headed to the hallway. Her mother's bedroom door opened and out walked the most gorgeous man her mother had ever brought home. For a split second, a black mist swirled around him, obscuring his features. Darkness hid behind his brilliant eyes. He strode towards her wearing tented boxers and a smile.

"Welcome home, Belle. We've been waiting a long time for your return."

She stared in disbelief. "Who are you?"

"Someone you hate. Something you crave."

What has the King's Dark Cloak done to the Queen?

Isabelle tried to clear her thoughts. She wanted to run away, but instead, she stood frozen. He grabbed her hand. His touch sent tendrils of horror and shameful lust pulsating through her body. She pulled away, the spell broken, and staggered backward. His nasty smile brought her back to earth.

"Don't you touch me! Ever!" Isabelle gripped the knife tighter.

"Do you want to touch me like your mother does?" He licked his lips and grabbed his crotch. "I promise you'll enjoy it as much as she does."

Isabelle jabbed at him with the knife, nicking his thigh. A bead of blood trickled down his leg. He touched the spot gingerly and brought the bloody finger to his mouth. "A little too close for comfort, my dear." His smile faded. "Put the knife down before you hurt yourself."

Isabelle swung the knife at his chest. He staggered backward to avoid the blow.

"Don't make this harder than it has to be."

"I'm not like my mother!"

The man sprang forward. Sidestepping him with the grace of a swordsman, she backhanded him across the face. The blow brought color to his cheek.

"Well done, Princess Belle. They taught you well," the man said, his voice steady.

Who taught me what? And what the hell did I just do? The man made no sense. "Why are you doing this?"

"We have plans for you."

"Plans?"

Isabelle slipped further into the dark, violent place. If she stayed much longer, she would kill this man. Maybe her mother too. She took a couple steps towards the door. "This is your last warning. Go now and leave my mother alone."

"I haven't finished enjoying her."

"If you don't leave, I will kill you."

He chuckled. "You can run away, but no matter where you run or hide, we will find you."

Isabelle. Leave. Now.

Stabbing pain shot through her brain. Isabelle slammed the door on her way out. As she ran a voice in her head laughed, and fear tore through her veins like the hot touch of the devil.

***

Carson had pulled open the curtain and watched as Isabelle appeared at the end of the block. An aura of blackness ringed her head.

"Isabelle." Had she heard him? "Isabelle, be careful."

She hesitated before entering the house, then let the door shut behind her. Carson rubbed his neck and watched. With the Black Cloak inside, he needed to make sure she stayed safe. He wanted to go across the street and verify, but John blocked the doorway.

"Where the fuck do you think you're going?"

"Isabelle's."

"The hell you are."

Carson flinched and went back to the window, hoping to find a different way.

"This can't be good," he said as Bob's green sedan squealed to a stop at the end of the block. The man with the scar jumped out, followed by Bob. They opened the rear passenger door. An otherworldly creature of darkness and shadows rolled out. Its features swam in front of Carson's eyes. He could not identify what kind of Wight it might be, but every inch of his body screamed a warning. His soul shivered in fear.

A staff appeared in the creature's hands. Whispers pulsated from its mouth. The wretched being raised its arms, and a dark mist billowed from its sleeves. The fog expanded and slid along the ground. A tendril wrapped around Bob's ankle slithered up his pant leg, and encircled his torso. The murkiness snaked into Bob's mouth, choking off his scream. His eyes bulged, blood poured from his nose, and his face turned ghost white. The Wight left Bob in a withered, lifeless heap. The man with the scar pulled a short sword from his belt. The darkness circled his feet but advanced no further.

The cloud drifted down the block, covering everything in a murky twilight. Residents walked by as if they couldn't see the creature. Most stepped over Bob and kept moving. As the Wight approached Carson's apartment, a profound silence filled his room. The air inside cooled, the window pane rippled. Outside, phantasms danced in the darkness. Threads of the mist sought an entrance. Carson needed to hurry. If he succumbed to the spell cast by the Wight, no one could protect Isabelle. His mind raced for a solution.

He pulled books from the hidden space in his closet, quickly paging through the Table of Contents. Not finding what he needed, he slammed the book on his desk in frustration.

On the brown grass outside Carson's apartment, the Wight's thin, long fingers drew in the air. Straight, thick black lines materialized in the outline of a door.

Isabelle! Leave. Now.

Isabelle had rushed out of her house, a knife clutched in her hand, the creature flicked its wrist, and the door swung open, a dark void directly in Isabelle's path. Two large black birds burst forth and headed straight toward her. If Carson didn't react, Isabelle would be lost. The last words his mother said before the Dark Ones killed her filled his head. "The fatal curse of magic: for every reward, there is great loss."

Isabelle was worth it.

He pulled his violin from under his bed, drawing the bow across the strings until a heart-piercing beautiful tone filled his room.

Isabelle slowed to a stop. The open door beckoned. The two large black birds swooped down, talons ready. She turned towards Carson's second-floor window, her head cocked.

"Follow the music," Carson said, projecting the sound into her backyard.

Isabelle followed the sound toward the back of her house, her body fading with each step until she vanished.

A hideous wail filled the air. The Wight's ice-blue eyes glared in Carson's direction. The window to his room exploded. Carson turned and covered his face, but a few of the deadly missiles pierced his arms. A frigid wind blew through, coating his room in a thin layer of frost. The two blackbirds studied him through his missing window, then with a flap of their wings, they flew into the dark void of the door.

Something worse than death would visit him soon.

# Chapter 13

Sharon sat up in bed and reached for her cigarettes. Her breasts spilled from underneath the sheet, which Tom eyed with lust. Her drink on the nightstand, empty except for a couple half-melted ice cubes, needed refilling. And where were her matches? Didn't matter. She needed vodka more than a light.

"Tom, could you be a sweetheart and get me another drink?" she asked, an unlit cigarette dangling from the corner of her mouth. "We left the bottle on the kitchen counter."

Tom grinned. "I was good, wasn't I?"

Sharon smiled and placed her hand on his thigh. "I'm thirsty." She jiggled her glass. "Hurry back."

Tom snorted. "I was good." His feet tangled in the rumpled blankets, he lost his balance, tottered, and fell to the floor.

Sharon laughed at his clumsiness. Tom pushed himself to his feet and pulled on his silk boxers, covering up that perfect ass. His gaze caressed her body from head to toe until she blushed. Sharon shuddered and sighed as he turned away and left the room. How could a man built like a Greek God be manipulated so easily?

Sharon gazed down at her slightly sagging breasts. When did that happen? Even if they were no longer perfect, they still caught men's attention, didn't they? She lifted them up and together, and sighed as she released them. Why was time so cruel to a woman's body? She lit her cigarette and inhaled deeply.

Sharon took a couple more puffs, snuffed the butt out in the ashtray, and rested her head on the pillows piled against the headboard. Sleep came nudging in among her thoughts, but she perked up when Tom returned with two glasses of vodka.

Her body ached for more of his touch. Would he be ready for more? The front door slammed as he handed her the drink.

Sharon glanced at the clock. "Oh my God." She tossed Tom's clothes at him. "Get dressed. Isabelle's home."

"No, she just left."

"What…you let her see you like that?"

"Like what?"

"Are you kidding?" Sharon raised her arms, palms up. "Virtually naked and …." She shook her head.

Tom took a long swallow of his vodka. "Aroused, yes, but you should have seen the look on her face as she stared at my manhood. Your daughter drooled."

"You son of a bitch, she's only sixteen." Everything made sense now. Tom had lied to her about the affair at the office. "You're fucking our high school file clerk, aren't you?"

"Aw…not all of them are as innocent as they seem."

"You're sick."

"I'm tortured by the desire for young nubile flesh and have no desire to control my urges." Tom set his drink down and crawled back into bed.

"What the hell are you doing?" Sharon squirmed to the farthest edge of the bed. "Get out."

"I'm not done with you yet." He pushed Sharon back into the middle and forced her knees apart. In one swift motion, he pinned her wrists above her head. His smug expression revealed an air of conquest

"Does your wife know about this little perversion of yours?"

"Your daughter wanted to touch me so badly, wanted to be just like her mother."

A sense of dread and concern filled her with self-loathing. What had she done? His erection pressed against her thigh. Her brain begged for the vodka on the nightstand. Within eyesight, but out of reach. Against her wishes, her body responded to Tom's touches.

"Please...Tom," she said, uncertain if she was asking him to stop or continue.

Her mind begged her to stop. She shouldn't be doing this.

Tom grunted.

"Tom...." With each thrust, she trembled, and her body gave into the pleasure.

He ran his hand over her breasts and pinched her nipples until they turned a deep scarlet. He forced her mouth open with his own. Sharon moaned in protest; ragged whimpers of sheer need escaped her lips.

The sickening sensation of her life plunging into a great void engulfed her. Every time she seemed on track, her plans derailed. Her mind numb and paralyzed by fear, she peered into his lust-crazed, blue eyes. For a split second, Tom's eyes changed color. His dark evil soul, the midnight black eyes that filled her nightmares, the eyes she had spent so many years trying to escape, stared back at her.

Tom leaned down and whispered into her ear, "Did you think you could run away and hide? Did you think he wouldn't find you?"

Sharon screamed.

Tom slapped her. "Stop it. I'm here to take you and Isabelle home. Everything will be alright. I promise," he said, now caressing her cheek.

Sharon stopped listening. The door to her past stood wide open, an ancient set of keys clanked to the floor. If she didn't close this door, and get rid of the keys, many more would open. Somebody from her past uttered that same phrase as Tom, and it echoed again and again. Everything will be alright, I promise. As Tom grunted above her, she searched her memory for the person who lied to her.

The unwanted memories came rushing back.

Sharon screamed and sat straight up in bed rigid with terror. "Beware of the man with the dark eyes."

"Hush, my darling," the older nun said as she brushed the hair out of Sharon's eyes. "I'm here."

Wrapping her arms around the nun, Sharon whimpered. "The man with the dark eyes is getting closer. Every night he's getting closer. He wants me."

"Why does he want you?"

"He wants to do bad things, horrible things."

Sharon followed Sister Ann through the dark halls. The nun knocked on Mother Superior's door and stepped inside. Peeking through the keyhole, Sharon saw the young priest, Father Abrams, reclining on the sofa.

"Sharon dreamed of him again," Sister Ann said.

"Did she wet her bed?" Mother Superior asked.

"Yes."

"Punish her."

The older nun nodded.

After morning prayers and breakfast, Sharon followed directions and wrapped the soiled sheet around her head. After finishing the sign they'd made her wear, deep shame, and embarrassment turned her cheeks crimson and her stomach sour. She would rather feel the strap. At least the pain faded away. The sign she wore around her neck stated, "I'm a pig." The humiliation would never fade.

The first "oink" of the day, she ignored; the second she cringed, but the third proved too much. Sharon pushed the girl to the ground and stood over her, hands on her hips, "What did you say?"

Like a steel trap, a hand clutched her shoulder. "Sharon!"

The nun hauled Sharon to Mother Superior's door. Sharon searched the nun's face for any sign of compassion. Finding none, she wondered how the nuns behaved as children. Did they pull off the wings of flies? Kick stray dogs?

As they approached, the door stood ajar. Sister Mary raised her hand to knock but stopped. She pressed her finger to her lips. Voices from inside drifted to where they stood.

"Do you know much about her mother?" Mother Superior questioned.

"Too much," Father Abram's answered. "Her mother was young, poor, and untrustworthy. Sharon was born out of wedlock, an illegitimate child, the daughter of sin. The mother wouldn't reveal who the father was if she even knew. She abandoned the child and left her at our door. I found her mother morally inadequate."

"That explains a lot. I should have asked more questions when you brought her to us."

"Her mother was a Protestant."

Mother Superior snorted. "If I had known, I wouldn't have been so easy on the girl."

"Idle hands are the work of the devil."

A chair scraped against the floor; footsteps followed. Sharon squirmed. Sister Mary squeezed harder. Sharon bit her tongue so she wouldn't cry out. As the footsteps approached, Sister Mary placed her other hand over Sharon's mouth.

"Why are you here today, Father?" Mother Superior asked. "It has been too long since your last visit."

"Just here to remind you, he doesn't want Sharon to be adopted, ever. He has special plans for her."

Tears welled in Sharon's eyes. She needed to get away; she couldn't bear to hear any more. They didn't want her to have a family or be loved. Didn't she deserve to be loved? Didn't all God's children need love?

Sharon stomped on the nun's toes and kicked her in the shin several times. Sister Mary gasped, her fingers snapped open, and Sharon yanked herself free. The nun grabbed at the air as Sharon dodged capture. The nun lost her balance and crashed into the door.

As the door swung open, Father Abrams and Mother Superior broke their kiss. Sharon, her mouth agape, stood riveted in the entryway. Mother Superior's granite hate-filled eyes locked onto hers. If Sharon hadn't sinned before, striking one of the nuns was like sinning against God. Her blasphemous actions frightened her more than the strap. She would go to hell.

Blocking out everything around her, Sharon ran as if Satan nipped at her heels. She searched for the quickest way outside. Her only hope would be to reach St. Elizabeth's before they caught her. Apologize to God directly. Only then might her soul be saved from the fires of hell. She flew across the yard and pounded up the steps. She reached the sanctuary doors, pushed them open, and leaned against them as they closed.

Sharon walked down the center aisle and knelt in front of the cross. "Dear God, if you forgive me for the terrible sins I have committed today...." An arm wrapped around her shoulder. Relieved to find Sister Ann by her side, she finished, "I will become a nun."

The doors opened behind them. Sister Ann took Sharon's hand and they stood together. A scream built in Sharon's throat. The man with the dark eyes stood wrapped in the vestments of a priest.

Sister Ann held her close. "Everything will be alright. I promise."

***

Tom rolled off after he finished. Sharon could never return home to Pine Bluff; death waited for her there. If she allowed them to capture Isabelle, her daughter's fate would be worse than hers.

"Just a pair of sinners, aren't we, Sharon?"

# Chapter 14



*An Excerpt from Isabelle's Composition Books*

Princess Belle found her mother alone in her chamber, standing in front of a roaring fire. She held a mug of mulled wine, her gaze far away. Its exotic aroma of cinnamon and cloves permeated the room.

"Who is he, Mother?"

This drew her mother out of her reverie. "Is it right for the King to spill his seed with any common peasant girl, while his wife, his queen, is locked away becoming dry and brittle with age?"

"It doesn't matter what you want. You're his queen, not a common harlot!"

Anger flashed across the Queen's face. She flung the mug at the fireplace with a grunt, sending shards of pottery and flecks of wine across the mantle, then stumbled. When Belle tried to steady her mother, she slapped her daughter across the face. Belle rubbed her cheek. The heat of her mother's slap lingered.

"I may be the Queen, but I am still your mother. You will respect me and so shall the King. He'll find out soon enough; I'm more than just an object."

She ladled more wine into a new mug and pointed towards the door. "Go now and let me be. Your father shall be back soon. He will expect his ladies to be ready for the feast."

Princess Belle left rubbing her cheek. In her room, she changed out of her riding clothes, slipped into a gown befitting the occasion, and headed to the Great Hall.

She sat at the end of the King's table. Preparations were well underway. Flames licked at the crispy skin of the two large pigs rotating on a spit spun by two young boys. Fat sizzled and dripped into the fire. The smoke swirled around their heads and drifted upwards out through the louver. The aroma made her stomach grumble with hunger. She hadn't eaten since before her ride north.

Industrious workers came and went across the expanse of the Great Hall. Bakers filled a large table with loaves of different varieties. The smell of freshly baked bread wafted across the room, making her mouth water. Not able to resist, she stole a fresh yeasty bun from one of the trays. Breaking it in half, she dipped a piece into the large bubbling pot containing rabbit stew. The other pot held large chunks of beef, onion, and garlic floating in a dark gravy. One of the kitchen servants glared at her before she had a chance to dip the rest of her bread. Princess Belle glared back and displayed her knife to the servant before piercing a piece of meat out of the pot. She licked her fingers clean of the hot juices. Servants placed pewter platters loaded with cheese and fruit on the banquet tables.

Guests trickled in, and the hall grew noisy and crowded. A horn sounded, and the doors to the Great Hall opened. Everyone rose to their feet. The Castellan, a man named Bierger, entered with the Queen on his arm. She wore a deep scarlet dress made of pulled wool, its collar lined with snow-white ermine fur. The dress seductively flowed with each of her steps. An intricately woven gold and silver circlet, which sat upon her brow, shimmered in the candlelight. Eyes gleaming, cheeks flushed, the Queen waved to the guests. Her calm demeanor was a sharp contrast to her earlier mood.

Bierger, a handsome man except for the scar which ran from mouth to ear, carried himself with confidence. He helped govern the northern lands until the King, who had been orphaned at the age of twelve, turned sixteen. Bierger still served as a trusted adviser.

Bierger escorted the Queen to the table. She leaned close to his ear. "Thank you, Commander. May God grant you health, honor, and joy."

His eyes sparkled with amusement, but he grew pale and bewildered when the doors to the Great Hall opened and the King stormed in, followed by a group of men dressed in black, their faces obscured by their cloaks. A hush settled over the hall.

As the group approached the dais, the princess kept her eyes on the scar-faced man. She saw Bierger covertly reach for his dagger, and she wondered why. Is he my mother's secret lover?

The Queen stood and gave her husband a warm embrace. The King turned to his guests and pronounced, "Let the feast begin!" Princess Belle saw Bierger let out his breath and clap along with the rest of the guests.

The Princess wasn't enjoying the festivities. Besides the drunken guests and their excessive merriment, the men who accompanied the King concerned her. Rigid as posts, they neither ate nor drank. Her father spoke to them in hushed tones. Why did they hide their faces? Could they be the evil that the old crone in the village warned her about?

After an event-filled day, Belle should have been tired, but she needed to move, to find a cure for her restlessness. She pushed her way across the expanse of the Great Hall to the porch overlooking the Lower Bailey. She stopped in front of one of the large windows and her gaze drew upward, like the strings of a marionette. The moon high in the night sky filled the Lower Bailey with dancing shadows. One of the shadows suddenly moved, and a dark figure glided into view from behind the well. A shaft of moonlight illuminated the Queen's face, but she ducked back into the darkness along the walls and disappeared. Concerned where her mother had gone, Princess Belle followed. She didn't get far before someone grabbed her arm.

Princess Belle spun around and faced Freyja who stood with hands on her hips, her eyes narrowed into tight slits. "Princess Belle, don't follow your mother. Trust her. She's dealing with issues you wouldn't understand."

"I'm not a child. Don't treat me like one," Princess Belle said between clenched teeth.

"Belle, trust me, please."

Unable to tolerate Freya's gaze, Belle stepped backward and collided with her friend Jeppe. He lost his grip on the keg of beer he was moving. "Belle!"

Partygoers scattered and did their best to avoid the rolling barrel.

"Sorry, Jeppe," Belle said.

They caught the barrel of beer before it exploded against a wall. Once they righted the cask and averted disaster, Princess Belle grabbed Jeppe's arm and pulled him back into the buttery, a storage area for wine and ale. The room reeked of sour, vinegary wine and stale beer. "Jeppe, I need your help."

Amusement lurked in his eyes. "I'd love to."

Princess Belle punched him in the shoulder. "This is serious. My mother snuck out of the castle. I think she's meeting someone. I need to find her before the King discovers she's gone."

"Are you sure?"

"I watched her leave." Belle pulled at the hem of her dress. "Do you know a way out of here? Where nobody can see me leave."

"I know a way."

"We need to hurry. Do you see Freyja?"

Jeppe squeezed Princess Belle's hand and peeked around the corner. "She's by the main entrance."

They stepped out of the room, Jeppe in the lead. "She's watching us."

Princess Belle made a snap decision. She pulled Jeppe close and pressed her lips to his, long enough to ensure Freyja had witnessed it.

"That should buy us some time," she said and pulled Jeppe back into the room. "She always thought I should be more interested in boys." Princess Belle wiped her mouth with the back of her hand.

Jeppe stood with his mouth hanging open.

"Don't read too much into that kiss. How do we get out of here?"

A crooked smile preceded his chuckle. "There's only one way out and, in my humble opinion, it's not fit for a lady like you."

Jeppe went to the sink and pulled the copper basin away from its base. A dark hole appeared. "The only way out is through there. The sink drains into the river below."

Belle peered down the chute, sickened by the smell. The latrine down the hall also drained into this portion of the river. She kicked off her slippers and pulled up her dress. "What are you waiting for?"

"Ladies first."

Belle wriggled into the chute, her shoulders scraping against the bricks. Her fingers sought purchase but kept slipping off the slime-covered walls. Her stomach churned, and the bile rose when she thought about what coated her hands. Past the first few feet, most of the bricks were missing grout and made for natural hand and footholds.

They progressed in silence until Belle's foot slipped. She dangled there, holding on with only her fingertips. Perspiration beaded on her forehead; her hands cramped. Below her, water gurgled and spit as it rushed by. She swung her legs until her feet caught.

Jeppe grunted when his foot struck her shoulder. "Why did you stop?"

"How far is the water below?"

"I don't know. I've never done this before."

Belle peered between her feet into the murky darkness. The water below sounded close. She took a deep breath, released her grip, and fell. Eyes closed, she hit the water and went under. The frigid water took her breath away. She gasped, inhaling the murky, dank water. Her feet hit bottom, she pushed off and kicked hard. After what felt like minutes, she sputtered to the surface. The current wasn't strong, but the cold water caused her teeth to chatter. In the dark, the outline of the castle walls on the other side of the channel appeared featureless. She swam to the ledge and pulled herself out of the water. Shivering, she examined her filthy and torn dress. The Queen would not be happy.

A splash followed, and Jeppe soon joined her on the platform. The squeaks of vermin echoed in the dark expanse. A long tail brushed up against her. She shoved the rodent away. "Where are we?

Jeppe pointed to his left. "That door leads to the cellar where the barrels of wine are stored. If we follow this ledge, it will take us to the docks. I know the guard. He won't say a word. Which direction did your mother go?"

"I'm not sure," Belle said, but then changed her mind. "She went north."

"We'll need to cross the river." Jeppe pulled a key from around his neck. "I'll be right back."

Belle wrapped her arms around her torso in an attempt to keep warm. "Okay, but hurry up. I want to get out of here."

Several minutes later, Jeppe returned clutching multiple leather pouches. "We'll need these."

As they approached the deserted docks, a guard stepped out of the shadows holding a sword. "Who goes there?"

"Elo, my good man." Jeppe wrapped his arm around the guard like a long-lost friend and handed him a skin of wine. "This should keep you warm tonight. Speaking of warmth, do you have a blanket my lady could use?"

Elo nodded and gave Jeppe a knowing wink.

Jeppe placed the blanket from Elo around Princess Belle's shoulders. They boarded one of the flat bottom skips tied to the dock and, without ceremony, paddled north.

Once out of earshot, Belle smacked Jeppe in the arm. "So, you have done this before. I'm not one of the simple peasant girls who trail after you like a bitch in heat."

Jeppe laughed, eyes sparkling. "Who kissed who?"

"Just paddle."

They battled the current for twenty minutes. The further north they traveled, the trees along the shore changed from sentinels standing at attention to grotesque, twisted figures. Their arm-like branches reached out to them in the darkness as if waiting for the opportunity to attack. Belle and Jeppe remained quiet, saving their energy to fight the current. The cold fall night air settled heavily on the river. Even with the blanket draped over her shoulders, Princess Belle shivered. Nearing a bend in the river, she laid the paddle across her lap, ready to give up and let the current drag them back to the castle. The faint sound of music in the distance stretched like a tight wire through the air, its melody plucking at her soul. At first, she thought it was the wind blowing softly through the trees, but as they edged closer, the music came alive inside of her. What started as a shiver transformed into humming nerves. The electricity in the air trickled into her pores, igniting her spirit.

"Did you hear that?" she asked Jeppe. "Do you feel the excitement in the air?"

"What are you talking about?"

"Don't you hear the music? It's everywhere."

"I don't hear anything, but I'll admit, something is odd about this place. I've never been this far north. I've heard many tales. My father's customers say the North Forest is enchanted."

"I need to go ashore." She jumped into the river, her body wedded to the music.

"Belle, what the hell are you doing? Get back here."

Princess Belle crawled onto the bank. Water dripped from her hair. Her tattered dress clung to her curves like a second skin. She gazed at her bare feet. Wet, cold, mud squished between her toes. When did she lose her shoes? She slipped on the torn hem of her dress, sat down hard, and waited.

Jeppe paddled to the bank. He dragged their small boat onto shore, hurrying over to Belle.

The North Forest was wild and unruly, made up entirely of brambles, briars, and thorns. Isabelle searched for animal-made trails away from the river but found none. With nothing to follow, she closed her eyes, opened her mind, and let the music guide her steps. Thoughts of finding her mother vanished.

Jeppe grabbed hold of her shoulders. "You're wet and cold. We need a fire to dry our clothes. I have another skin of wine we can share to warm us up. I also need you to tell me what's going on."

Princess Belle nodded, ignoring the pull of the music.

They gathered kindling and started a fire. Between the fire and the wine, warmth inched its way through the Princess's veins. Jeppe slid closer and draped his arm over her shoulder. She leaned into him, closed her eyes, and let the night music pulse in her veins.

"When those four men came into the Great Hall tonight with my father, the Castellan's face grew pale, and I saw him reach for his blade." Belle shivered, though if from the memory or the cold, it was hard to tell. "There was something dark and sinister about them. When I was in the village earlier today, I ran into a strange old woman who sniffed the air proclaiming evil was on its way."

"An ugly old woman?" Jeppe asked.

"Yes."

"Do you know who she is?"

"No."

"You need to open your eyes. There's a different world out here, one which those living in your reality don't see. The old woman is my aunt, my mother's sister Bergljut. The most beautiful woman I've ever seen."

"Really? Beautiful? What happened to her?"

"It's a long story. I'm not sure you would like to hear."

"Why wouldn't I?"

Jeppe pressed the wineskin to his mouth, then threw a large branch onto the fire. "Because there's much you don't know about your parents."

# Chapter 15

Heather, Ms. Dahl to her students, sat back in her chair and breathed a sigh of relief. She had survived her first quarter. Even with her successes, Sarah's behavior frustrated her. She talked to the administration, but their lack of support disappointed her. No wonder Sarah and her friends thought they ran the school.

What about her other problem child—Isabelle? Had she lit a fire under her today? She shook her head. Isabelle displayed the same defeated demeanor she did the first day of class. Heather blinked back tears as memories of her father spilled forth. How would he, as a teacher, have handled her most challenging students? She grabbed a tissue and wiped the tears from her eyes. She missed both her parents.

A pile of tests sat on her desk. Should she start grading them? Tonight and Sunday were her only nights off. As she dived into the first test, a knock on the door interrupted her. The other first-year teacher, Adam Hendricks, popped his head in. "Some of the teachers are heading over to Bennigan's to celebrate the end of the first quarter. It's tradition. Do you want to join us for a few drinks?"

Her heart fluttered just seeing Adam's curly brown hair, broad shoulders, and sparkling brown eyes. She blushed. They had gone on one date during their freshman year in college. He possessed all the physical attributes she desired, but she needed something more than the party boy could provide.

Why did she have such a reaction to seeing him today? Maybe her long day had played a part. She deserved to relax, let her hair down. Why not join the other teachers for a night out?

"Let me put my stuff away. How about I meet you there?"

He flashed his gorgeous smile. "Great."

***

The evening went better than expected. No awkward silence or forced conversation. Heather and Adam spent the time reconnecting. Their first date could have been last week, not five years ago. At the end of the celebration, after most of the other teachers left, Adam expressed a desire to get better re-acquainted. She agreed. Silently, she wished for more.

Buoyed by the conversation and a couple glasses of wine, she was excited to call her grandmother, a Friday night priority since college. Back at home, she dialed the number.

"Hello?"

"Hi, Grandma. It's me, Heather."

"God kveld, Heather. Have you met a man?"

Heather chuckled. Her grandma knew everything and didn't waste any time getting right to the point. "Have you been spying on me?"

"Your bestemor knows all the secrets of your heart, my dearest one."

"You're so funny. Will I marry this one?" An uncomfortable silence settled over the telephone line. "Grandma, are you still there?"

A few seconds of unresponsiveness turned into an unbearable minute. "Grandma, is everything okay?"

She hung up and dialed again. Busy. She tried a third time. Same results. The phone rang, and Heather grabbed the receiver. "Grandma, is that you?"

"No, it's Avery. Is everything alright?"

"Are you at home?"

"No, I'm at a friend's house. Is something wrong?"

"I was talking to Grandma, and the phone went dead. I tried again, and the phone was busy."

"You've been gone too long. Did you forget about the trouble we have with the phones in the fall and winter? It's probably nothing. I'll be home soon and will have Grandma call you."

"I just have an uneasy feeling."

"Heather, you always think the worst," Avery said. "Kevin said the new boy's going to ask me out!"

"The stud hockey player, the one you think is such a hunk?"

"Yes. Jacob Neely."

"Great news, sis, but when you get home, make sure you call."

Heather headed to her bedroom. For pajamas, she chose a simple T-shirt and dance shorts. Her thoughts drifted to all the compass points of her life. Sinking into her pillow, she couldn't find a comfortable position. She tossed and turned, thinking about Adam, her parents' death, and everything in between. Why didn't Grandma call back?

Her eyes snapped open in the dark room. She didn't remember when she'd fallen asleep but wished she could return to her dreams of Adam. In the stillness of her apartment, beads of perspiration slid off her brow and into her hair. She waited for the reassurance, the silence of nothingness, the presence of nobody. The floor creaked. She sat up, goosebumps rising on her arms, and shivered. All she wanted to do was to burrow back under the safety of her blanket. Something wasn't right, an uneasiness invaded her room. Someone watched her. "Hello?"

None of the shadows moved, but she couldn't shake the feeling she wasn't alone. Fear gripped her insides like a vise. Whatever hid in the darkness of her apartment crept closer. Her mind encouraged her to flee.

She pushed the covers back and placed her foot on the floor. A large, dark shadow fell across her window. A strangled cry leaked from her pursed lips. She scrambled from her bed to the window.

Outside, the dark waters of the Red River flowed under the Main Avenue Bridge. Thin fingers of ice formed along its banks as new-fallen snow disappeared in the frigid waters. The heavy snow swirled and drifted, covering the ground with an unblemished blanket of white. Frost-covered trees stood like soldiers at attention. Dark silhouettes against the luminous sky, they peeked through the fog. The large ominous shape, too high and out of focus in the foggy, snowy night, circled above.

The dark shadow headed south and glided above the bridge which spanned North Dakota and Minnesota. Like a spider's egg sack, it broke apart, scattering its offspring across the sky. Thousands of tiny specks dotted the night. Their shrieks became one and as if they had murderous intent, the flock of blackbirds descended on the bridge, landing on the guardrails. Like a firing squad, they stared in her direction. Behind the birds, snow-covered mounds littered the bridge deck. Were those cars? Her mind couldn't grasp the possibility. If an accident occurred, why hadn't she heard the collisions, the metal tearing, the glass crunching, the people screaming? No movement or sound, just snow settling over everything.

Heather picked up the phone to dial 911 but heard no dial tone. Slamming the phone back into its cradle, she pulled on her sweatpants and stepped into her Sorels. Her fingers fumbled with the door chain, not grasping the urgency of her thoughts. With the lock undone, she flung the door open, working her feet to completely seat her heels. After failing the one-footed bunny boot-hop several times, she sat and finished the job. Extreme cold greeted her outside the lower level. She rushed back to her apartment and grabbed her jacket and gloves.

The door closed behind her with a groan, like the finality of a casket lid being shut. She stood in the middle of Main Avenue, whiteness swirling at her feet.  The landscape, whitewashed in gray, cast a gloomy aura upon her soul. The abandoned buildings were mere outlines; shadows roamed their empty shells. Nothing alive wandered the streets. A sense of loneliness crept up on her. She had never experienced this depth of solitude and despair. Could this be a dream?

Bad memories and whispered stories filled her head. Secrets and sinister words lingered upon her lips, and a bitter taste seeped into her mouth. She spat a mouthful of black phlegm to the ground. A hard fist of fear grew in her stomach as she sensed something or someone matching her pace, stride for stride. An icy presence followed her westward to the bridge. When she stopped, it poked and prodded her forward. What awaited her beneath the blankets of snow?

Besides the nightmare qualities of her surroundings, something was amiss, but she couldn't put her finger on it. If this wasn't real, how could it be staged? Car accidents scared her. The victims in the vehicles needed her help. She wasn't going to let them down. If somebody had helped her parents, they might be alive today.

A slight movement to her right made her turn. Two large blackbirds perched atop the streetlight.  They stared at her with beady eyes. Even in the cold, a light sheen of sweat covered her body. Her nerves leaped and shuddered. She grabbed a handful of snow and tossed it at the birds. "Get the hell out of here!"

The birds screamed back at her.

In unison, they swooped from the streetlamp and glided to rest on the bridge deck. Heather followed. One of the birds fluttered onto a snow-covered mound. It pecked twice, and the snow fell away, revealing a boy's face.

Heather pressed her gloved fist to her mouth.

As the boy's scream pierced the air, the bird plucked his eye from the socket, flipped the nugget into the air, tilted back its head, and swallowed.

Heather ran toward the first mound and waved her arms. "Go away! Get out of here."

The birds, with an almost human gaze challenging her, cawed a warning.

The surface of the bridge, slick with snow, made running difficult. Slipping and sliding, Heather fell to her knees and brushed away the snow. She pulled the boy from the pile of children's bodies haphazardly stacked on top of each other and rolled him onto her lap, cradling his head. She wiped the blood and snow from his undamaged eye and, with a voice racked by pain, mumbled, "Are you alright?"

The shadow that followed her onto the bridge touched the boy's chest. The boy convulsed and gripped her hand tighter. With his functional eye closed, he took a deep, rattling breath. Blood bubbled between his lips. "Oh, I hurt."

Heather put her finger on his lips and lied. "Don't try to speak. Help is on its way."

He coughed; a bloody mist sprayed from his nose and covered her hand. He convulsed once, then twice. Hot tears streamed down Heather's face. What did all this mean? She ran from mound to mound. Each one the same, the bodies of the innocent piled together. She raised her arms, looking skyward, beseeching God for answers. Everybody was dead. She turned in a full circle and took in the whole nightmarish scene. "Where is everybody? What's going on?"

In the middle of the bridge, one last mound remained, a shape she recognized. Rushing to the car, she wiped the snow from the window and peered in. Empty. She scanned the bridge. Who owned this car? Warning bells clanged inside her head, but she opened the door anyway.

Cobwebs of time undulated in the gloom, and the smell of the past hit her head-on. Her father's Old Spice and the fragrances from her mother's kitchen: cinnamon, cloves, thyme, and rosemary, filled her nostrils and wrenched her soul. Another scent lingered in the background, but her mind pushed it aside. Impossible. Could this be her parent's car when …? "Oh, God… Oh, God… No!"

Stuck on the glove compartment, a big yellow smiley-face sticker stared back at her. Heather slid inside. In a daze, she pulled open the latch and found a faded envelope inside. Placing it against her heart, she pulled her mother's memories close. She hadn't seen this card, shaped like a pair of pointe shoes, since her parents' funeral. Inside the card, her mother had written: Dance like nobody's watching. Drive safe. We will see you soon. Love you always. She had placed it under her mother's hands right before they closed the casket.

Heather pressed her forehead against the dashboard. "God, why do you torment me so?"

The car door slammed shut.

Heather startled, hitting her forehead so hard on the rear-view mirror that blood trickled into her eyes. The snow slid off the front window. Four dark riders, their faces obscured by their hoods, sat motionless upon their mounts.

Did they just laugh? She listened closer.

"Beware the King. Thou shalt not suffer a witch to live."

# Chapter 16

"**B**eware the King?"

The entire scene seemed surreal. Blurred shapes rushed around the car, their laughter growing louder and closer. Heather could take no more. Her anxious fingers fumbled with the lock on the door.

"Damn it, come on."

Breathing deeply until her hand no longer trembled, she wiped her hands on her pants and pulled on the lock. The mechanism clicked but would not open. Her shoulder pressed against the door, she pushed harder. Nothing.

"God damn it!" She slid across the front seat and tried the driver's door. Still nothing. When she crawled into the back seat to try the other doors, her sweatpants caught on the parking brake. Panic kicked in as an imagined hand wrapped around her ankle. Her feet hit the radio. A sound erupted from the speakers, white noise penetrating her fragile mind. Several attempts to turn down the volume yielded nothing. She laid her head on the cold vinyl of the seat as tears rolled down her cheek.

The radio shut off. The sudden silence a welcome reprieve, she wiped her face with the back of her jacket sleeve.

The car accelerated forward. The radio began blasting AC/ DC's "Hell's Bells." Vertigo struck. She grasped at air. The car fishtailed.

Flung across the backseat, she grabbed the headrest to stop her momentum. The car recovered, but the tires spun on loose gravel.

What the hell?

She tried to comprehend this new reality as the car swerved once again. Clutching the front seat with both hands, she squeezed her eyes shut.

"Teddy! What are you doing? Stay on the road."

A lump formed in Heather's throat. "Mom?"

"It's alright, I'm alright," her father mumbled.

"What's wrong?" her mother asked. "Is it too dark? Do you need me to drive?"

"I don't need you to drive!"

The swerving car picked up speed. Heather grabbed the handle above the door. This can't be happening. How could the car be moving?

"Teddy, please slow down," her mother begged. "You're scaring me!"

The car thumped the side of the road, shuddering on the ruts the road grader had left behind. Tires screamed to find traction. Heather gripped the handle tighter. The stench of alcohol filled the car.

"My God, Teddy, have you been drinking?"

"Heather, are you listening?" her father asked.

Heather opened her eyes. Her parents, looking just like she remembered them, sat in the front seat. Her dad in his favorite cardigan, her mother's hair perfectly styled.

Her father pulled a small flask from his jacket. Both hands off the wheel now, a wicked grin plastered on his face, he uncorked the bottle and held it high. "Yes, I have!"

Her mother yanked it from his grip.

The car left the road again, teetered, and skidded along the edge of the ditch.

"Please stop the car! I want out!" her mother said. "What about the girls?"

Teddy glanced into the rear-view mirror. "Heather, tell the bitch, your grandmother,  he wants what's his--the books and the girl."

Heather pinched herself. Please wake up.

Teddy laughed, ripped the flask from her mother's hands, and shoved her. He brought the flagon to his lips and with his best Rod Serling voice said, "Next stop, Hell!"

He stomped on the gas. The car rocketed forward and as it came around the curve, he glanced into the backseat. "Hold on, the landing's going to get bumpy!"

The car leaped into the air.

Heather squeezed her eyes shut and braced for impact. "I don't want to die."

The car struck the surface of the black water of the pond and bounced. Her head snapped back then hurtled forward on impact.

The car settled, the front end submerging first. Stunned, Heather fell backward onto the seat. Her parents no longer in the vehicle, silenced filled the space.

Was it over? Condensation covered the windows. With the cuff of her jacket, she wiped a spot clean. Pressed against the window, the white, lifeless eyes of a child stared back. Heather screamed. She wiped the side window. More faces. One by one, their vacant visages surrounded the car. The car trembled as tiny feet stomped across the roof. Small faces now upside down, their death grimaces unchanged, gazed into the vehicle as if waiting for something to happen. Their unblinking eyes peered into her soul. A rush of dread whirled inside her as the water pressed down upon her. She needed to get out.

Could she roll down the window enough to escape? Jumbled thoughts made her second-guess her options. Left with no other choices, she tugged at the window crank. It wouldn't budge.

"Son of a bitch." She pounded on the window. "No!"

A wet, putrid stench seeped into the car. She put all her weight against the handle and pushed. "Come on, damn it. Move."

It snapped off in her hand.

"Shit."

One of the children tried to reach through the window but couldn't get his fingers into the small gap. Heather hammered at the white curled digits. The window slid down a fraction of an inch. Freezing water trickled in, but within seconds it became a small stream. The window slipped farther down. She tried to hold back the onslaught, but the water surged in, spraying the backseat. Tiny black worms writhed in the water covering her hands. The sensation of millions of insects crawling over her skin filled her with disgust. She swatted and beat at them. Peeling off her wet clothing, she scratched at her violated skin.

"Go away!"

She pounded at the window, hoping to scare the children. Water lapped at the top of the seats. The entire bottom of the car vanished; the murkiness of the water, absolute. She sat shivering. Instructed by some unknown force, she submerged her hands into the icy water. The water wanted to control her, wrap its frigid arms around her neck, and drag her into its depths. The effects of the contact burned through her like wildfire. She lifted her feet onto the seat. An invisible touch made her skin crawl. A feeling so vile; a corruption so complete.

"Please let me out!"

The water poured in like a firehose filling an aquarium. Heather didn't have much time to figure out how to escape. She pressed her back against the ceiling as the water inched upward.

"Oh my God," Heather screamed. Her thighs disappeared into the inky blackness of the water. "Mom, is this how you died?"

Overwhelming exhaustion settled over Heather. She wrapped her arms around herself and let herself float. If she closed her eyes, all this would be over and she would find peace.

The water only inches from her face, warmth settled over her body. It didn't matter anymore, did it? She closed her eyes. Best friends, hypothermia, and death approached fast. Under the water, a hand slid up her thigh and rested on the lace of her panties.

"No!" She pushed at the invisible hands. Her face dipped under water.

"Don't fight. It will be over soon."

Heather broke the surface. She sputtered and spit out a mouthful of water. Her sister sat in the front seat. "Avery, why are you here?"

"I'm here to save you. How are you getting out of this one?"

"I have no fucking idea." Heather spat the water at her lips.

"You know, Dad's a monster."

"You might be right. I think he killed Mom."

"He wants us all dead," Heather's mother said, taking Avery's place in the front seat. "Your father isn't who he pretends to be."

"Mom, what am I to do?"

Her mother disappeared. Despair filled Heather with hopeless thoughts. What was the point of fighting any longer? She would be dead soon.

Violent tremors rocked her body. She took one deep breath and plunged underwater. The children screamed and begged her to join them on the bottom of the pond. She tried to get her feet underneath her, but they didn't respond. As her lungs reached their bursting point, death inched closer. Outside the window, surrounded by the children, her father beckoned.

"Come to me," he commanded.

He reached for her, but she wasn't ready for his embrace – she wasn't prepared to die. A bright light appeared in the distance. The bottom of the car faded, bones glowed on the murky bottom. She swam.

"As you sow, so shall you reap," her father said, slipping deeper into the thick gloom of the pond.

Warmth wrapped itself around Heather as she kicked harder toward the light. The back door opened, and the car spat her out. She hit the ground, gasping for breath. On her knees, she gagged and expelled mouthfuls of black, dank water.

On the bridge, the piles of dead children had vanished. The presence from earlier slinked across the bridge. Heather brushed off whatever crawled along her cheek then she jumped to her feet. Her cold, numb feet tangled, she stumbled and fell face-first in the snow. She had no concrete proof, but her intuition pounded the warning drums. Whatever approached meant business.

Something heavy lay across the back of her legs. She shook her foot to no avail. Using her other foot as leverage, she pushed with more force. That didn't help either. She shoved the snow away to reveal what weighed her down.

She jerked her leg away. A body rolled over, its fire-blackened face stared back at her. The sweet smell of burnt flesh filled her nostrils. After several attempts, she untangled herself from the body. Crab-walking up the slick ramp, she encountered a cold, solid object. She froze and clamped her lips shut to stifle a scream. She slipped on the icy pavement and fell backward.

Her heart leaped into her throat as another scream built deep inside, but she couldn't look away. A burnt arm stuck out from a mound of twisted bodies, its hand gripping scrunched papers. She lifted each blackened finger until the documents came free.

***

Beep... Beep... Beep.

Heather rolled over and grabbed her phone. "Yeah?"

"Is this Heather Dahl?"

"Yes."

"This is the Fargo Police Department. The alarm at your dance studio has been activated, and we need you to let our officers into the building to investigate."

Her brain kicked in a moment later. "Ahhh....Give me fifteen minutes."

When Heather arrived at her studio, a patrol car sat in her parking lot, the lights off. Two officers, one of them Sarah's father, walked up to Heather. She started to get out of her car.

"You should just sit tight. We'll take a quick look around the building. Make sure it's safe."

Heather handed the keys to Sheriff Erickson. She stayed put while the two officers walked toward the building. After a quick trip around, they approached the front door. The faint sound of music wafted from within.

Against her better judgment, Heather followed them into the lobby. The music came from a back studio. The officers pulled their weapons and proceeded down the hallway.

A female figure danced in the shadows. Her arms were beautiful and fluid, her toes pointed, she flowed as one with the music. Absorbed in her dance, the trespasser didn't notice Heather or the officers standing in the doorway. Heather, astonished by this dancer's skill, watched in awe. Who was she? She didn't dance at this studio. A night light illuminated the far corner of the room and when the dancer passed into the glow, Heather gasped.

"Isabelle?"

# Chapter 17



*An Excerpt from Isabelle's Composition Book*

J eppe poked at the fire. "At the age of fourteen, while the Castellan tended to the affairs of the kingdom, your father fell in love with a peasant girl, my aunt, Bergljut. She was a beautiful young woman; hair of spun gold, her eyes ablaze with the hues of the sky, and her cheeks freckled, as if kissed by the sun. So innocent, so full of life.

"Although amused by the attention the future King bestowed upon her, she didn't yearn to be his queen or mistress. She already loved a peasant farmer and intended to wed him and fill his house with many children. This was what God had ordained for her.

"Your father, obsessed with her beauty, couldn't stay away. The Castellan and the priests made it clear; he was forbidden to soil his reputation and consort with an ordinary girl from the village. Your mother would be his first, their marriage blessed by God."

Belle's blood still thrummed with the sound of music, every cell in her body finely tuned to the sensation. She gazed past the fire and into the darkness beyond. What was out there? Would the music disappear before she found its source? Could she sit here much longer before the lure of adventure became too unbearable?

"He's a handsome man," someone said.

Belle peered into the darkness to see who had spoken. Two large ravens were perched on a branch behind Jeppe. Could they have uttered the words she'd heard?

"Your mother lived in a convent, but not by choice," Jeppe said.

The birds cackled. Their small heads and beady eyes bobbed in the glow of the fire. "The girl sees us," they screeched in unison.

The hairs on the back of Belle's neck lifted. Her gaze moved from the birds back to Jeppe. Something wasn't right.

"Jeppe, what did you say?"

"Your mother was raised in a convent."

"How do you know this?"

"It's common knowledge in the village."

Then why didn't she know about this? Her mother wasn't a stranger. They spoke to each other daily.

Jeppe pulled out the wineskin and tossed it to Isabelle. She threw it back to him without taking a sip, her gaze never leaving the branches where the two blackbirds perched.

Jeppe moved closer to Belle. "Your father became King on his eighteenth birthday."

Caw. Caw. Caw.

One of the birds swooped toward the ground. Small pinpricks of light danced in the air. Belle blinked. When the lights died, a mirror image of the princess stood on the other side of the fire, a mischievous glint in her bright green eyes.

"Jeppe?" Belle said, pointing at the girl.

He stared into the girl's green eyes, his story forgotten. "Umm...Princess Belle, how did you get...."

"Jeppe, listen to me," Belle said as she grabbed his shoulders. "That isn't me."

"Belle, do you hear the music?" Jeppe asked.

The green-eyed girl beckoned. A smile sprang to Jeppe's lips as he reached for her hand. Princess Belle stepped in between them, and the air whirled around her like a tide pool. It spat her out and spun her to the ground.

The strange girl's eyes flashed a warning, and she hissed. "Child, don't interfere."

Jeppe brushed Belle aside. The emerald-eyed temptress pulled him into an embrace and pressed her lips to his. Wide-eyed, Princess Belle watched the kiss linger. A tinge of jealousy pecked at her heart.

The kiss ended. The imposter's eyebrows rose in obvious pleasure, and she smiled cruelly at Belle. "All that's yours is mine, and all that's mine is mine."

The other bird launched itself into the night sky. Belle reached for Jeppe's shoulder. "Leave him be." The green-eyed girl squinted in amusement and with a flick of her wrist, drew Princess Belle close. "It wasn't I who trod upon our path or burnt our trees."

Belle stared into the poison-colored eyes and grew faint. Her feeble mind struggled. "Who are you?"

"Like your mother, a queen." The imposter raised her arms wide. "All of this is mine." She pushed Belle to the ground and plucked a cloth bag out of the air. "I see you care for this boy. Nonetheless, I plan to keep him." She dropped the bag at Belle's feet. Coins jingled inside. "Payment for your troubles."

One of the blackbirds landed on the log next to where Belle lay. Without provocation, it pecked her. "Ouch," Belle protested, pulling her hand back, a bead of blood sprouted from her skin. Her mind clouded with sleep and collapsed. As the green-eyed girl walked away with Jeppe, her face took on angelic qualities of mythical perfection. Belle drifted into a vague half-sleep.

Caw, caw.

Belle willed her eyes open, but they were too heavy with sleep. When she finally pried them open, the bird sat next to her, its eyes bold and defiant.

"What did you do with Jeppe?"

Caw.

The fire had died. A few burnt embers flickered in the moonlight. Her damp clothes clung to her body and the crisp night air nipped at her skin. She tossed a couple sticks on the fire and blew onto the coals. A small flame flickered. With the addition of a few larger sticks, the fire leaped to life.

What a failure. Belle set out to find her mother and ended up losing Jeppe. All she had to show for her adventure sat on the log: a half-empty wineskin and a bag of coins. Her stomach growled. Where did the girl take him, and why? Questions without answers piled up. First things first, she pulled out the plug of the wineskin with her teeth and drank deeply.

Belle picked up the bag of coins, which weighed less than she thought it should. She untied the bag and dumped out the contents. Gold and brown leaves fluttered to the ground. She kicked the dirt in disgust. What kind of creature was that girl?

She circled the fire. Think, Belle, think. It might be too late to find her mother, but she needed to find Jeppe. She had dragged him out here.

No, he came on his own.

Her father warned her to stay away from the North. Why hadn't she listened? Tears spilled down her cheeks. She didn't even know how to get home. Her only option was to follow the music still pulsing through her veins. Kicking dirt on the fire, she closed her eyes and let the passionate mournful rhythm of the music's pull lead her.

Each step drew her deeper into the forest. Her body responded, swept away as if carried by the tide. As one with the music, she didn't need to follow the ravens to get to her destination. Late into the night, when the night was darkest and dawn approached, Belle entered a clearing. As she neared the top of a small knoll, guided by a soft glow, the night came alive. She kicked off her shoes, wiggled her toes in the greenest, sweetest-smelling grass her feet had ever trod upon. Her soul awakened, full of endless energy. In the middle of the glen, in a circle of stones, fairy folk danced and played their pipes. Mixed among the tiny people, other young adults danced with them. The girl with the emerald eyes watched her approach. Jeppe skipped toward Belle. She grasped his offered hand, closed her eyes, and danced.

"No." Someone hissed. The crone's bent, arthritic fingers clutched the sleeve of Belle's dress, stopping her from stepping into the circle of stones.

Belle twisted and turned but couldn't break from her grasp. "Let me go," she ordered as only royalty could. "I need to save Jeppe."

"My nephew is already lost. Such a silly boy."

"Let me go, I beg of you."

The crone cackled. "Your mother would be sad to lose another child. Wouldn't she?"

"What did you say?"

The witch drew her close, her putrid breath scalding Belle's senses. "Didn't I warn you once? Evil loves innocence."

# Chapter 18

"**I**sabelle?"

Isabelle turned toward the voice, a voice she recognized. She raised her hand to shield her eyes. "Hello, who's out there?" Shadows shifted behind her. "Where am I?"

Another beam joined the others, this one brighter. Pain knifed behind her eyes. Wincing, she recoiled from the light. As she brought both arms in front of her face for protection, hard calloused hands grabbed her from behind. Cold steel bit into her wrists.

"Ouch! What are you doing? Why are you hurting me?"

"Don't struggle. It'll only make things worse."

Isabelle opened her eyes. Two male police officers and her history teacher, Ms. Heather Dahl, stood in front of her. What's going on? She remembered racing from her house after she cut the man, but nothing after that. Would she be arrested? Her mother would be pissed.

Sarah's father, Sheriff Erickson, turned to her teacher. "Do you know who this is?"

"Yes, she's one of my students. Isabelle Gunderson." Ms. Dahl flipped a light switch. The overhead lights flickered for a second then stayed on.

Sheriff Erickson circled Isabelle. Mirrors lined the front; bars lined the back. She still didn't know where she was or how she had arrived. The sheriff gave her the once over. A smile crawled to his lips and his eyes lit up. "Don't I know you? Your mother is Sharon, right?"

Isabelle nodded.

He motioned to the other officer to take her away then sighed.

Ms. Dahl, hands on her hips, responded, her voice laced with irritation. "What did that look mean?"

"I've had a few incidents with her mother, and it doesn't surprise me the daughter would follow in her footsteps." He turned to leave. "Let us know if anything's missing. You can come to the station in the morning and give your statement."

"I don't plan to press charges." Ms. Dahl's gaze wavered between Isabelle and the officers. "Isabelle is one of my dance students. I gave her permission to dance here whenever she wanted. I have trouble opening the door as well."

"Are you sure?" the other officer asked.

Sarah's father raised his eyebrows. "Sarah hasn't said anything about a new student."

"I'm giving her private lessons, trying to get her caught up. She'll be joining regular classes on Monday."

"I hope you know what you're doing, Heather."

"I do."

The sheriff shrugged. "Alright, take the cuffs off."

"Thank you for your quick response officers, and sorry for any misunderstanding," Ms. Dahl said.

"I assume you'll give her a ride home?"

Ms. Dahl nodded.

The sheriff eyed Isabelle. "I look forward to the next show."

Isabelle rubbed her wrists and wiped off a spot of blood that dotted her hand. Her shitty day had only gotten shittier. Was she losing her mind? No matter what the sheriff thought, she wasn't like her mother.

Monday would be hell. Sarah would tell the whole school she broke into the dance studio. Just like she told them about her mother and the incident earlier this summer.

Ms. Dahl stood in the doorway with a pained expression, as if she had been wounded. "Don't just stand there, Isabelle. There's a broom in the closet by the front door. Clean up your mess."

Isabelle found the broom and swept up the glass without saying another word. How would she explain this to her teacher when she couldn't even remember how she got here? A memory rippled through her mind like the wind on water. What did dancing children, green grass, and music have to do with any of this? Ms. Dahl disappeared into an office and came out carrying cardboard, duct tape, and a plastic bag.

"Ms. Dahl...."

"Yes?"

"Umm...I'm sorry."

"It's late and I should get you home. Your mother will be worried. We can talk on the way to your house."

Once they were seated in the car, Isabelle asked, "Can I ask you a question?"

"Yes, go ahead."

"Why did you lie to the police?"

"I didn't lie," Ms. Dahl said, handing the plastic bag she had taken from the studio to Isabelle.

"What's this?"

Ms. Dahl smiled. "A leotard, a pair of tights, and dance slippers."

"I don't understand. Why do I need this stuff?"

"You will start classes on Monday, just like I said."

"I can't attend dance classes!"

"Oh, I think you will."

"My mother will never let me. We don't have the money."

"We have scholarships. What's your next excuse?"

Isabelle stammered under her breath, her eyes wide with apprehension.

"Isabelle, you're a talented dancer. A little rough around the edges, but talented." Ms. Dahl adjusted the volume on the radio. "Where did you learn to dance?"

"I've been to the hill and danced to the fairy music."

"What?"

Stunned by her own proclamation, Isabelle turned away from her teacher. She didn't know where the words had come from. They had appeared in her mind, and she couldn't stop them from escaping.

They drove in silence, unasked questions dangling between them. As they neared Romkey Park, Isabelle directed Ms. Dahl to take the next right then sank lower in her seat. The shame of living in her neighborhood weighed upon her. Her fellow students passed judgment on the clothes people wore and the community they lived in. The single mothers on welfare, the drug dealers, and those with a different skin color, all resided in Isabelle's neighborhood, Moorhead's slum.

Two blocks down, they turned onto her street. Her house stood dark and the strange car from earlier no longer sat on the road. Ms. Dahl pulled into the driveway.

"Do you want me to come in and talk to your mother?"

"Why?" Isabelle asked. "She's sprawled out in her bed, drunk."

"Is your mother's drinking out of control?"

"Yes."

"Have you found her stash?" Ms. Dahl asked. "When my father's drinking was at its worst, he hid his bottles all over the house. Find her stashes, confront her demons."

Ms. Dahl didn't know her mother too well.

Isabelle climbed out of the car. Her steps to the house were slow and deliberate, her hands stuffed into her pockets. Pausing at the door, she turned. "Thanks."

Carson glanced at his watch. His nerves paced like an expectant parent. If everything went as planned, Isabelle should be returning soon. Above his head, the streetlight cast a soft, yellowed halo. The symbolism didn't escape him, but he needed more than that. He turned to the next page. His work on creating a plant stone needed to be successful.

Bob's green sedan drove past, did a U-turn at the end of the block, and parked. The hi-beams flashed. A minute later, John walked out of the apartment building, showing no signs he had shot up heroin earlier. "Where's your little girlfriend?"

Carson clenched his jaw. "It's late. She's in bed."

"The Princess isn't back yet, is she?"

Words failed Carson. He turned away, covering his mouth.

"Your little trick fooled no one. Where did you send the princess?"

Carson's brain struggled to understand. How did John know about Isabelle or Princess Belle?

John snarled, eyes rolling back into his head. "They know who you are, boy. They will be coming for you...Shit, I'll be coming for you." Fangs sprouted from his gums.  Fingers transformed into claws. The stench of death covered him like a wet blanket. "You won't escape this time."

Carson leaped backwards, his fingers already working a spell. The words he needed sprang to his lips, but he held them back.

Bob's green sedan squealed to a stop in front of their apartment. The man with the scar jumped out and grabbed Carson's father. "You fool, not now," The man said and dragged him back to the car.

Carson's father leaned out the window, spittle dripped from his incisors. "You little fuck. You're as good as dead."

Carson rushed across the street and up to the second floor. His feet barely touched the stairs. He went straight to his parents' bedroom and ripped open the closet doors. Inside, drawn with thick black lines, another door.

He collapsed onto his parents' bed, his insides writhing with frustration, humiliation, and failure. A curse spread through his world at an alarming rate. The fairy tale would end soon. The Friar and his followers, the Dark Ones gobbled up innocent lives, growing fat on lost hope.

When he stepped out of the room, the ancient odor of rot and decay licked at his face. Tears ran down his cheeks. How long had they deceived him? They had played their parts well.

Opal waited on the living room couch, her eyes poisoned with bitterness. "John is gone."

"I know."

"He left you this." She handed him a needle and a note.

Carson unfolded the piece of paper.

Use it wisely, John wrote. A better death than you deserve.

Carson's footsteps grew heavier as he approached his room. He grabbed the doorknob, and it fell apart in his hand. The door swung open. Shredded pages torn from his precious books lay scattered across the room. Tomes of knowledge that could never be replaced. His mirror, broken into a thousand pieces, lay atop his desk.

Carson roared. Using his arm, he swept the desk clean. Tiny shards of glass pierced his skin, but he didn't care. Outside his window, a hostile wind blew. How could he have been so blind? He pounded his fist against his forehead. His foster parents played their simpleton roles quite well. The signs had been clear, and he missed them. The enemy had lived down the hall.

Across the street, Isabelle climbed out of a car parked in her driveway. Carson placed the syringe on the desk. He needed to protect Isabelle for as long as he could. He hoped destiny would give him a second chance.

# Chapter 19

"Sometimes it is hard to separate church and state in history," Ms. Heather Dahl told her class. "So, don't go home and tell your parents I maligned your religion. I'll try to stick to the facts and not give my opinion."

Everyone giggled.

"When we talk about the reign of Nero, we talk about contradictions—what was real and what was a myth. History has portrayed him as a monster, a sadistic man of greed and excess put on the earth to warn mankind of the grave tumult the world was in. On the other hand, the Greeks revered him and so did the populace of Rome. He lived in a dream world of art and theater."

In the back, a student raised his hand. "Didn't Nero play his fiddle while Rome burned?"

"No, he couldn't have played the fiddle. It didn't make an appearance until the eleventh century. Most historians believe he was so moved by the fire he donned his singing robes and played his lyre while the city burned. It was rumored Nero set the fire so he could clear the land to build his Golden House. None of the rumors found any footing in fact. Because of the accusations, he needed to find a scapegoat."

Isabelle spoke up. "Wasn't it the Christians?"

"Correct, Isabelle. Nero needed to divert attention away from himself and found it convenient to fasten onto the most unpopular and defenseless group he could find, the Christians. At the time, they were a strange cult that most Romans believed hated the human race. Nero dressed them in wild animal skins, and they were torn apart by dogs. Others he dressed in tar shirts, set on fire, and used their burning bodies to light his garden at night. Because of his persecution of Christians, historians believed Nero to be the Antichrist mentioned in the book of Revelations."

Sarah raised her hand.

"Go ahead, Sarah."

"My uncle is a collector of rare coins," she said, retrieving a coin from her book bag. "The image on this coin is believed to be Nero. I thought the class might want to look at it."

Ms. Dahl glanced at the clock. The bell would ring soon.

"Can you bring the coin back tomorrow?" she asked. "We'll finish our discussion on The Last of the Caesars tomorrow. Listen up. Make sure you read the rest of the chapter."

Sarah handed the coin box to her teacher. "I can trust you not to lose this, can't I?"

"Yes, I'll take good care of the coin."

Ms. Dahl touched Isabelle on the shoulder. "Do you have a moment?"

Isabelle shrugged. "Sure."

"Are you excited about Dance class tonight?"

Isabelle fiddled with the strap on her book bag. "Yeah, and a little nervous, too."

"That's understandable. Can your mother give you a ride?"

"I'm not sure."

"Did you tell your mother about my offer?"

Anger flashed in Isabelle's eyes. "My mother and I didn't speak much this weekend. She had more important things to do."

"I can give you a ride to dance." Ms. Dahl smiled. "Remember, I know where you live."

Isabelle's eyes never left her shoes.

"I can take you home to change, then I can wait for you. We can spend a few minutes before class to discuss what classes I think you should take, ballet terms you need to know, and answer any questions you might have."

"I guess, but I need to go to my locker first."

Ms. Dahl nodded. While she waited for Isabelle to return, her thoughts returned to Friday night's dream.

After she dropped Isabelle at home on Friday night, she had struggled to fall back asleep. Every time she closed her eyes, she recalled the vile memories of the pond. She would wake, choke out a scream, and fall back into a fitful slumber.

When she could clear her mind of the visions, her father's words echoed inside her mind. "Tell the Bitch he wants what's his, the books and the girl." What did her father mean? She knew who her father considered a bitch. Her grandmother's and father's mutual animosity simmered out in the open for all to see.

She couldn't sort out the meaning of the overpowering and too-realistic dream. Was it a warning? A thought gnawed at her. Would her grandmother know what her father meant? Heather would try to remember to ask.

A chair scraped the floor, and Heather glanced up. "I didn't hear you come in. Are you ready?"

Isabelle sat at one of the desks in the front row, chewing on her thumbnail. She nodded.

"Before we go, I want to talk to you about your issues at home."

Isabelle turned a deep scarlet.

"Or we could discuss Friday's test?"

Isabelle slumped in the chair. Heather sat down next to Isabelle and placed the test in front of her, a red "F" front and center. "I know being a teenager at a new school can be difficult. At times, I struggled in high school, too. I can understand the pressures and uncertainties, especially dealing with a parent who has a drinking problem."

"Leave my mother out of this," Isabelle said, gripping the edge of the desk.

The intensity of Isabelle's voice shocked her. Heather chose her next words carefully. "You had some interesting answers on your test. Wrong, but interesting. Would you like to explain?"

Isabelle shrugged.

Heather would have to find another way to break down the barrier.

"I'm not the enemy. I'm here to help. You're a smart young woman. Don't waste your time being angry. Don't worry about everyone else; concentrate on what you can control." She placed the test in front of Isabelle, sat back, and waited for some indication the girl cared. "Like this test."

Isabelle leaned over and read the answers. She quietly handed the test back, but her eyes told a different story. Hers were the frightened eyes of a child who screwed up and waited for her punishment: not just a stern lecture, more than the raised voices and harsh words of an unhappy parent, but the psychological jabs and punches of abuse.

Isabelle sat silent.

"I can be more than just your teacher. Over the past few months, and watching you dance on Friday night, I see so much potential, glimpses of how special you are. You're intelligent and caring. When you smile, you brighten up the room. You reminded me of me when I was younger." Heather ran her fingers through her hair. "Isabelle, look at me. I can be your friend."

"I'm sorry I've disappointed you." Isabelle's voice quivered as tears as big as raindrops rolled down her cheeks.

Heather scooted her desk closer and took Isabelle's hand in hers. "I'm not disappointed, just concerned. Are you on any medications or doing drugs?"

"No. I would never drink or do drugs. I'm not like my mother."

"Then tell me what's going on."

"I don't know," Isabelle said, confusion written all over her face. She tugged at her ear. "Most of Friday is blank. I woke up with a headache. I remember the walk to school, first period, and part of lunch. I don't remember anything else until the bell rang. This test and those answers? I have no clue who wrote them or what they mean."

"Why did you break into the dance studio?" Heather asked, unsure if she believed Isabelle. She hadn't lied outright, but had she purposely omitted segments of her story?

"I don't know."

"I need a better answer than that." Heather glanced at her watch. "We need to leave. Don't think this conversation is over. You owe me some answers."

Once in the car, Heather's exuberance returned. "Your first class will be Ballet I. You're more advanced, but you need to work on your technique and learn the language of dance. You should only have to take the class for a couple of weeks."

Isabelle nodded.

"You should work yourself out of this class quickly. I would like you to try Advanced Ballet too."

"Advanced ballet?"

"You will be challenged...Not only with the dancing, but Sarah is in this class."

Isabelle's eyebrows knitted into a frown. "Sarah...Okay, I'll try."

They came to the stop light at Twelfth Avenue and Twentieth Street.

"I had a fight with my Mom's new friend after school on Friday. I couldn't stay any longer, so I ran."

"What kind of fight?"

Isabelle stared out the passenger window and took a deep breath. "He wanted something he couldn't have."

"What did he want?"

"Me."

"What do you mean he wanted you?"

Heather's anger flared. Isabelle's home life was worse than she imagined. When her parents argued about her father's drinking, their fights became too much for Heather to bear. At least she could turn to her grandmother for support. To the best of her knowledge, Isabelle shouldered them alone.

"He was aroused. I think he wanted sex. So, I pulled a knife, made him bleed, and ran away."

"Where was your mom while this happened?"

"I never saw her. Probably passed out in her room."

"You need to go to the police."

Isabelle shook her head, the message in her eyes clear. No police.

"He wasn't like the guys my mom usually brings home. He was younger, clean-cut, and didn't smell of old man's aftershave. I've seen him before, at my mom's office. I think he's one of the partners. He isn't somebody you'd accuse of anything."

If Isabelle was telling the truth, Heather was more concerned about Isabelle's welfare. How could she not get the authorities involved?

They pulled behind the other car in the driveway. Isabelle's shoulders stiffened, her face grew white.

"Is everything alright?" Heather asked.

"My mother should be at work. I didn't expect her home."

"Do you want me to come in and wait for you?"

"No, I can handle her."

Isabelle stepped out of the car and walked to the front door. Once she was inside, chaos erupted. The sound of shattering glass and screaming alerted Heather to a heated battle raging inside the house. By the time Heather reached the front door, the argument had ended. She hesitated then walked back to the car, but made a mental note to talk to the principal and the counselor. Isabelle needed changes in her home life to survive. If not, she would be another statistic in a sea of statistics; a teenage suicide, an unwanted pregnancy, or she could follow in her mother's footsteps and turn to drugs or alcohol.

A few minutes later, Isabelle emerged from the house, eyes bloodshot, cheeks flushed. She reminded Heather of her sister Avery.

Isabelle wiped her tears, opened the car door, and slid in. "Sharon wasn't happy, I found her stash."

Happy that Isabelle had at least taken a stand, Heather backed down the driveway. The curtains opened, and Sharon peeked out. Heather removed her foot from the gas and the car rolled to a stop. The face in the window could have been her mother's, possessing the same fine bone structure, the same elegant style. Heather closed her eyes.

Heather turned to Isabelle. "Have I ever met your mother?"

"I don't think so."

***

Heather drove away, but she still had many unanswered questions.

At the dance studio, the glass man was busy repairing the broken door.

"Ready?" Heather asked.

"Sure."

Heather held the studio door as her newest student entered. Isabelle tried to hide her smile, but nervous excitement leaked from her pores.

"The first thing we need to talk about is the basic vocabulary of ballet. We will start with the five-foot positions. All ballet movements begin, pass through, or end in one of these five positions."

In front of the mirrors, Heather showed Isabelle all five positions, surprised at the deftness with which she learned. They had progressed to her arms when her students for Ballet I walked in. Heather gave Isabelle a quick hug. "You did well."

Heather took her young dancers through their warm-ups. They pranced around the floor to get their blood flowing, did toe raises at the barre, and stretched to loosen and lengthen their muscles. Moving onto the dance floor, Isabelle helped the girls with their arm movements. When class ended, Isabelle's smile lit up her face. The excited girls gathered around Isabelle, giving her a hug before they left.

Heather smiled at the interaction between Isabelle and the girls. Maybe she could hire Isabelle to teach this class, though it would involve more babysitting than teaching technique. She had hoped to hire another instructor before Christmas anyway.

As Isabelle glided and leaped across the floor, Heather wondered if maybe her Grandmother was right. To become a great dancer, you needed to hear the fairy music.

# Chapter 20

Sharon spent most of the weekend sick. After Tom left on Friday, she drank until the dark eyes disappeared from her mind. She paid for her bad judgment on Saturday, praying to the porcelain god. Sunday, she burrowed under the covers, too hungover to care about the world around her. When sobriety held her hostage, and the pictures in her mind became too recognizable, she drank more until the edges blurred. She suffered and wished for the world to end. Not once did her ingrate daughter check to see if she needed anything. Not a glass of water or a slice of toast offered.

Tom's call pulled Sharon out of bed. He said it would be best if she didn't come back to work, not yet anyway. She didn't think she could if she wanted to. He told her he had scheduled a meeting with Andrew to discuss his new case and planned to request her as his paralegal. He promised he would let her know when she could come back to work.

Once her call with Tom ended, Sharon considered taking a shower, hoping it would wash away the last remnants of the weekend. No such luck. Her head spun, her stomach lurched, and she lay curled up on the bottom of the tub. She crawled out and leaned against the toilet until the bile settled. She needed food.

In the kitchen, she gasped and held onto the counter. Empty vodka bottles lined the kitchen sink. "Isabelle, what did you do!"

Sharon waited in the kitchen for Isabelle to arrive home. Her anger bubbled and spilled over once her daughter walked in.

"You little bitch," Sharon yelled, an empty bottle clutched in her hands. "You had no right." A sob racked her body. "You don't understand."

Isabelle stood in the doorway, her jacket half off, as the empty vodka bottle her mother threw exploded against the door frame. Shards of glass, like glinted missiles, sprayed in all directions.

Her anger still simmering, Sharon grabbed another empty bottle. "Who in the hell do you think you are, little girl?" she screamed. The frustrations from the past few days spilled forth. "You had no right."

Her daughter glared at her with such disdain, Sharon hesitated mid-throw. Isabelle stared at her with icy contempt. Sharon expected her daughter to run to her room in tears and slink out with an apology later.

"You don't understand, I need ..." Sharon's arm fell limply to her side.

Isabelle stopped in the middle of their small living room, dropping her book bag and her jacket. She spun around and faced her mother. "You need what? You need, you need. That's all I ever hear. Do you know what I need? I need a mother."

Tears rolled down Sharon's cheeks. She needed to pull herself together. If she didn't, her life would collapse around her like so many times before, the past and present horribly mixed together. She blindly searched her purse for a smoke, lit one, and took a deep drag.

"You lied to me again. Didn't you, Mother?"

Sharon stood there, stunned.

"You never did stop drinking. Did you?"

"I...."

Isabelle walked toward her bedroom. "Do you think he's the only man you've brought home that I've seen naked?"

"What did you say to me?" Sharon yelled as she stumbled after her daughter.

"Do you know how many men have stood naked by my bed? Do you know, Mother? What about the men who have crawled into my bed, men too drunk to find their way back to yours? You disgust me!"

Sharon shook her head. Hadn't she kept her sex life hidden from Isabelle? Anxiety gnawed at her. Could she be wrong? Her mind, sputtering, and misfiring, begged for a drink to smooth away the rough edges and allow her to think clearly. Isabelle's behavior wasn't what she expected.

"I didn't know."

"You didn't know? You're too drunk to care!"

"You can't talk to me like that!" Sharon screamed.

"Not only is my mother a clueless bitch, but a drunken whore too. Who will you sleep with tonight? The same asshole as this weekend? I do admit he wasn't one of your typical bar buddies. How much did he pay you?"

Like a rabid dog, Sharon leaped and snarled. "You little tramp. What did you do to turn him on?"

"You saw how much I wanted him. I left my mark with a knife."

"He came back to me. Do you hear me? He came back to me!"

Isabelle shook her head. "Someday you'll be old and gray, and no one will want that. What else will you have to offer? Fond memories?" Isabelle pushed open her bedroom door.

"You little bitch. Don't leave your room until you can apologize."

"I'm getting ready for ballet." Isabelle slammed the door behind her.

"What do you mean?" Sharon pounded on the door, her anger beyond control. "We don't have money to waste on dance. Isabelle, open this door right now."

No matter how hard Sharon tried, she couldn't walk away. A lifetime of pain and guilt ran unchecked through her soul. She could no longer stop the offensive words that spewed from her mouth.

"I should have never kept you. I should have let him have you. Such an ungrateful little bitch. I should have listened. I should have listened!"

Sharon lit another cigarette and struggled to the couch. Plumes of smoke swirled around her head like a crown of doom. Would the nicotine be enough to appease her shaky nerves? Apparently not. A deep-buried rage raced through her veins. How dare Isabelle speak to her like that? Pain and resentment ate away at her core. The thirst of her demons begged for something stronger. She lit another cigarette and waited.

Isabelle's door opened, and her daughter walked out, eyes puffy. She wore a black leotard and pink tights, a pair of sweatpants clutched in her hand. Her hair was pulled back into a high pony. She grabbed her jacket. "Mom, I'm scared."

So am I.

Isabelle left the house and stepped into a car Sharon didn't recognize. Did Isabelle lie about dance? Was it a boy or maybe Tom who waited outside? She let out a breath, relieved to see a woman driver.

On the couch, she closed her eyes. What upset her the most? The vodka poured down the drain or her inability to cope with life sober? Could she make her daughter understand the demons who plagued her every waking moment when she couldn't confront them herself? Hadn't she tried? Could she ask God for help? She tried once, but He didn't listen.

One night, at the age of eight or nine, she wondered if God existed. Every night she prayed for a mother and a father, but He never answered. Why couldn't she be loved?

Even after confession, when the priest absolved her of sin, and the church forgave her, Sharon felt unclean. When she peered into her own heart, she saw nothing worthy of God's love. The terrors of hell ruled her soul.

Drifting in and out of sleep, Sharon found no comfort in her dreams, so she paced the house like a caged animal. The urge to drink overwhelmed her common sense. In the kitchen, she dug through the cupboards and tossed everything to the floor. After attacking the hall closet Sharon moved on to the bathroom. She even pulled the cover off the toilet. No bottle.

Damn you, Isabelle. Her daughter's uncharacteristic behavior surprised her. Isabelle never pushed back.

Her body craved a drink. Her mind desperately needed a drink. For her sanity to stay intact, she needed to push back those childhood memories.

She paused at Isabelle's closed door before pushing it open and peering in. Neat and tidy. Bookshelves lined one wall. Her desk, uncluttered. Piles of clothes littered the closet floor. In a corner, the cute sweaters she purchased Isabelle lay wadded up in a ball. This was why Isabelle didn't have any friends, no fashion sense. Books were Isabelle's friends.

Sharon swallowed three ibuprofen, chewed two berry-flavored antacids, and slunk back into bed.

A sudden knock on the door startled her from sleep. She kept her eyes closed and ignored the sound, but the knocking continued.

"This better be good." Sharon pulled on her robe and headed to the front door.

Tom stood on the steps, his blue eyes gleaming with hunger. Sharon blushed, pleased to see how much he wanted her. The cold November air hardened her nipples. Goose pimples covered her body. Tom took the sight as an invitation and stepped into the house.

He tugged at the belt of her robe. "A present for me? It's so nicely wrapped, it's almost a shame to open."

Tom slipped the robe off Sharon's shoulders and pulled her naked body tight against his. The wool of his jacket, like sandpaper, rubbed against her erect nipples. He kissed her hard, his tongue dancing at the entrance to her mouth. She knew she should stop. Isabelle was who he wanted.

But he had come back to her.

Tom's kisses trailed down her neck. His strong hands grabbed her ass. A small sound of wonder came from her throat. She ran her fingers through his hair, and she urged his kisses lower. He had other ideas. Stepping back, he unbuckled his pants, smiled, and guided her head down. Oral sex–not her favorite activity, but she was talented.

After a couple of minutes, Tom pushed her away. He kicked off his shoes, stepped out of his pants, and folded them. "I talked to Andrew about your job. At first, he had no desire to compromise." He loosened his tie. "Until I shared a secret, one of his dirty little secrets, and he changed his mind. It seems we all have dirty little secrets. You can come back to work tomorrow." He unbuttoned his shirt. "I have thirty minutes."

Sex was different this time; a little rougher, a distinct sense of urgency. The piston-driving strength of Tom's body possessed her. Afterward, they lay in silence. He dressed without words. He kissed her forehead and left the room.

A couple of minutes later, he stood in the doorway. He pulled a small flask from his jacket pocket and tossed it on the bed. "I thought you might need this."

# Chapter 21

Ms. Dahl clapped her hands, the signal for dance class to start. The girls split into their respective social groups. The Moorhead High girls (Sarah, Michelle, and Jordan) mingled in one corner, and the four Fargo girls gathered in another. Isabelle stood alone, her face flushed from her earlier class.

"I would like to introduce our newest member, Isabelle Gunderson. She's a junior at Moorhead High School. Please make her feel welcome."

The two groups clapped along with Ms. Dahl. Isabelle met Sarah's scowl with a smile. This wasn't school. She wouldn't be pushed around.

Earlier with the Ballet I dancers, Isabelle danced on air. Electricity she couldn't describe pulsed through her limbs. She fed off the children's boundless energy and their willingness to please. They seemed unafraid to make mistakes. Butterflies fluttered inside her. Anxious to dance, she wanted to show Sarah she was more than her equal.

"I want to start today with the combinations we worked on last—"

"Can I give a demonstration on how the combination is supposed to be performed?" Sarah said.

"Go ahead."

Sarah moved into position.

In the third position, her feet should be turned out, parallel, partly overlapped, with one foot in front of the other. One of the key fundamentals Ms. Dahl taught was that the heel of each foot should touch the middle of the other. Lazy like her arms, which routinely dropped below her shoulders, Sarah's heels didn't touch either.

Sarah moved across the floor and performed the combination.

Isabelle nodded. Good but not perfect.

"Thank you, Sarah. First group ...ready?"

Sarah strutted over to where Michelle and Jordan huddled and assumed the prominent spot. One of the Fargo girls fell in behind. Ms. Dahl started the music. The group performed the combinations.

"Next group."

Ms. Dahl leaned close to Isabelle and whispered, "Do your best."

Isabelle moved to the back of the group, her mind focused on her technique. No lazy arms. The music started. Her group, not as talented but technically sound, danced across the floor. She concentrated too hard on her arms, and her feet betrayed her. A slight miscue, a stumble. If she noticed, so would Sarah.

The girls from the first group whispered, laughed, and pointed. Sarah rolled her eyes and smirked. Her body language told Isabelle all she needed to know.

"You're a worthless piece of crap. Is that the best you could do?" Isabelle's father whispered.

Isabelle gritted her teeth.

"Dad, I don't know what you saw, but she isn't good enough to share the same stage with me." Isabelle imagined what Sarah would tell her father.

"Again," Ms. Dahl said.

The first group stepped it up, performing with more precision, more energy. Their bodies radiate confidence. Sarah wanted her to fail, to rub her nose in it. If Isabelle messed up again, Sarah would bury her at school tomorrow. Isabelle set her jaw.

"Isabelle," Ms. Dahl said, "please move to the front and lead your group."

Isabelle blushed. Her group did a better job, but tonight, she only cared about her performance. She wanted perfection. She needed to be better than Sarah.

"Jordan, please change places with Isabelle." Ms. Dahl requested. "This time, immerse yourself in the music."

Isabelle took a spot behind Sarah. The music started and she squeezed her eyes shut. The space behind her eyes became prickly. No! No! No! Not a headache. She opened her mind and in between the notes, fairy music played, wild and capricious. She stood on the hilltop with the children and Jeppe. She wiggled her toes in the cool green grass. The crisp, clean night air invigorated her. She immersed herself in the music and danced. The song ended, and she opened her eyes to the stunned faces of the other dancers.

She stood in the silence, her heart racing with excitement. All the girls except Sarah patted her on the back. On the inside, she wanted to do cartwheels, but all she did was smile. The girls accepted her. For the rest of the class, she belonged.

Isabelle waited for Ms. Dahl's last class to finish. She sat in the reception area, worked on homework, and wished the night would never end. The minute she walked out those doors, life's hardships would return. The dream would end. Life could be different at school.

The two other Moorhead dancers, Michelle and Jordan, talked to her after their class ended. Sarah glared and stormed out. Isabelle had proven her point, but at what cost?

When Ms. Dahl came out of her office, Isabelle sat alone, books propped on a table. "You danced great tonight."

Isabelle smiled. "Thanks."

"Are you ready to go?"

"No, not really," Isabelle said. "I want more. The studio feels like home, a place where I belong. As soon as I walk out those doors, my life will revert back to the way it was. I'm tired of that life."

"Do something to change it."

"What can I do?" She scrunched up her forehead and groaned. "I'm only sixteen."

"Have you thought about living with your dad?"

Isabelle had. She even replayed the conversation in her head several times. What would it be like to live with him? Not good. The outcome never changed. Her mother needed her, and her dad didn't. He'd started a new life that didn't include her.

"He doesn't have time for me." Isabelle shoved her books into her backpack.

"Have you talked to your mom about the issues you have with her?"

"What good would it do?" She flung her backpack over her shoulder, turned her back on her teacher, and walked toward the door.

Her mother hid secrets, but so did she. She had never told anyone about the night that changed everything in their lives. Closing her eyes, she pushed those memories deeper, but they spilled forth anyway.

Isabelle lay in bed and listened to the restless activity of the night. A dark shadow slid in front of her window. A familiar face appeared, outlined in the moonlight, and hauntingly blurred. The kind you remembered but couldn't remember where it came from. His visage drew her out of bed.

The floor creaked. Faint footsteps sounded outside Isabelle's door, and the shadow glided past. She counted to ten then followed.

She inched her way down the hall and avoided the squeaky boards. She paused, but the need to know pushed her forward. Her mother's doorway beckoned. One more step.

Isabelle's breath caught in her throat. She forgot about the man's face as her mother's arms wrapped around the stranger's neck. Her mother guided his hands to the straps of her dress. He slipped the gown over her head. The white cloth fluttered to the floor. The stranger stepped back and admired her mother's naked body. She opened her arms, and he accepted. Isabelle turned away. Like rain, tears flew down her cheeks.

Isabelle crawled back into bed. Unanswered questions haunted her sleep and dark secrets roamed the corridors of her mind. Her mother's infidelity filled her with guilt and shame. How could she ever trust her mother again? Her mother could never know she knew.

Her father scared her the most.

Isabelle and her father had never been more than careful strangers. What had she done to create such a large void in their relationship? Maybe she'd never know, but no lie escaped him. He could see her soul through her watercolor blue eyes. When he caught her in a lie, his belt sought the truth.

What could she do? She was too young to leave and had no place to go. Only one place to hide such crucial information, and it had to be someplace where nobody could look.

Isabelle grabbed all the incriminating memories and images, bunched them into a ball, and crammed them into the nooks and crannies of her mind. She stopped and gazed in the mirror for the last time at the old Isabelle, the one she knew so well. "Goodbye, my friend."

She took a deep breath, wiped her arm across her face, and disappeared into the tangled mess of her subconscious. She immersed herself in her new story.

"Oh, Mother. Why?" she cried.

"Isabelle?" Ms. Dahl asked.

Isabelle blinked several times and rubbed her forehead. "Um…what did you say?"

"Did you see Sarah's expression as she left?"

"Yeah, she wasn't happy."

"A little competition won't kill her. If she wants to be the best, she'll have to work a little harder."

"I'm not the best. I have so much to learn."

"But you have a gift. If you work hard, you can be the best."

Isabelle blushed. "I'll try."

As they climbed into the car, Ms. Dahl said, "Your situation at home isn't healthy. Your mother needs help, and so do you."

"I know...." Isabelle wiped the tears with the back of her hand. "I know."

"Would you talk to one of the school counselors?"

Isabelle swiveled in her seat. "Why can't you just be my teacher?"

Ms. Dahl pulled away like she had been slapped. "Because...I...I want to be more than your teacher."

"Why do you care?"

Pain filled her teacher's eyes. "We have a connection."

"Can't I just go to bed one night with a smile on my face?"

"Isabelle."

"Teach me to dance but stop meddling in my life."

Sadness clouded Ms. Dahl's face. "I'll try."

They pulled into the driveway. No strange cars.

"When's the next class?"

"Wednesday at seven," Ms. Dahl said. "Make sure you do your homework tonight. You need at least a 'C' in all your classes if you want to dance."

Isabelle acknowledged the comment with a nod and exited the car

Another day of ups and downs, a roller coaster ride of emotion. She didn't want the day to end. When she pulled on her dance slippers, her worries and troubles vanished. Except maybe for Sarah, but the studio leveled the playing field. The music brought to the surface the girl who hid inside, the Isabelle she searched for but never found.

Excited to tell Carson about Dance, she scanned the block in search of him. At the corner, under his favorite streetlight, she found nothing but darkness. An uneasy feeling intruded into her happy thoughts. She would have to stop by tomorrow and tell him everything.

# Chapter 22

This time, Tom left before Isabelle arrived home. Sharon's argument with her daughter had brought on a stronger urge to drink. Her hands shook as she rifled through the sex-scented sheets, searching for the flask Tom had brought. She hoped enough would be left to stifle the memories and keep her past at bay.

Sharon unscrewed the cap and tilted back the bottle. A few drops reached her tongue. She rattled the container, trying to coax out a few more.

"Fuck," she screamed, throwing the flask against the wall. She put her head in her hands. Her body craved more. "Oh God," she whispered. "Help me."

The telltale signs of a headache announced itself. A shadow flashed in Sharon's dresser mirror. She turned, but nothing behind her could have caused the dark shape. In the mirror, a pair of eyes, dark and menacing, stared back. Her hands shaking and lips quivering, she buried her head in a pillow, wishing the eyes away.

With dread, she counted to ten before opening her eyes. She blinked several times. In the mirror, a door appeared at the end of a long dark hallway. Etched onto its surface, a single blurred word. She leaned closer, the word shifted into focus. SHARON written in capital letters.

A dark figure appeared inside the mirror. Sharon fell forward, and her fingers disappeared into the glass. An icy chill enveloped her hands. She yanked them back. The door to her room slammed shut.

She grabbed the doorknob. She needed out. Right now.

Everyone warned her about her drinking and the health consequences that continued abuse could cause. This must be a hallucination, but she hadn't drunk that much today, had she? What else could this be?

A dark shadow figure inserted a key into the lock. A sudden coldness filled Sharon with desperation. "Please don't. I beg you."

She backed away, hands trembling. She shoved and yanked, but the door refused to open. "Isabelle? Anyone? Let me out!"

Sharon tried the knob again. This time the door swung open. "Yes, thank you, God, thank you."

She staggered out of the room straight into another.

She turned around. Her bedroom appeared in the mirror. She rushed forward, but the cold glass stopped her progress. Her guttural scream pierced the room as she backed away in quick steps. "No...no...this can't be real."

In her mind, the lock clicked open. She was the dark figure, and this was her nightmare. She dropped the key, and the heavy door swung open. Through the threshold, her past waited. Her mind told her to run, but her feet refused to listen. She inched forward. Her future slammed shut behind her.

Sharon stood rooted. The pitch-black darkness had swallowed all her senses. "Hello?" The single spoken word disappeared into the cavernous void. She pushed herself forward, using her arms for balance. "Is anybody there?"

Her hands searched for substance. Her heart raced to new anxiety levels. A gust of air slashed against her face, blasting her nostrils with the reek of decay and the stench of stagnant water. The demon from her past touched her. She spun around and scrubbed at her body, trying to rub away the iciness of his touch. His breath was at her neck, caressing her skin with his moist lips. She prayed he would disappear. He spun her around, and his dark, menacing eyes sent chills up her spine.

She ran, fell, got up, and ran some more. Memories snapped at her heels. As she roamed the darkness, terror pushed her forward and kept her on her feet. A speck of light appeared in the distance. Another door materialized, glowing under the light of a single bulb. An ancient set of keys dangled from a nail. She couldn't go back because he waited for her. Happiness, sadness, love, hope, and devastation singed her memory.

She slid to the floor, her back pressed against the door. The keys ridiculed her from above. Darker shadows crisscrossed in front of her. Soft giggles pierced the silence. The hairs on the back of her neck stood like tiny nails.

She grabbed the keys, inserted the first of seven into the lock, and pushed the door open. A well-lit corridor waited. She stepped in. The door closed without a sound.

The mirrored walls echoed with her past. Memories of faces and voices nipped at her skin. The hunger to leave gnawed at her heart. She searched for a handle, but none existed. She wished for the darkness. The bright lights ate at her skin and revealed too much of her soul. The walls shimmered with the reflection of her true self. Swallowing the lump in her throat, she knew the only path was forward.

The walls never changed. As Sharon followed the corridor, her visage traveled alongside. At the first intersection, she needed to choose a path. Being left-handed, she decided on left turns. For the next ten minutes, she continued turning left. With no end in sight and no idea if there was a way out of the labyrinth, she pressed on.

Birds chirped somewhere in the distance. The strong smell of a pine forest prevailed. Sharon rounded the next corner and found herself surrounded by trees, the corridor gone. A simple two-story white farmhouse stood in a clearing.

A dirt path led to a small porch. The house, the air she breathed, and the dirt she trod upon seemed vaguely familiar. The house pulled her closer. The planks creaked as she stepped onto the porch. The murmur of voices inside paused then continued. She peered in the window at an ordinary couple sitting at the kitchen table. He read the paper, and she sipped from a cup, an apron tied around her waist, Bernice embroidered on the top. The image faded. Sharon moved on before the tears flowed.

At the back of the house, a small stream flowed by a large garden. On tiptoes, she peeked inside another window. A woman with a kind face knelt on the floor in front of a large blanket. All the pain of childhood resurfaced when she realized the possibilities. Could this be her mother? Sharon followed the young woman's gaze. Two small children rolled together on a blanket. If she was one of them, could the other child be her sister?

An unseen force pulled her from the window. "No," Sharon begged. "Let me stay."

An empty space formed around her heart. She wanted to understand more about her younger life and the people inside the home. Was Bernice her mother? Why had she given her to the nuns? What had happened to the other child?

The orphanage, cold and loveless, left scars on her soul. On her seventh birthday, she asked Mother Superior why she didn't have a mom and dad. Her answer? The church was her family. God was her father, and the nuns were her mothers. If she wanted to see her parents in heaven, she needed to follow God's word. Had Mother Superior lied, like so many times before?

Sharon glanced back at the babies and the woman one last time. Her heart ached to the point of bursting. The strings of time pulled her further away. She followed the stream. The longer she walked, the more familiar the landscape. Rounding the bend, she arrived at its source. The pond's black velvet waters glistened in the twilight. Memories came flooding back.

The Evangelical Sisterhood of Mary, an orphanage and a religious refuge, sat atop the bluff. The nuns believed everyone sinned daily. Repent, and you will have a foretaste of heaven. Sharon struggled with her religion then and now. Mother Superior told her that God reveals His glory to the eyes of the faithful. She tried to be faithful.

Sharon continued towards the convent. Her entire body wedded to the sounds of the woods. After a couple of steps, the voices returned. They directed her through the stillness of the night like they did so many nights as she was growing up.

She found his voice beyond the scrim of the dark mist radiating from the pond. She felt his presence before he whispered her name.

The scars and the painful memories of the past had festered, causing misery to control her life. She had no desire to confront them tonight – or any night. She ran, but his laughter followed. The forest disappeared, and Sharon ran down the mirrored corridors again, passing through a lighted doorway. She fell to the floor and curled into a ball, her soul lost and tormented. Many parts of her life, pushing at the corners of her subconscious, wanted to be recognized. She closed her eyes, not caring if she ever found her way out. Death would be preferable to the life she led.

When she opened her eyes, she found herself on the floor in her room. The image of the door faded. She had no trouble reading the words written on the mirror this time. HOME. She pulled too hard on the knobs of her top dresser drawer, and the dresser teetered and crashed to the floor. Her panties and bras fell in a heap. The clink of glass echoed as a bottle hit the floor. She dug through the pile until she found what she craved. The bottle of vodka wasn't full, but it might be enough to silence the words she had heard as she ran away.

The warm liquid burned, lighting a fire down to her toes. She tried to ignore all sensations, to just be an empty vessel, but she failed.

His words reverberated. "Bring me my child!"

# Chapter 23

In the dark quiet of the living room, Isabelle found her mother sprawled on the couch. She helped her stand then sat on the edge of the bed, gazing at her mother's face. Sharon had aged ten years since they moved to Moorhead. Her mother mumbled, her mouth twisting into a grimace. Even at rest, her face appeared troubled. Isabelle brushed a strand of hair away from her mother's eyes. How long before their lives crashed into a million pieces? Where would they go this time?

Isabelle went to her room to finish her homework. Tonight was one of the rare nights she completed it all. Tired and a little sore but the glow from her dance class lingered. Wednesday couldn't get here soon enough. She closed her eyes for a moment's rest.

The fairy mound appeared, filling her mind with the joyous notes of their airy music. She smiled, but the nagging certainty that something dark lurked in the woods never left. A figure watched from just outside of her peripheral vision, partially obscured in a patch of shadow. A cold sweat dotted Isabelle's forehead, her chest constricted. The nameless creature, with eyes bright, nodded and disappeared.

The sensation of two red hot nails pierced her eyes, and the headache started with a roar. She rushed to the bathroom.

She dropped to the floor, grabbed the toilet seat, gagged, and expelled this round of vileness. She rested her forehead on the cold tile, waiting for her stomach to settle.

"Oh, God." The vise grip of pain intensified. The dark thoughts that she had been keeping at bay took advantage and slipped back in. There was no escape. A sense of futility rocked her to sleep.

***

The sound of the shower woke Isabelle. She pried her eyes open to daylight and wondered how she had made it back to bed. She winced at the foul taste in her mouth and the remnants of last night's headache and rolled over to check the time.

Dirt rained down on her damp pillow. She ran her fingers through her hair, pulling out small broken sticks and leaves until a pile formed on her bed. What the hell?

"No way."

She held up her dirt-encrusted hands, turning them over, unable to fathom the possibilities.

She threw back the covers. Her legs from the knees down were covered in mud. Large globs of mud littered the bed.

What happened last night? How could she explain to her mother why she was covered in filth?

When her mother finished in the shower and closed the door to her room, Isabelle darted across the hall, sheets wrapped around her feet. Safe in the bathroom, she leaned her head against the door and waited for her heartbeat to slow.

Setting the water as hot as she could stand, she laid down in the tub and let the water cascade down like rain, thrumming in her ears. This was enough to clear her mind and impose order on her thoughts.

Isabelle inspected her red, raw feet. She traced one of the angry scrapes with her fingernail and pain flared in response. Where had she gone last night? What was wrong with her? She hoped Carson could answer her questions. If anybody knew, he would.

"Carson's dead," someone said with a giggle.

"Why do you say that?" Isabelle snapped back. "It's not funny!"

"You know it's true. I'm only speaking the truth."

"Shut up! Carson isn't dead." A quiver of fear grew in her stomach.

Pain surged and twisted behind her eyes. The familiar shadows of Romke Park filled her mind. She could see a young body lying on the ground behind the basketball courts and tucked into a corner. The coppery, metallic taste coated her mouth. Thick, clotted blood covered everything: splashed against the building, splattered across the white snow, and a scarlet pool under the body. In the dim light, a message was written above the magic-marker-drawn door: Take away the eyes, and the body dies.

Is that what I did last night?

Isabelle opened her eyes, but all she saw was red splashed against white. She shook her head until the world around her returned to normal. She turned off the water.

Did I kill my best friend?

Isabelle grabbed a towel and wiped off the fogged mirror. As the condensation beaded, she glanced at her reflection, horrified by her bedraggled appearance. She swallowed the bile that crept up her throat, took a deep breath, and opened the door. Her mother stood, hands-on-hips, haggard and unsteady.

She walked to the bus stop, hoping to find Carson already there. Should she stop at Carson's apartment to see if he was home? Maybe he caught a bug and stayed home sick?

Or maybe he's dead?

Isabelle hurried north and, within minutes, reached the edge of the park. A patrol car, its lights on but no siren, drove past and headed behind the pool. Two large pine trees blocked her view of the basketball courts and the restrooms. She took a large breath and focused on being positive.

"Caw, caw, caw."

Two large ravens sat high in the branches. Their beady eyes scrutinized her as they hopped from branch to branch.

"Death, death, death," the two birds said in unison.

Isabelle's next steps took her past the trees. Behind the yellow crime tape wrapped around the restroom, police scurried everywhere. Her arms and legs started to shake. If she didn't hurry, she would be late again, and this time would mean detention and the possibility of no dance. She told her feet to continue down the sidewalk to school, but this morning they had a mind of their own. She stepped into the ankle-deep snow and made a beeline to the basketball courts. One of the officers glanced up and tapped another officer on the shoulder.

"Oh, shit," Isabelle muttered.

Sheriff Erickson's eyes locked on her and followed her approach.

Her fear of the unknown outweighed her stupidity. She needed to get closer to see the words written above the body and prove to herself that she didn't kill Carson.

Carson's voice drifted from the restrooms. "Isabelle..., Isabelle.... Why did you let them kill me?"

"Who killed you, Carson?"

Her legs wobbled when she stopped in front of the yellow police tape. "This is no place for you, Isabelle," Sheriff Erickson said.

Isabelle and the sheriff stood at the edge of the basketball court and studied each other like two gunfighters. The sun peeked through the clouds like a spotlight, illuminating the corner where the body lay covered. Isabelle read the words written over the body. Unbearable pain and anguish washed over her. She turned to hurry back the way she came but the sheriff grabbed her arm and spun her around.

"Why are you here?"

Isabelle forced a smile and pushed her panic deep within herself, someplace the sheriff couldn't see it. She needed to calm down and understand the meaning of the words written above the body.

"Is it Carson?"

"The body hasn't been identified," he said as he led her to his patrol car. "If your mother found out I drove you to school, she would be pissed, but let me give you a ride anyway. I think we need to talk. Get in."

Isabelle waited for the sheriff to open the back door.

"The back seat is for criminals. Sit up front."

Sheriff Erickson pulled away from the curb, and as the yellow crime tape faded in the distance, something green flashed in the side mirror.

"Where were you last night?" Carson asked. "I needed your help. I waited but they...."

"What?" Isabelle asked.

"I said you must have danced well last night," the sheriff repeated. "When Sarah came home, she was pissed as hell."

Isabelle tried to listen to what Sarah's father said, but her overwhelming grief muffled his words and Carson's accusations reverberated. He had always been there for her. Where had she been when he'd needed her the most?

He was dead because she failed him.

"Competition is good for her," Sheriff Erickson said. "If she wants to be the best, she needs to work a little harder. Most things come too easy for her."

No shit!

"Sarah's a great dancer. I could learn so much from her."

"You'll be a wonderful addition to the studio."

"I hope so."

"We talked to the tenants who live in the apartments adjacent to the park this morning. Do you know what they told us? A girl who fits your description dances most nights in the park....a girl who can really dance."

The police cruiser pulled up to the front doors of the high school. Isabelle shifted uncomfortably, anxious to get out. The sheriff had an accusatory tone she didn't like. Her hands trembled. If she hurried, she could make it to her homeroom before the bell rang.

"Thank you for the ride. You saved me from detention."

The sheriff turned the car around in the parking lot as Isabelle headed to the front door. When she was twenty feet from the safety of the school, the sheriff's voice rang out. "Do you know why your friend was in the park last night?"

Isabelle didn't need to look back to know the sheriff watched. His eyes burned a hole in her back.

# Chapter 24

If death ever came knocking, Sharon would have flung open the door and embraced him like an old friend. An epic hangover assaulted her: an unsettled stomach, an angry head, and a mouth dry as sandpaper. The clock read six a.m. She dumped three ibuprofen down her throat, guzzled a glass of water, and went back to bed.

Sleep evaded her. She forced open her eyes, thankful the curtains were closed. Even in the dim light, her eyeballs begged to be covered. Exhausted, she lowered her lids. With no way of escaping herself, her mind churned in the darkness.

Sharon sat up. Her hands fumbled with the alarm, her nerves stretched taut with worry. She remembered bits and pieces of last night, but the rest was lost in a hazy black fog of alcoholic fumes. She crawled to the bathroom, only to spend the next ten minutes with her head propped on the toilet.

Last night, after Isabelle left for dance, Tom called. They agreed to meet in the conference room at nine a.m. to review the files for his new case and devise a game plan. He would provide coffee and rolls. She hoped for something stronger: vodka and orange juice, the ideal liquid breakfast.

The floor of the shower supported her head. She vowed never to drink again. A wishful thought. With slow and measured movements, she struggled to prepare for her day. She ate a dry piece of toast to calm her stomach, but that didn't work. She wanted to go back to bed, pull the covers over her head and die.

Her arrival at the office seemed to surprise her co-workers. Sharon agreed with them; she thought last Friday would be her last day too. Her presence today would be the topic of several rounds of gossip. On her way to the conference room, she ignored their curious stares and whispers. She passed the office of Andrew's eldest daughter.

"Good morning, Sharon."

Surprised by the greeting, she stopped in the doorway. "Good morning, Mrs. Erickson."

"You don't have to be so formal. Call me, Jenny. I watched your daughter dance last night. Why didn't you tell me Isabelle was a terrific dancer?"

How should she respond when she didn't even know her daughter could dance? She only learned yesterday of her daughter's desire to dance. "Thank you."

"Sarah dances at the same studio," Jennifer said with a wide grin. She pointed to a picture on her desk of her daughter dressed in orange and black. "Is Isabelle interested in the Highlights?"

Sharon didn't know what or who the Highlights were, but she heard enough about Sarah to know Isabelle didn't like her. She blushed, embarrassed by the fact she knew so little of what interested her daughter. "We haven't talked about the Highlights. Thanks. I'll discuss the opportunity with her."

"I'm the parent adviser. If you need more information or have questions, give me a call." Jennifer scribbled her phone number on a notepad and handed it to Sharon. "We would love to have Isabelle on the team."

Jennifer's excitement grated on Sharon's fragile nerves. Who in the hell did she think she was, telling her what Isabelle should do? Sharon needed to get away before she said something she would regret. "I need to go, Tom's waiting for me."

At the end of the corridor, the conference room loomed. Sharon collected her thoughts, took a deep breath, and entered. Tom handed her a glass of orange juice.

She took a small sip and handed it back. "Oh, God, no."

"How do you feel?"

"Rough."

Sharon watched as Tom pulled files from a banker's box. Why did he save her job? Could his kindness be a ploy? Did he appease her because he wanted Isabelle? He exhibited a dark side, a secret obsession for teenage girls. She should just walk away, but he possessed qualities most men didn't.

Tom dropped two stacks of files on the table in front of her.

She flinched, torn from her thoughts.

"This is what I need you to do. Read through these profiles and briefs. Jot down your initial thoughts. Understand?"

Sharon nodded.

"We can discuss them when I get back."

Sharon opened the first file, read the bio, and paged through the relevant information. As she jotted her notes, she found a rhythm. The stack in front of her grew smaller. The work kept her busy but didn't stop her from dreaming of a dark corner where she could sleep off the previous night. Nonetheless, the morning slipped away. She grabbed the last file and flipped it open.

A grainy picture of a dead German Shepard, its throat cut and missing an ear, sat on top. Her stomach lurched, and a bead of sweat formed on her forehead. She wasn't a pathologist, but the dog's cuts were performed with surgical precision. What did this have to do with Tom's current case?

Unable to resist, she flipped over the next picture and gasped. A skinned dog hung from the rafters, its fur piled in a heap below. She took a deep breath and turned over the next picture. She gasped at the image of a man sprawled on the floor, his face blown away, a shotgun near his feet. Blood smudged the wall. Letters, maybe numbers, covered the baseboard. Clearly visible on the dead man's hand, the figures 666 were written in dried blood. Someone had written Wheaties-Rapist, Suffocator of Young Girls in black marker at the bottom of the picture.

Wheaties. Why did that name sound familiar?

Sharon flipped to the next picture. "Oh, my God."

What had she gotten herself involved in?

"Sharon! What do you think you're doing?" Tom slammed his fist on the desk full of files.

Sharon jumped backward in her chair and quickly closed the file. "What the hell? You scared me to death!"

Tom towered above her, venom leaking from his pores. He snatched the file off the table and shot her an eerie smile.

Sharon inched further away.

He sat down and lined up the pictures. A moment later, he reshuffled them and laid them all out in front of Sharon as if he were dealing a game of Blackjack.

"You couldn't leave well enough alone, could you?" Tom shoved the file in front of her and pointed. "What does it say right here?" Spittle flew from his mouth.

Written on the outside of the file, PRIVATE AND CONFIDENTIAL.

She squirmed in her chair. "Then why was it with the files you gave me?"

Her mind reeled with possible explanations as Tom's angry eyes bore into her soul, He ran his cold finger down her cheek. Visions of her past came into focus. She pulled from his touch.

Tom pointed to the first picture, his tense face softening. "The first dog had to be a stray, a mutt nobody would miss. We were just kids, dabbling in things we didn't understand. We had killed smaller animals, but nothing this big. Excited to make the first cut, I slid my knife across its throat. The hot blood sprayed in long arcing streams, and as the life ebbed out of the dog, it slowed to a trickle. We learned death could be patient."

Sharon squeezed her eyes shut, refusing to listen to Tom's descriptions of the pictures laid out on the table. Her mind told her to run. The job no longer mattered. The man who sat next to her, the man who wanted to have sex with her daughter was clinically fucking insane. What did that say about her?

"Wheaties, my man, Wheaties," Tom said. "Wheaties had to die. My friend John had to die because he knew too much."

Tom grabbed another picture from the table and thrust the image in Sharon's face "Open your eyes, Sharon. Look at what I'm showing you," he said.

"Wheaties' brother, Michael, died in this crash. Michael never drank, he abhorred alcohol. We were involved in some serious shit. His conscience bothered him. He crashed into a bridge going seventy-five miles per hour. Pretty ugly." Tom shook his head and stared into space; his eyes glazed. "He didn't act alone. The police in Queens had no idea what hit them. They closed their eyes to the truth, blind to the evil that walked the streets."

Frozen in her seat and disgusted by the images, Sharon tried to focus her gaze on something else in the room.

"Do you know why Michael had to die?"

Sharon had no idea what Tom was talking about. She was too afraid to ask any questions and terrified of what the answers might be.

"Because he knew too much," Tom said.

Tom set the picture down and grasped her chin roughly, squeezing until tears formed in her eyes. His hot breath slid down her neck. She tried to pull away, but Tom tightened his grip.

"I hope I've painted a clear enough picture. People...even those we care about...die. Some are sacrificed. Some, like Andrew Dupay, are forced to commit suicide." Tom pulled a grainy picture of a postman out of the file. "I can't protect you if you tell anyone any of this."

He forced her head to nod in agreement. "I'm glad you agree with me. Nobody would believe a drunk like you anyway. Your death would be painful. Not short and sweet like those of my friends."

Sharon swallowed hard. "Does your wife know how fucked up you are?"

Tom's entire face lit up. "I am sure she's caught a glimpse of my darker side. We all have our darker sides; hidden secrets we don't reveal to our spouses...or our children." He winked at her and said, "Some just do a better job of hiding their secrets."

Tom picked up the file, kissed Sharon on the cheek, and adjusted his tie. He kept his voice low, but his words cut deep. "Should we talk about your dark secrets?"

He set another picture on the table. A large brick building stood on a bluff overlooking the dark waters of a serene pond.

Repulsed by more than his kiss, she wiped her cheek.

"I'm having lunch with my wife today. We can meet back here." Tom checked his watch. "Let's say one-thirty. We can go over your notes."

An uneasy silence filled the room as Tom left, but a battle raged inside Sharon. She knew the consequences of talking. Tom made that point perfectly clear. But if she brought the files to the police and told them everything Tom had said, would that give her enough time to disappear? No, they would find her. She didn't need a drink; she needed the whole god damn bottle. The only way to silence the noise in her head was by drowning it. She grabbed her purse and headed to the restroom to regroup.

The quiet welcomed her. She leaned against the counter, her body racked with tremors. She turned the cold water on and cupped her hands to fill. The water slipping through her fingers mesmerized her and caused an ironic laugh. Kind of like my life. After a few deep breaths, she rubbed her face, trying to massage the strain from her eyes.

Her face dry and make-up reapplied, she tossed the wet paper towel in the garbage. An image of a long hallway appeared in the mirror. The door labeled HOME mocked her.

"No!" She struck the mirror again and again with her fists. A spider web of cracks spread across the surface. Blood dripped from the many cuts, leaving bright red streaks in the white porcelain sink.

"No."

The door in the mirror creaked open.

# Chapter 25

Heather collapsed on the couch. She kicked off her boots and slid her arms out of her jacket. Ballet classes went better than she expected. Isabelle danced well and seemed to fit in, especially with the younger dancers. They'd loved her. The older girls had tolerated Isabelle, except for Sarah, who gave her the cold shoulder. No surprise. Sarah hated anyone who challenged her reign at the top.

She checked her messages. Listening to the sound of Adam's voice made her feel warm and fuzzy inside. He wanted to go out again this weekend.

Supper consisted of a frozen pizza which she ate while watching the ten o'clock news. The pile of tests sitting on the table needed to be graded and her outline for tomorrow's lecture reviewed before bedtime. Unpacking her tote bag, she found the coin Sarah had brought to class. She placed the case on the coffee table in front of her. Something about the relic bothered her. A rush of anticipation and dread whirled inside.

Heather returned from the kitchen with a glass of red wine and found two large blackbirds perched on the deck railing. She raised her glass to them. "Look at you guys."

A memory gave her a nudge and pushed her thoughts to Nero and the coin. She pulled out a book her father had written, paging through it until she found the passage.

Heather read out loud, "'During the dark ages it was believed crows were demons serving Nero's wandering spirit.' Can you believe that?" she asked the birds on her deck. "'His spirit would continue to wander until the time came for Nero's return to earth when Christ himself would hurl the Anti-Christ into the bottomless pit.' He was talking about the end of the world."

A second glass of wine didn't relieve her growing apprehension concerning the coin. She turned her thoughts to a more pressing problem. The animosity between Isabelle and Sarah had escalated. Did she allow Sarah's bullying to go too far? How could she get them to form a truce?

Loud cawing from the two boisterous blackbirds outside her patio doors drew her attention. She pounded on the door. "Knock it off."

The birds hopped closer and inspected her with mild curiosity.

The living room was filled with the odor of smoke. Heather jumped up to her feet. Did she leave the oven on again? At this rate, the papers would never get graded.

She stood in front of the stove, perplexed. All the burners and the oven were off. Had she imagined the smell of smoke? Heather returned to the living room with another glass of wine and a half-empty bottle, ready to attack the pile of tests. But the coin intrigued her. Her father, an expert in Roman coinage, had written several books on the subject. She plucked another one of his books off the shelf and took a seat on the couch.

The passages she read would make for an exciting lecture. She added the information to her notes. Unable to resist the pull of the past, Heather opened the ornate box. Her hand hovered inches from the relic. She chastised herself because she knew better than to try to handle the coin with her bare hand. In Archaeology 101, they learned about the corrosive properties of sweat. She set it back in its box and retrieved a pair of cotton gloves from the kitchen.

Heather turned the box on its side, and the coin rolled into her gloved hand. She wiped her forehead with her sleeve, gripped the edges of the coin, and inspected for any irregularities. At first glance, it appeared authentic, but when she compared it to the dozens of pictures in the book, she found no match. The coin glowed red hot in her hand.

The chorus of caws grew louder and more agitated.

"Shut up!"

A strange, vexatious sensation radiated from her palm and inched up her arm. She didn't have the strength to drop the coin. A warm glow spread throughout her body. She closed her eyes, too sleepy to keep them open. The nightmares of her youth began again.

A full moon sat high in the sky. A brilliant beam of light reflected off the dark waters and blinded her. Heather wanted to cover her eyes, but a line secured her arms. She twisted her hands, but the bristly rope dug into her wrists. The gag in her mouth stifled a scream. A noose shaped shadow dangled above her head and danced in the moonlight.

Tap, tap. Tap, tap. Tap, tap.

Heather woke, her hands resting underneath her head. She must have dreamed about the rope. The thought drifted away as quickly as it had come. More birds sat outside her window. A black curtain moved painfully at the back of her mind. She needed to finish the tests. Her eyes fluttered for a second before sleep forced its way back in.

Horrid images of death filled her with such grief, she tried to scream herself awake.

Someone laughed. "Scream all you want. Nobody can hear you."

"Where are all the people?"

"There's nobody else. You're the last."

A crimson moon slid out from behind the clouds. Heather stood at the edge of a reservoir, innocent blood lapping at her feet. Her face glistened from the heat of the fire dancing upon the inky surface of the pond. Tongues of flames licked up in defiance and challenged the heavens.

A wooden throne rose from the blood and fire. A false prophet, dressed in black with a fearsome horned mask made from the flesh of martyrs, sat on the chair. He laughed. Fury hid behind his smile.

"Behold," he raised his arms, fists balled, "this is my kingdom now and until the end of time. The innocent are doomed to my eternal flame, their young bodies ravished by fear. Their pain is my comfort. Their screams are ageless, hoarded for eternity within my grasp. The land shall revel in my wickedness. The darkness shall be mine."

Lightning ripped the sky apart. Bodies of children, stacked like cordwood, burned and illuminated the night. Trees grew from their ashes. A whole forest of grotesque, twisted trees, nurtured in hell and raised on the sorrows of man.

The children, soaked in blood and wrapped in death, rose from the pond. Their gurgled lamentations haunted the air.

Heather closed her eyes and pressed her hands over her ears. The screams leaked between her fingers and wrapped tightly around her mind.

"Caw, caw, caw."

Midnight-black birds, their beaks and talons dripping blood, gorged on the flesh of the young. Soon the carnivorous birds had picked the bones clean. The ghost-white remains rippled dreamily against the bloody background. The birds flew away into the endless night, fading into the phantasmagoria of her cluttered mind.

"Please, no more," Heather begged.

Something stirred deep within the pond. The surface rippled.

She ran, chased by the river of blood, and fell. The blood seeped over her, burning her flesh black. Blisters erupted.

She screamed in agony...

Her alarm, a high-pitched shrill sound, pierced the quiet of her apartment. Thrown from a landscape of horror back into the reality of her life, Heather lay frightened, the coin still clutched in her hand.

A layer of cold sweat covered her body. Panic enveloped her, and she gasped for air. She needed to escape the madness inside her head. When she stood, the coin fell out of her hand and rolled out of sight. Whatever spell she'd succumbed to had vanished. She crawled back onto the cushions and laid there in silence. The dreams of the last few nights had been so vivid. A journey into the dark depths of her mind. She thought the nightmares that plagued her before and after her parents' death had faded into a figment of her imagination. But she was wrong. The faceless bogeyman of her youth grew into a fleshed-out monster.

No more wine or Nero before bed again. She glanced under the couch in search of the coin. No such luck. She would look for it after her shower.

On the way to the bathroom, she stopped mid-stride. What the hell was she doing? She had her morning rituals. To deviate would mess up her whole day. She did an about-face and headed to the kitchen to start a pot of coffee. Maybe a blast of caffeine would make her feel human. If she took a shower before she made coffee, she would forget and would have to settle for the sludge dispersed from the vending machine at school.

She finished in the kitchen then washed down a couple aspirins. She sat naked on the edge of the tub and turned on the water. She waited until the steam billowed out before stepping in. The hot water scalded her skin at first, but it gradually melted away her uneasiness. She put on her robe, wrapped her hair in a towel, and went to fetch the morning paper.

At the front door, she stopped and listened. The pitter-patter of small feet echoed in the hallway. No one in the building had children. She stepped into the hall to get the paper, and the door slammed behind her.

"Oh, shit." Her nerves were more fragile than she thought.

A child laughed.

Heather pivoted.

Nobody.

Feet pounded down the stairs.

Faces of the zombie children flashed in her mind, sending a shiver through her. A cold uncertainty crept into her heart. She loved children, but she'd have to complain to the management. She didn't like parents who let their children run wild. She opened the door and ducked back inside.

# Chapter 26

The snow-covered roads made the drive to the school an adventure. Heather, her patience wearing thin, slammed on the horn and her brakes. The car fishtailed. Fortunately, she stopped before she plowed into the vehicle that slid through the intersection. "Goddamn idiots," she blurted.

She parked in her regular spot. The car's locked door swung shut before she remembered the coin. "Oh shit."

She could hurry home but wouldn't make it back in time to prepare for her first class. A trip home after lunch would have to suffice.

A fluffy blanket of snow carpeted the grounds of the school. Heather made the first footprints to the main entrance; the only doors open at this time in the morning. Stomping the snow from her feet, she headed for her classroom. Her steps echoed in the empty building. When she stopped in front of the door to her homeroom, the same snickering she heard in her apartment building's hallway reverberated down the dark corridor.

"Who's there? This isn't funny anymore."

Erie giggles continued.

Heather rushed forward, but the dark shape disappeared around the corner, the sound of the footsteps fading in the distance. Cold air wrapped her in a blanket of fear.  She quickly unlocked her classroom door, stepped in, and relocked it.

Her heartbeat thrummed. She leaned against the door until the spots in front of her eyes disappeared. Was she foolish for being scared? She flipped on the lights. They sputtered, and a cold, harsh light filled the room. The words written on the chalkboards made every hair on the nape of her neck stand at rapt attention. The boards had been erased before she'd left the previous day.

The first question from Friday's history test was written on the chalkboard behind her desk. Written below, word for word, was Isabelle's answer. The same response she said she hadn't written.

What Caused the Downfall of the Roman Empire? Cite examples.

Meddling- You have meddled in matters too exalted for you, things beyond your nature to comprehend

'I will not meddle in the affairs of others, '

Her eyes darted to the next board. 'I will not meddle in the affairs of others.'

The same answer was written on all the chalkboards around the room.

She collapsed into her chair and shook her head. No one else knew Isabelle's answers. Did the girl have more issues than she knew about or understood? Isabelle had started to open up, hadn't she? Maybe her student didn't want her help after all.

The door rattled.

Heather jumped to her feet, an icy plume of fear slid down her back. She glanced around the room in search of protection and found a pair of scissors on her desk. She grabbed them and advanced towards the door.

The door rattled louder.

She gripped the scissors tighter and inched closer to the door.

A knock. "Heather, open the door."

She opened the door just enough to peek out.

Adam stood there, a weak smile splayed across his lips. She hoped his smile would take away the uneasiness, but his smile did not last long enough. Worry was etched across his brow.

"Adam, what's wrong?"

"They found a body this morning.... a high school student.... dead, in Romkey Park."

"Oh my God, was it one of your students?"

She pulled him into an embrace. His body quivered.

"I'm not sure. The police haven't released any information. They just notified the administration to make the schools aware. I'm sure Principal Swanson—"

The intercom buzzed. "All teachers please report to the commons area."

"Are you alright?" Adam eased the scissors from her hand. "What's this about?"

She shrugged and gave his hand a squeeze. "Yes, everything will be alright."

Adam dropped her hand as they walked to the commons in silence.

Hushed whispers greeted them. They found separate seats and waited for someone to speak.

Principal Swanson stood and raised his hands. "One of our students was found dead in Romkey Park last night. The police have not made the name public or given the administration many details. When they release the name, we'll have additional counselors here and at all the other schools to help those grieving."

One of the counselors, Tammy Anderson, stood and addressed the staff. "Right after homeroom, we'll gather in the gymnasium and break the news to the students. Remember, the counselors are here not only to help the students but teachers and staff as well. If you know of any student who has questions or requires assistance, please inform the counselor's office."

Principal Swanson cleared his throat. "Before you go back to your classrooms, I have one last thing to say. The kids are our number one priority. Give them whatever support they need."

After everyone left, Heather walked up to Tammy Anderson. "Do you have a moment?"

Tammy nodded.

"I have some concerns about one of my students. Isabelle Gunderson."

"What type of concerns?"

"She's having issues at home. Alcohol issues."

"Isabelle has issues with alcohol?"

"No, her mother. Can I bring her to your office after the seventh period?"

"Funny you should mention Miss Gunderson this morning. Sheriff Erickson asked if I would sit in on a few of her classes and observe her behavior. How about we talk to her together after the seventh period?"

Heather nodded, but all the way back to her classroom, she second-guessed her decision.

After taking attendance, she led the students to the gym. Sarah and a group of girls whispered the entire way. For some reason, this irritated her. She stayed close and listened to their conversation about the dead body found in the park.

The students sat subdued as the principal delivered the news. Not a raised hand or question asked. They shuffled back into their own worlds. Between classes, hushed conversations filled the hallways. The students were nervous. Heather did not blame them. No matter how it happened, the death of a student hit hard.

Arriving home at lunch, Heather moved the living room furniture and crawled around on the floor searching for the missing coin. It had simply vanished. Tonight, after ballet class, she would rip the house apart. How could she explain to Sarah she had lost the relic?

While she searched, she thought more about Isabelle. Why would the sheriff want the counselor to keep tabs on Isabelle's behavior? Was Isabelle in trouble with the police?

Heather was not prepared for her World History class at the end of the day. She let the students work on their reports. She decided that if Sarah brought up the coin, she would tell her she left it at home. Not an outright lie. Every time Heather glanced up to check on the students, Sarah gave her a look like she already knew.

As the final bell rang, Tammy walked in and sat at the back of the class.

When Isabelle passed her desk, Heather asked for a moment to talk.

Tammy rose from her seat and moved towards them.

Isabelle studied Heather apprehensively and glanced at the school counselor. "What's she doing here?"

Tammy answered. "Ms. Dahl had some concerns about your home life and the current situation with your mother."

Heather could see the hurt in Isabelle's eyes. She tried to diffuse the situation before it escalated. "Isabelle, please understand I'm concerned about how your mother's drinking affects you."

"Why don't the three of us sit down?" Tammy suggested.

The two teachers took seats, but Isabelle stood and glared at them.

"Isabelle," Heather said. "Please sit."

She shook her head and refused to sit or speak.

"Have you gone to an Al-Anon or Ala-teen meeting to help you cope with your mom's drinking problem?" Tammy said.

"Yes, a couple of times," Isabelle answered in a cold, flat voice.

Heather realized from Isabelle's fidgeting how uncomfortable and maybe unfair this encounter would be to her student. She listened as Tammy reinforced all the benefits of the support group: the opportunity to learn about one's self and the effects of someone else's drinking on the individual.

They had ambushed Isabelle. No wonder she seemed leery and defensive.

Heather's mind drifted as she listened to Tammy's one-sided discussion with Isabelle about her mother's disease. Her thoughts returned to the dream she had of her father's alcoholism and the painful memories it dredged up. Was he drunk, like her dream suggested? Did he miss the curve on purpose?

If she gave any credence to her dream, then maybe her father had been a ticking time bomb. His fuse waited for someone or something to set him off, to give him a reason to start again. She would have to talk to Grandma. She didn't know if she could wait until her regular Friday call. She might need to talk to her tonight. Too many unanswered questions swirled inside. Grandma believed all dreams served a purpose. The past and the future could be gleaned from what you saw while you slept.

The conversation between Tammy and Isabelle concluded. After the counselor left, an agitated Isabelle turned and said, "Are you happy now? You didn't have any right to tell her about my mother! You had no right to interfere in my life."

"Relax, Isabelle. I didn't tell Mrs. Anderson anything. The sheriff wanted her to keep an eye on you today, not me. I know something else is bothering you. I can see it in your eyes."

Isabelle crossed her arms and stared belligerently at Heather.

"What did you do after dance class last night?" Heather asked.

Isabelle's face paled. Her eyes dropped to the floor. "My homework... and I went to bed."

"Okay." She pulled out Isabelle's homework from the file on her desk and scanned the papers. Heather wanted to make sure the homework had been completed.

"Okay. That's it?" stammered Isabelle. "That's all that you have to say?"

"I see you turned in your homework."

"I told you I did my homework." The pitch of her voice grew higher. "Why did you ask me what I did last night?"

"You really want to know? Okay, I'll tell you. Somebody came into my classroom, this classroom, last night, and left me a little present on the board. A warning to quit meddling!"

Isabelle stared at her teacher in disbelief, fidgeted with her hair before she answered. "You think I did it?"

"It crossed my mind."

Heather understood Isabelle's internal struggle, the battle of wills. Would the truth finally spill forth? Would Isabelle ask for her help? Like a big sister, Heather wanted to take Isabelle in her arms and tell her everything will be alright.

"I didn't do it," whispered Isabelle, her hands clenched together, her knuckles white. "I'm not sure what I did last night, but I know I didn't come to school."

"What did you do last night?"

"I don't know." She glanced up at Heather. Her eyes pleaded. "That's the problem. I don't remember."

"I'm not sure I understand."

"Last night, after doing my homework, I had one of my headaches. I blacked out. I woke up this morning with leaves in my hair, and my feet were muddy, red, and sore."

"You walked in your sleep?"

"Ms. Dahl, it's more than that. I know who died in the park. My best friend, Carson." Tears streamed down her face. "And I know too much about the crime scene. I think I'm involved somehow."

# Chapter 27

Ms. Dahl walked towards Isabelle, a look of concern on her face. She held out her arms and Isabelle melted into them. Squeezed tight against Ms. Dahl's chest, she went limp. Isabelle needed to be protected, needed to feel safe.

"Are you alright?"

Isabelle did not have the strength to shake her head. No lights flashed before her eyes, no sounds exploded in her mind, but Ms. Dahl's memories tugged and pulled at her emotions more than the first time. The stench of decay overwhelmed her nostrils, smoke irritated her eyes, and a gust of wind pushed against her face. The taste of fear and panic sat bitterly on her tongue. She experienced a sense of falling from a great height. Blurred shapes flew past her eyes.

Heather and Isabelle stepped apart and a chill swept over Isabelle. Her throat itched and burned. Her neck ached. As anxious as a child who stumbled upon something they did not understand, she didn't want Ms. Dahl to see the terror in her eyes. The same dark shadow she saw before Carson's death appeared for an instant behind her teacher. Death had put its mark upon Ms. Dahl. Isabelle didn't know the when, where, or how, but her instincts told her it would be sooner rather than later.

"It's been a long day. I'm getting a headache." Isabelle massaged her temples. "Can you give me a ride home?"

"Yes. Are you sure you're okay? You don't look well."

"I'll be fine. A few aspirins should do the trick," Isabelle said, though she suspected she may never be alright.

Neither of them spoke on the drive home; an uneasy truce had been reached. Isabelle guessed Ms. Dahl knew she had lied. Isabelle intruded like a thief into a part of her teacher's life she would not have shared otherwise. How could any of this be her fault? Still, she felt guilty. Questions lingered in her teacher's eyes, a tenseness clearly visible in her body language. Ms. Dahl teetered on the edge of a cliff and Isabelle did not want to be present when she fell, and didn't want to answer the questions she knew Ms. Dahl would ask. Isabelle couldn't sit any longer. She needed to get out.

"Do you and your mom have plans for Thanksgiving?" Ms. Dahl asked.

Isabelle plopped back down on the seat, surprised by her teacher's question. "I don't know."

"Would you join my family for Thanksgiving?"

"I'll have to ask," Isabelle said as her heart raced. "I'm sure mom is excited to pop another turkey loaf into the oven this year."

"Please do." Ms. Dahl hesitated. "This is going to sound crazy, but I think we're related."

"Why would you think that? Where are you from?"

"Pine Bluff. It's an hour or so west of Duluth."

"I've never been to Duluth." Isabelle stepped out of the car then leaned back in. "I promise I'll ask about Thanksgiving," she added. "Thanks for the ride. See you on Monday."

Isabelle fought back tears of happiness and sadness as her teacher drove away. Could Ms. Dahl be right? Could they be related? Having a family was one of Isabelle's greatest dreams. Most Thanksgivings, not to mention the rest of the holidays, she spent with just her parents. Since their divorce, it had only been her and her mother. She was jealous of the kids who had large families, Thanksgiving feasts, and cousins to spend time with. Maybe a Grandma to hug too.

Life could be cruel. This could be Ms. Dahl's last Thanksgiving. The Lord giveth and the Lord taketh away. Isabelle needed to find a way to stop Ms. Dahl's death. But how?

The hairs on the back of Isabelle's neck prickled and a heavy uneasiness settled on her shoulders. Somebody watched her. She stopped at the bottom of the steps and turned. Carson's mother, Opal, stood in the window of her second-story apartment and glared down at her. She ducked from view when they made eye contact.

Isabelle walked up the steps. The sound of a door slamming shut made her turn around. Opal, eyes wide, barreled towards her, fists balled, arms rigid at her side. Hostility rolled off her in waves. She stepped into the street and pointed one of her meaty fingers at Isabelle. "You little cunt! Carson's dead because of you."

The accusation struck Isabelle like a brick to the side of the head. *Why would she blame me for his death?*

"I didn't kill Carson." Isabelle fired back. "He was my friend."

Tears blurred Isabelle's vision. Her hand shook as she inserted the key into the lock. Opal tossed accusations like hand grenades, and Isabelle didn't want to be hit with another one. Behind her eyes, the darkness of another headache crept closer. *Hurry, Isabelle, hurry.* The harder she tried, the more she fumbled with the key.

"God damn it." The key slipped from her fingers. She picked it up and used both hands to line it up. Behind her, Opal huffed and puffed as she crossed the street.

Isabelle closed her eyes and tried to concentrate.

The key slid into the lock. She scurried inside and leaned against the door, her forehead pressed into the wood. Safe. Opal stood on the other side, verbally assaulting her and her mother. She could rant and rave all she wanted; Isabelle stopped listening..

Reality became all too real. Carson was dead. Isabelle brushed the wetness from her eyes.

"Isabelle...Do you hear me?" shouted Opal. "You let my boy die."

Cold icy fingers clutched Isabelle's shoulder. The butterflies in her stomach froze. Her knees wobbled.

An image of Carson rippled in the middle of the room, his face etched in sorrow. "Why did you let them kill me?"

"Carson?"

"I kept you safe. I watched over you." His face flickered in the shadows of her living room.

"Don't leave. Carson...No."

He reached out for her. "Come with me."

The air around him radiated a frigid uneasiness, but she grasped Carson's hand. Loss and despair filled her heart. She tried to let go of him, but he held on tight. "Isabelle, I don't want to be alone."

As Carson pulled her towards him, his body started to disappear. Her hand flickered and became invisible. Panicking, she pulled herself free.

"You were supposed to be my friend, but you let them kill me."

Did he speak the truth?

Isabelle shoved the curtain aside and peeked out. Opal had crossed the street and was pacing the sidewalk in front of Isabelle's house, talking to herself.

Opal stopped in front of the window. Her face red and swollen, the tendons in her neck rigid, she flared her nostrils like a raging bull. Their eyes locked. Isabelle saw in Opal's eyes an indescribable pain. which Isabelle thought was a natural response to losing a child.

Oh my God, Carson died because he was my friend.

Opal's face twisted into a mad leer. "Are you a whore like your mother? Wrapping those skinny legs of yours around anything with a dick."

Did she actually just say that?

All the sympathy Isabelle once felt for Opal died with this last accusation. Anger rose inside her like bile. She flung the door open and raced to the bottom of the steps. Electricity bubbled from her core. Her fingers tingled. Her head buzzed. Blue sparks popped and crackled from her fingertips.

She flexed her hands and, with an audible pop, the electrical storm which raged inside of her stopped. In its place, a headache raged. Fury poured from Isabelle's mouth. She jabbed her finger at Opal. "You fat bitch! I heard what you said."

Opal stumbled backward.

Isabelle took a step towards her. "Do you have a job?"

Opal mumbled something and shook her head.

"If you don't have a job, how do you pay your rent, put food on the table, and...buy your drugs?"

Opal stood rooted in the street, struck dumb.

Isabelle turned to go inside, thought twice about it, and said, "That's right, you get paid for sex, don't you? Doesn't that make you a whore?"

Opal stared at Isabelle with hatred in her eyes.

"You disgust me. Close your mouth, it makes you look stupid."

Opal obeyed.

"You weren't much of a foster mother, were you?" Isabelle asked. "Carson deserved better."

Opal dropped to her knees, a large pile of miserable flesh. Sobs racked her body.

The last comment had been over the top, but it was too late to take it back. Isabelle knew she should put her arm around the grieving mother.

She took a tentative step outside to do so but hesitated when Opal looked up, defiance in her eyes.

"How dare you pass judgment on me. You don't know me," Opal said through clenched teeth.

Isabelle's knees buckled as one of Carson's memories poked through.

"Get your ass over here," Opal said, tucking her large breast back into her nightgown and adjusting her robe. Finished for the night, she hoped. The last man's desires disgusted her. She sat down, damp and dumpy, slouched against the lumpy cushions, and rubbed her reddened eyes. She shook out her last cigarette and took a deep drag as though her life depended on it. A wad of sweaty, crumpled bills sat on the scratched coffee table. She began to straighten out the money only to find that half of them were food stamps.

"Fuck." She flung the food stamps at Carson. "How many times have I told you to make sure they pay in cash?"

Carson cringed. He slipped the book Isabelle lent him under a magazine. "I'm sorry, Mom. He seemed to be in a hurry. He threw down the bills and left."

Opal grabbed the book Carson had tried to hide. "You were reading, weren't you?"

He nodded.

"Where did you get this? Did you steal it?"

"No."

"Speak up. You got this from that girl, didn't you?"

"Yes," Carson whispered.

"Fuck! Fuck! Fuck!"

He stood up and slowly walked towards his mother.

Opal grabbed him around the bicep. "I can't pay the rent with food stamps, can I?

"No."

She squeezed his arm tighter. "Take off your shirt."

"No... Please?"

"You know what your punishment is," Opal said, taking a long slow drag until the tip of her cigarette glowed red.

Carson took off his shirt and stood stoically, his already scarred back turned towards her. Opal took her lit cigarette and smashed it out on an open spot between earlier burns. Carson's flesh sizzled. The sickly sweet aroma of burnt skin filled the room. He didn't dare flinch. The punishment for that was far worse.

Opal handed Carson the food stamps. Her night might not be over; she needed to pay rent tomorrow. "Get me a bag of chips and a coke."

Isabelle wiped her eyes to rid herself of the memory and glared at Opal.

Yes, she could pass judgment. Opal deserved no mercy.

"You're right. I don't know you. But I know all the terrible things you and John did. Those are things I'll never forget. And, just so you know, I'm nothing like my mother."

# Chapter 28

Blood dripped from the many cuts on Sharon's hands. In the spiderweb of cracks, six doors lurked in the mirror instead of one. Frantic to escape, she dropped her purse. She bent to pick it up but accidentally kicked it instead. The pocketbook skidded across the floor and bounced against the garbage can with a metallic clang, scattering the contents across the ground.

"Shit, shit, shit."

She grabbed the keys and her wallet. The rest could stay behind. She would retrieve her purse after lunch if she came back at all. Heavy and clunky, the keys dangled in her hand. Memories of the door with the word HOME written above it overwhelmed her. In the mirror, the door swung open.

Smells of the pond filled the bathroom. Crickets chirped. Frogs croaked. Sharon dropped the keys, scampered out of the restroom, and headed for the front door. She made a mistake coming to work today. Her relapse was more than a problem. It was a symptom of another failed attempt at sobriety. She should check herself back into rehab before she loses all control.

Sharon rejected those thoughts as soon as she reached the safety of the parking lot. She didn't need help. She needed a drink. The nearest bar which sold off-sale was Duffy's, the local watering hole for the business class. She pulled out several napkins from the glove compartment and wiped the blood from her hands.

Within ten minutes, she sat at the bar with a double shot of their best vodka. Two large gulps emptied the glass. She slammed it on the counter and motioned to the bartender. "Do it again."

The first drink had warmed her insides. Her hands now rested peacefully on the bar. The bartender poured the second, and she knocked it back.

"Ah." Sharon sighed. "Much better."

What the hell could she do about the things Tom had told her? The pictures horrified her. His words scared her even more. If she revealed what she knew to anyone, nobody would believe her. When the bartender placed her third drink in front of her, she glanced up at the large mirror lining the back of the bar. Like yesterday, reflected in the mirror, she stood in front of a door, keys in her hand. She grabbed her drink and searched the room. She needed to get away from the image. She spotted an isolated corner in one of the dark recesses, far from any mirror. She ordered a bottle and walked to her table.

Sharon nursed her next drink. The taste of vodka lingered. Exquisite. She scanned the room. A group of well-dressed men, their ties loosened, were playing pool. The drinks set fire to her libido. Which one of these young professionals could she seduce?

The barmaid arrived with Sharon's to-go bottle wrapped in a brown paper bag. To pace herself, she ordered a Greyhound, a sipping drink.

What would fucking one of those men prove? It would be a pleasant diversion, a way to spend the afternoon and keep her thoughts occupied, but it would only delay the inevitable. She needed to find a way out of the hole she had dug for herself. She never made great choices in the men she entertained in her bed. Tom went beyond bad. This mistake could change her life and not for the better. He possessed all the physical assets any woman could dream of, but he was broken inside. Pure evil. What did she really know about him? She grabbed a napkin and a pen from her wallet.

She paged through her mental notes of their previous conversations and picked out a couple tidbits she could fact-check. One- Tom grew up in Minot, two- he attended Minot State University for undergrad, and three- he went to the University of North Dakota for his Juris Doctorate. Sharon could do a criminal background check or run his name through LexisNexis and see what she could find. The rest she considered hearsay. He admitted he enjoyed sex with teenagers. Yes, she'd believed him. Tom was a man of his words, a man of action. Could she find evidence to prove his dalliances with teenagers? She could talk to their high school filing clerk. Her name was Sarah, wasn't it? Sarah might be Jennifer's daughter and Tom's niece.

What about the file she examined this morning? Could Tom be a killer? Sharon shrugged. What bothered her most about Tom? How was he connected to the man with the dark eyes? What could they want with Isabelle?

Sharon shivered and remembered what Tom said earlier. He painted a clear picture: his friends died because they knew too much.

"Oh Isabelle, what have I done?"

The barmaid arrived at her table with her drink. "Rough morning?"

Sharon nodded. "Do you have children?"

"Yes, two grown boys." The barmaid sat on the chair across from her. "What's the matter, honey?"

Sharon hadn't been a perfect mother. She couldn't lie to herself any longer. Facts were facts. Her body sagged against the chair. "I've done the best I could."

The barmaid looked like anyone's grandmother: silver-haired, full-bodied, a soft, caring face, and kind eyes. She patted Sharon's hand. "I'm sure you have."

Sharon shook her head. Time and time again, she put her own desires and needs before Isabelle's. The space behind her eyelids felt hot. A lump formed in her throat. "I was dealt a shitty hand," Sharon said. She had a right to be angry, didn't she? She gulped the last of her drink. The alcohol was winning, but she didn't care. "I never had a mother."

"Poor child."

"I was raised in an orphanage by nuns."

"I'm sure they did the best they could."

"They taught me how to be a nun, not a mother."

The barmaid offered a wide, warming smile. "Don't be so hard on yourself. I read someplace, not sure where, that your background and your circumstances influence who you are, but you are ultimately responsible for who you become."

The barmaid was right. Most days, she didn't like herself, or who she'd become. She wasn't ready to forgive herself for the mistakes she made. She couldn't even look in the mirror anymore. Maybe it was time to put Isabelle's needs first.

"Thank you."

"If you need to talk, you know where to find me. My shift's over."

Misty brought over another drink. "Deloris said you're having a rough day. This one is on the house."

Sharon tried to smile. "Nothing an afternoon with one of those well-dressed hunks couldn't cure."

Misty nodded and giggled. "I know what you mean. The kitty needs to be scratched when it has an itch!"

"Hey," one of the hunks yelled. "Can we get our tab?"

Sharon looked at her watch. Only fifteen minutes before she had to meet Tom back at the office. Could she handle an afternoon working with Tom after what she had learned? Did she have the willpower not to have sex with him? In her present state, she didn't think so, but if she wanted to do right by Isabelle, she needed to stay away from temptations. Tom could go fuck himself.

She would go home and finish drowning herself in her sorrows there. The noise in her head, far outweighing the itch between her legs, needed to be quiet. She left her unfinished drink, grabbed her liter, and headed for the door.

A dark mist clouded the mirror behind the bar. The outline of an open door appeared. She needed that door closed, and to stay closed forever.

She rushed outside, turned the corner, and crashed into a human pile of filth.

The man staggered. His dark eyes barely visible beneath the rat's nest of a beard, his body covered in a thick layer of grime, he glared at her. "Whatcha running from, lady?"

Sharon took a couple steps backward.

The man smiled and lifted his own brown paper bag to his lips. "A toast." He stepped to the side and blocked her path then took a big swallow and wiped his lips with a dirty sleeve. "Here's to staying one step ahead of the devil."

His laughter filled the air as she sprinted towards her car. She threw open the door and collapsed onto the seat. She cracked open the bottle, gulped until the burn gripped her throat and set fire to her insides. The noises in her head stayed silent for the moment.

Rosary beads dangled from the mirror. Sharon yanked them down and held onto them. They once comforted her, but not any longer. It had been a long time since she prayed to the Holy Mother. She rubbed a bead between her fingers. The prayer Hail Mary filled her mind, but her heart no longer opened to the mysteries of the faith. Dejected, she dropped them into the passenger seat.

"Oh, God. I have sinned," she said, cradling her head.

The homeless man stood at the edge of the parking lot and raised his bottle in the air. "He will find you, the Dark Ones will devour your soul."

Sharon's hands shook all the way home. She took another long swig from the bottle. The current buzz would have to hold her over until she finished a project. Getting out of the car, she grabbed the mirror to keep from falling. Her stomach lurched and beads of perspiration formed on her forehead. She stopped to catch her breath, to force down the nausea that threatened.

She pulled herself the rest of the way up the stairs and made a beeline for the linen closet. She removed all the sheets, blankets, and towels from the shelves and proceeded to cover all the mirrors in the house. She couldn't take any chances.

Finished with her project, she cozied up to the bottle of vodka she'd brought home. A couple shots later, she melted into oblivion, the bottle tucked under her arm.

# Chapter 29

Isabelle slammed the door on the confrontation with Opal. Her stomach heaved, and she sprinted to the kitchen. The school's mashed potatoes and turkey surprise splattered the inside of the sink. During a short respite, she rested her forehead on her arms and took small ragged breaths. It did not take long for her stomach to expel the rest of lunch. She washed the detritus into the disposal and flipped the switch. She grabbed a kitchen towel, wiped the sweat off her face, and blew her nose. Stopping in the bathroom to discard her soiled cloth, she pulled off the towel covering the mirror and caught a glimpse of her reflection. Dark and puffy, her eyes radiated pain and torment. Clumps of sweaty hair stuck up randomly. A grayish pallor clung to her cheeks. Her appearance concerned her.

Isabelle went to her room and opened her Algebra 2 textbook. The numbers and words blurred and ran together. She banged the book closed and gazed at her hands. Did she imagine her fingers turning into sparklers, spitting out streaks of blue lightning? Yes, what other explanation could there be? But what about Carson's memories, or any of the memories that filled the recesses of her mind? Could those be real?

She pushed away from the desk, crawled on top of her covers, and snuggled underneath the quilt. Her thoughts turned back to the strange events outside. She drew the only conclusion she could. Insanity, a brain meltdown.

Her hands trembled. "Please make it stop."

Her lips quivered. "Can anyone help me?"

Grief and uncertainty clutched at her heart. What was happening to her? She buried her face into her pillow. Drifting into a restless slumber, she wept. When she woke from a short nap, she winced from the light streaming into her room. A headache grabbed hold and burrowed itself deeply.

She closed her eyes, but the image of her mother with a drink in her hand flashed before her. The clink, clink sound of ice dropped into an empty glass magnified the pain. She rolled over, and the sounds in her head increased. Blowing out a puff of frustration, she sat up and leaned against the wall. Her mother would never quit drinking, never keep her legs closed, and never be the mother she needed.

Like an uninvited guest, wicked thoughts made themselves at home. Her mother would be better off dead, wouldn't she, the voices said. Put her out of misery, they whispered. Those violent thoughts scared her. She wrapped the quilt tighter. Most nights, despondency swallowed her whole. Could she kill her mother? No, she loved her.

"Yes," the voices answered in unison. "We will help."

Isabelle paced the room. Tendrils of pain reached out and captured more territory. The taste of bile crept up the back of her throat. She needed to get this under control. She crawled back into bed to the comfort of her favorite blanket. The voices whispered more deadly promises.

"Please leave me alone." Isabelle pleaded.

She pushed the voices into a corner of her mind and locked the door. The hinges squealed but held. It was time to deal with the pain head-on. The best method she found to control her headaches was not a pill or any medicine but measured breathing. She curled into the fetal position and concentrated on slow, steady breaths. If she could relax enough to fall asleep, the odds were good, the headache would disappear. Shadows filled her room as she slipped into a shallow, fitful sleep.

"Isabelle?"

A hand rested on her forehead. She opened her eyes. "Mom."

Her mother raised a finger to her lips. "Shh.... Are you sick?"

"No. Just one of my headaches."

Her mother stroked her hair and kissed her cheek. "Shhh.... Go back to sleep."

The astringent tang of alcohol permeated her mother's breath. Isabelle decided not to push the issue because she had encountered enough confrontation and harsh words for one day. She smiled, closed her eyes, and melted into the cocoon of warmth she wrapped herself in earlier.

The aroma wafting from the kitchen pulled Isabelle from her slumber. Weak and tired, she wrapped the quilt around her shoulders and wandered into the kitchen. Her mother stood at the stove, stirring a pot. Whatever dish she prepared smelled wonderful and made Isabelle's stomach gurgle with excitement.

A vodka bottle sat on the counter next to her mother. The lid was twisted off, and a generous portion was already gone. Isabelle turned her attention back to the stove before her mother caught the look of disapproval. She could tell her mother teetered close to the edge between happy-go-lucky and a miserable drunk. She bit her tongue. The last meal they shared at home was a distant memory.

"Mom, whatever you're cooking smells great."

Her mother smiled. "I thought I would fry us up a couple of steaks and make your favorite mac-n-cheese. We can sit at the table and eat together. Go sit, it's almost ready."

Isabelle should have been excited about the meal and spending time with her mother, but the opened vodka bottle in the kitchen dampened her mood. The plink, plink of fresh ice cubes did even more to deaden her spirit. She filled her plate and picked at her food. They sat close to each other, but an endless gulf of tension hung between them.

Isabelle broke the uncomfortable silence first. "My history teacher, Ms. Dahl, invited us to her family's Thanksgiving dinner."

"Isn't she the one who thinks you can dance? Gave you a scholarship or something?"

Isabelle stabbed a piece of the steak and ignored the slight. "Yes, she's the one."

"We don't need her charity." Her mother took a healthy swig from her drink and with a glazed expression, stared back at Isabelle.

Isabelle needed to be careful. The wrong word could set her mother off.

"I've kept a roof over your head, and food on the table, haven't I?" her mother snapped. "We've survived without government assistance, and we're not going to start taking handouts now."

Her mother had drunk herself way past indignant and staggered straight to nasty. Tonight would not be the night to mention the possibility of being related to Heather. Her mother didn't talk about her family when she was sober.

"It's not charity. We're expected to bring a side dish or dessert or both. Her grandmother's old, and Ms. Dahl would like her to meet me... meet us."

Her mother finished her drink, and shuffled to the kitchen, using one hand for balance. The plink, plink of fresh ice cubes distracted from her mother's mumblings.

"Where does your teacher's grandmother live?" her mother called out, a little too cheerful.

"A small town west of Duluth. Pine Bluff, I think."

Her mother's silence smothered the sounds of the house. A cold chill permeated the room.

"No. No, we aren't going. You can tell your teacher we're not interested in her offer." Her mother stood in the doorway, a fresh drink in hand.

Anger flared inside Isabelle. Resentment bubbled to the surface.

Isabelle should have thanked her for the meal, cleared off the table, and went to her room. Instead, she asked, "Why?"

"I cooked you a nice dinner, and this is the thanks I get?" her mother said, pouring half the drink down her throat. "Instead of thanking me like a good daughter would, once again, you're selfish and think only of yourself."

"I want to know why we never spend time with anybody else."

"This isn't a debate. My final answer is no."

Isabelle's mother placed her empty glass on the edge of the counter. It teetered and fell to the floor. She took an uneasy step, found her balance, and grabbed her jacket from the front closet. "I had planned to spend the night at home with my daughter. Yet again, she ruined my plans."

With those words, she left. Isabelle knew that if she came back at all, she'd be drunk—even drunker than she already was.

Isabelle would be alone again tonight. She stood and dizziness overtook her.

"If you don't get this headache under control, it could get nasty," a voice reminded her.

With her hands pressed firmly against her eyes, she stopped at the bathroom. She shook out two more pills and with some trouble, gagged them down. In her room, she collapsed into a chair. Her composition book splayed open on her desk, an invitation she could not resist. She read what she wrote yesterday.

Princess Belle was in a conundrum. She stood in front of the door to her father's library and lower-level dungeons. Did she dare to enter? The King's private rooms were off-limits. Only his closest advisors had permission. But the King's daughter, his princess, should have access, shouldn't she? Her hand trembled with uncertainty. The cold metal brushed her palm, and she yanked it away as if bitten. The handle shimmered with frost.

Cold radiated out from her palm and fingers. The more she rubbed it, the more her hand tingled, and the faster the corruption spread. The tentacles of ice moved up her arm as the poison destroyed tissue. By the time the toxin reached her elbow, Princess Belle's fingers had turned black.

Isabelle tried to turn the page, but a cold numbness invaded her fingers, and they were slow to respond. She stared at her swollen blackened digits. "Holy shit."

The composition book tumbled off the desk. Isabelle's mind spun as she pinned it to the floor. Did she live inside duel dreams, juxtaposing between hers and someone else's?

Isabelle continued to read.

Princess Belle didn't feel any pain. Shaking her arm with vigor, she slapped her hand against her thigh, hoping normal sensations would return. The Princess wrapped her knife belt tightly above her bicep, right under her armpit. Inserting the dagger into the knot, she twisted hard.

Her skin, from fingertips to elbow, turned inky black. A chill radiated from her pores. She rushed to the bathroom. The darkness she kept at bay all night flooded her mind, and she fell into a shadow as bottomless and black as a well. Echoes of voices, fragments of stories, and remnants of the truth had been constant companions since puberty.

In the dark, the voices spoke louder. "Isabelle. Open the door. Let us in." They urged Isabelle forward into the dark void of her soul.

She crawled, pushing the darkness to the side. Bit by bit, the light returned and aspects of the room came back into focus. The gray shower curtain emerged, and a picture took shape above the towel rack. Isabelle found herself in front of the mirror. The headache pounding at her temples was too much. She vomited. The aspirin tablets she had taken earlier floated on the shiny surface. Her hands clasped the toilet, and neither one was black nor swollen. Had her imagination played tricks on her again? She flushed the toilet and put down the seat. Her hand and arm were both intact. She sighed and willed herself to her feet. She needed to go back to bed before the insanity returned.

Isabelle paused at her bedroom door, a prickling sensation at the back of her neck. She gazed down the hall but saw no one. A murky grayness lurked in every corner, under every chair. Who were they, how long they had watched, and from where?

A babble of sounds drew her back to the bathroom. A green-eyed girl stood in the mirror. She waited at the edge of a forest, her copper hair blowing in the wind.

"When one is nothing," the girl said, "one invents."

Isabelle reached for the face in the mirror. Her fingers brushed the surface and it rippled like the whisper of a breeze across a pond. The girl smiled wickedly and faded farther into the forest.

"Your love waits for you. Hurry."

The sound of crickets filled the bathroom. A breeze ruffled the shower curtain, bringing with it the scent of loamy earth and wildflowers. Isabelle rushed to her mother's room and threw back the drapes. Shadows danced in the backyard, but there was nothing more there. An image of something different lingered in the folds of her mind. She shook her head. There was no rational explanation for the hallucinations except insanity.

She went back to her room and returned to her reading. Losing herself in words kept her from reality.

The makeshift tourniquet worked. The poison had not advanced; the cold and numbness stopped at the Princess's elbow. She knew what poison was applied to the door handle. The ingredients needed to counteract the poison could be found at the apothecary. A trip to the market would be required. If she kept the poison at bay, she would be okay. Unhappy that she had wasted so much time, she was now more determined to enter the tower. She needed answers from her father. Why did he have her friend killed?

Isabelle hadn't spoken to her father in weeks, maybe a month. So many questions popped into her mind. What did she really know about her mother's previous life, or her father's? Most kids, at least, knew the names of their grandparents, sat on a parent's lap, and looked at family pictures. Most families owned a Bible handed down from generation to generation. Isabelle had neither a past nor a family history. She had been left on her own, to fend for herself, and find her past.

Isabelle needed to talk to someone. She didn't want to stay in the house by herself tonight. The school counselor's business card stared up at her from her desk, daring her to call. At their meeting, Mrs. Anderson had stressed anytime Isabelle required help, she would make herself available. Tonight, she needed her father, needed to be reassured that everything would be okay.

She picked up her phone from the nightstand, took a deep breath, and dialed her father's number.

"Hello."

"Dad?" Isabelle said, thankful his new wife Stephanie hadn't answered.

"Isabelle."

"It's been a bad day. Do you have time to talk?"

"Stephanie's getting formula for the baby and—"

"I know you have a new life and new responsibilities. And Stephanie doesn't want you to have reminders of your old life."

"Oh, that isn't fair."

"Mom's drinking again."

"I'm sorry to hear that."

"One of my friends is dead."

"I know."

"Can you come to get me? Mom's out again, and I don't want to be alone tonight."

"Isabelle, the police were here asking questions about you and...."

"And the timing just isn't right," Isabelle said.

"You need to understand."

"I understand all too well. When we needed you the most, you left."

"It wasn't like that. I tried. Oh, how I tried."

"I need my father and, once again, you've let me down."

I'm not his little girl anymore, not important enough.

Isabelle slammed the receiver down before he could say anything else to make things worse and flung the phone across the room. Her emotions were wrung out. She was done crying and feeling sorry for herself.

# Chapter 30

"It's a somber day for our community."

Heather turned up the radio.

"Earlier this morning, the body of a high school student was found in Romkey Park. The Moorhead Police Department and the Clay County Sheriff's office both responded. The student was pronounced dead at the scene. Based on the information from medical personnel, the death has been ruled a homicide. The investigation continues. An autopsy will be performed by the Ramsey County Medical Examiner's Office. If you have any information on this incident, you're asked to contact the Moorhead Police Department."

The body had a name: Carson. Wasn't he a friend of Isabelle's?

Heather turned into J.C. Chumley's, a neighborhood bar, and only found a handful of cars dotting the gravel parking lot. She didn't see Adam's small truck. She pushed open the double glass doors and stepped into the dimly lit interior. She found a dark corner, where she and Adam could talk in private.

With everything that is going on, Isabelle must think she's going insane, Heather thought, motioning the barmaid over. She pulled a five out of her wallet. "Something dark, please."

The barmaid grabbed the cash and returned a few minutes later with her beer.

Then there was this thing about Isabelle being related to her. Other than gut instinct, what evidence did she even have that Isabelle was a relative? She shrugged and took a sip. Maybe her grandmother could get this straightened out.

Adam walked in as Heather finished her first beer. He offered a thin smile. The strain of the day etched his face. She hurried to meet him. Kissing him lightly on the lips, she grabbed his hand. She led him to their table and ordered two beers. "Are you hungry?" she asked. "We could order pizza."

"Yes, I'm starving." Adam took off his jacket. "Sorry that I'm a little late. A deputy arrived just as I was leaving. He wanted to ask me some questions."

"About Carson?"

"Yes, how do you know his name?"

Heather gave his hand a reassuring squeeze. "One of my students was Carson's neighbor and friend."

"Isabelle?"

"Yes."

"The deputy asked if I knew her."

"Oh?"

"You should stay away from her. She's dangerous."

"Isabelle? Dangerous? Are you serious?"

"You don't know...."

"Know what?"

Adam shrugged. "Carson was a smart kid, conflicted, but one of my best students."

"Conflicted..."

The waitress placed the beers on the table. "Anything else?"

"We'd like the Deluxe, extra olives."

She scribbled their order on a napkin, smiled at Adam, and walked away with enough wiggle to flutter her skirt in alternate directions.

Really? Did the barmaid just flirt with her boyfriend?

Adam took a long swig from his beer, his gaze following the sashaying barmaid all the way back to the bar.

Heather frowned. A sourness burned her stomach. She needed to get him back on track and thinking about her.  "Losing someone close is hard. It took a long time for me to cope with the death of my parents. Some days the loss still hurts."

"Did I ever tell you it was your dad who helped me put my life back together?"

"My father?"

"My partying started in earnest during my junior year of high school. Too much booze, an occasional joint and presto, I was struggling in class. The teachers threatened to not let me play football in the fall."

"Would the star running back miss his senior year? Not a chance," she said, smiling. "The whole school knew it was an idle threat. The only athletes who got better treatment than the football players were the hockey players, and you were a pretty good hockey player too."

Adam chuckled. "Hockey players were treated like Gods, weren't they?"

"So how did my father help turn your life around? As I recall, you still partied just as hard, but you seemed to do a better job of not getting caught."

The pizza arrived. Adam dove in with gusto. After he gulped down two pieces, he wiped the pepperoni grease off his lips. "I passed all my classes, so they couldn't force me to go to summer school. There was a program at UMD that allowed incoming high school seniors a chance to enroll in some summer classes. I loved chemistry--."

"My dad was a history professor."

"Not just a history professor. He specialized in Medieval History. I looked through the course offerings and saw that your dad was teaching a course called The History of Medieval Chemistry 101." The weariness seemed to leave Adam's body as he spoke of her father.

Heather smiled at his enthusiasm.

Adam scowled. "You don't understand, do you?"

She shifted uneasily in her chair. "I know my father had a passion for anything old."

"Do you know what Medieval Chemistry is?"

"Yes. It's the study of Alchemy."

Adam beamed. "Do you believe in magic?"

Heather thought for a moment before answering him. "No, I don't."

"Alchemy is magic with results."

"So how did this change your life?"

"First, I had to hit bottom. That happened the summer after graduation. I was fired from my job because I came back drunk from lunch. My parents sat me down and chewed my ass for a while. I stormed into my room and tipped over my bookcase. After sleeping off the worst of it, I cleaned up my disaster and found one of the books your father suggested I read, The Alchemist's Handbook by Frater Albertus. I couldn't put the book down. I spent the rest of the weekend working on the experiments."

"So again I ask, how did this transform your life?"

"Reading that book helped me focus on something other than myself. It brought me peace of mind and a positive outlook on life. But most of all, it made me a better person. I decided to enroll at the university in the fall, changed my major, and began working toward my degree, this time in chemistry. It re-energized me, and I started volunteering to help area youth."

"My father would be on top of the world if he could hear you now."

"Would you like to go back to my place and see what the boys and I have been working on?"

"At your house?" Heather hoped the invitation would lead somewhere other than looking at beakers and tubes. "Isn't conducting experiments at home dangerous?"

"Alchemy is an ancient art," Adam said. "I've been teaching the boys to develop their potential, to awaken their inner light using science."

"To impressionable teenage old boys?"

"I thought you, being Teddy's daughter, might understand." He grabbed her hand. "We're making progress. You'll have to see to believe."

Adam dropped the uneaten crust onto the table and drank the last of his beer.

"Are you finished?" Heather asked.

He nodded, pacing like an anxious child while Heather boxed up the leftover pizza and paid the tab. He hurried outside. Heather hurried just to keep up.

They pulled in front of a 1950's gray rambler. Two large windows dominated the foreground. Inside, a wood-burning fireplace graced the living room. Heather pictured the two of them snuggled there, sharing a bottle of wine.

"Nice," Heather said.

Adam smiled. "My parents bought the house for me the summer after my sophomore year."

The shine of the beautiful hardwood floors caught Heather's attention. The rooms appeared tidy for a bachelor, but sparsely furnished. What the house needed was a woman's touch. Adam rushed her through the tour of the main floor as if anxious to show her the basement.

They stopped at a metal door. "The lab is down the basement."

Adam nodded and took out a set of keys.

Why would Adam need to lock the entrance to the basement? She ignored the alarm bells sounding in her head. Adam ushered her into the stairwell and turned on the lights. The low hum of machinery greeted her.

"Ora et labors," Heather read from a quote on the wall at the bottom of the stairs.

"Pray and Work," Adam said, locking the door behind them. "It's the first thing the boys see when they enter the lab."

Heather's warning bells rang in double time.

Adam grabbed a different set of keys. "We need to prepare ourselves before we start. Each of us spends time meditating and visualizing the successful completion of our day's work."

There was something creepy about all of this.

Another locked door waited at the bottom of the stairs. Once Adam unlocked that one and turned on the lights Heather followed him into the room. The gleam of stainless steel and the crisp sparkle of glass welcomed her.

"Wow, did your parents pay for all of this?"

"No. We have some generous supporters of our program. The boys have the best tools at their disposal. A state-of-the-art laboratory."

Along the far wall, written in large letters above seven doors was another quotation: Ora, Lege, Lege, Lege, renege labors et Inverness. A tableau was painted on each of these doors. The first door depicted a young girl being swallowed by serpents. The illustration on the second portrayed a crucified snake upon a Gothic cross. An ancient bronze key hung by each entrance.

What the hell was going on? This wasn't a suitable environment for teenage boys. She started to say something, but Adam cut her off.

"The quotation reads 'Pray, read, read, read, reread, and you will discover it.' It is a reminder to the boys that preparation is the key to success."

"What's behind the doors?"

"Individual labs. Sometimes the boys work in pairs, but mostly Alchemy is a solitary endeavor. Each of the rooms has a separate experiment."

"Which door did Carson work behind?"

"The most important, door seven. And Carson was close, so close." Adam stared at the wall. "He had so much potential. He'll be missed."

"What was he working on?"

Adam turned and walked away.

She studied the equipment and stopped at one of the tables. "Is this a distillery?"

"Same principle. It's called a Distillation Train." Adam said, now joining her at the table.

"Looks complicated."

"It's a simple process. In this beaker, the liquid is heated to boiling. The water vapor travels through this tube." He pointed to another area. "This is the cold-water intake for the condenser. The vapor travels through the condenser and is cooled. It returns back to a liquid state and drips into this other beaker." He pointed to the other beaker. "This is the distillate."

Next to the distillation train, a large book lay open. Adam closed its cover. "Time to go."

"How old is that book?"

Adam rubbed the back of his neck and looked from the book back to her, avoiding eye contact. He then sat down on a stool and closed his eyes. After a moment's reflection, he spoke in a subdued tone. "There's a reason why we can be nothing more than friends."

"Where's this coming from?"

"I thought it was time somebody told you the truth—about this book, about your father, but mostly about your grandmother."

"What are you talking about?"

"This book is old, but it's not the original. To achieve our goals, we need the original—the one your grandmother stole."

"You're kidding, right?"

"I'm dead serious. The book your grandmother Bernice stole is more than old; it's an ancient, sacred text."

"Okay, my Grandmother stole a book. What does this have to do with my father?"

"The only reason why your father moved to Minnesota and married—"

A phone rang. A gamut of emotions ran unchecked in Heather while Adam answered the phone. What was he talking about? Her parents loved each other.

"Yes, Tom…. Okay, I understand," Adam said and eased the receiver down. He ran his fingers through his hair as his expression hardened. "I have to leave."

"You need to leave now?" Heather shifted nervously. "When will you be back?"

"Actually, you need to leave too."

Gripping her upper arm, he led her out the same way they had entered. Each door was locked and double-checked. Assured all was well, Adam shoved the set of keys into his pocket and hurried down the front steps.

"What were you saying about my father?"

Adam unlocked his car door.

Heather grabbed his arm. "Please talk to me."

He peeled her fingers away. "I once told you that I loved you, but I lied. I never have and never will."

His car door slammed. Heather stepped back and watched him drive off until the taillights disappeared, her thoughts tangled in the awful truth of his words. He never loved her.

Heather studied the house and shuddered. The basement windows were blackened and barred. What could be so important? What did he hide behind those seven doors?

The relentless desperation and overwhelming sorrow she experienced after her parents' death returned. All the way home, she wondered if her life's questions would ever be answered.

# Chapter 31

Sharon left the house, slamming the door and blocking Isabelle's words inside.

That selfish little bitch! All Sharon wanted was a quiet night at home. Why did Isabelle have to ruin everything and ask about Pine Bluff? Her daughter was never satisfied with, 'Because I said so.' She always wanted to know why.

Why can't I go to Sunday school?

Why are you crying?

Why is Daddy leaving?

Why do we have to move again?

Like most of Isabelle's questions, tonight's question couldn't be answered either. She should have stuck around and explained why going to Pine Bluff was a bad idea. Not a subject she wanted to ever discuss, preferring to drown those memories in vodka. The only question she wanted to consider was where she should spend her evening. How about The Nestor? It was the right place to tie one on. She might even find someone to make her evening more exciting. If Isabelle confronted her in the morning, the hell with her. Sharon didn't care. Isabelle had ruined their evening and her desire to get drunk tonight was Isabelle's fault. Why should she stay at home with a sulking teenager?

Sharon's past and Pine Bluff had found her much quicker this time; however, it was Isabelle, not a faceless stranger, who had pulled off the covers. What if Sharon moved farther away? What distance would be far enough?

Sharon climbed into the car and slumped against the steering wheel, closing her eyes until her head quit spinning. Where could they move? She pounded her palms against the hard plastic, hating herself, her weakness, and what she had put Isabelle through. She took a deep breath and opened her eyes.

A girl resembling her daughter stood in front of the car.

"Isabelle," Sharon whispered.

The girl's green eyes fixated on her, accusing and judging without compassion or understanding.

Several images flashed in Sharon's mind. She shook her head, not wanting her first instinct to be correct. She concentrated on bringing her thoughts back under control, but a single picture came into focus.

The girl's face ignited memories of the night Sharon broke her wedding vows. She remembered the exact moment when Pine Bluff pushed its way back into her life. The thought made her chest ache with regret. She couldn't close her eyes tight enough to hold back the tears.

A door with the words BROKEN VOWS written above it appeared in the rearview mirror. Sharon turned the key in the ignition, but instead of the engine roaring to life, a lock clicked open. An ancient set of keys dangled from her fingers. Were these the ones she had left behind in the bathroom at work? How did they get in her hand?

The door in the mirror swung open, and the memory spilled out.

***

She lay in the darkness, pressed against him, ready to give in to her body's craving. She felt his impatience—and her reluctance. This was it, the fantasy which made her life bearable. The man hovered inches above her nakedness. This was not an illusion, a sanctuary where her mind could hide while her husband grunted and groaned above her prone body, but something she could wrap her legs around.

Was it wrong to want pleasure?

Was it wrong?

"……to rut lustfully with the common man like one of Satan's whores," a famous TV evangelist had preached during one of his fiery damnation sermons.

Sex outside of marriage was wrong, a sin—adultery, an unspeakable desire she craved until it became a reality. If not this man, she would have chosen another, trading the damnation of her soul for ecstasy. Love or lust, she could no longer differentiate between the two. Then why the tears and unwillingness to consummate this union?

Isabelle.

Everything she did was for her daughter: escaping Pine Bluff, attending college, and marrying Steve. Isabelle be damned, she guided this new stranger in. This was for her, one of Satan's whores.

With their urges satisfied, the man whom Sharon couldn't recognize exited the bed and dressed. Before he left, he pulled a wrinkled wad of bills from his pocket and set them on the nightstand. "If you ever get to Pine Bluff, look me up. I wouldn't mind another go."

A knock on the car window startled Sharon from her memories.

"Mother, are you alright?"

Sharon starred.

"Have you seen a ghost?"

The girl with the green eyes, her face pressed to the glass, wore a grin of utmost wickedness. Sharon slammed the car into reverse. The door in the rearview mirror closed. Grinding the vehicle into drive, she jammed her foot on the gas. The undercarriage shuddered as the squealing tires found purchase.  Heading towards Twelfth Street, she glanced in the side mirror. The girl with the green eyes stood alone in the driveway. She reminded Sharon of Isabelle, a little girl lost. The similarity tore at Sharon's heart.

The light traffic made for a quick trip. Sharon drove into Fargo, turned right on Second Street and crossed under one of the many railroad bridges. She stopped at the corner of NP Avenue, her left turn signal blinking. Cars zipped by. Her mind filled with thoughts of Pine Bluff.

Pine Bluff kept its secrets well. Unsavory information or people who escaped always found their way back. In most instances, they ended up on the bottom of the pond or locked away in an asylum.

A car horn blared, jolting Sharon from her thoughts. The traffic light had turned green.

The horn behind her blared again. She glared at the driver, raised her middle finger, and screamed, "Fuck off!"

It was going to be one of those nights.

***

The Nestor was a typical blue-collar bar. The interior, drab and ordinary as its patrons, offered a couple of pool tables, an L-shaped bar, a small dance floor, and an off-sale. Local country music, the smell of stale beer, a thick cloud of blue cigarette smoke, and obnoxious drunk men helped create the perfect environment for debauchery.

The band finished its first set as Sharon entered. At the bar, she ordered a shot, threw it down, and ordered a second. Drink in hand, she strolled through the crowd: a meat market smorgasbord of tight asses and flat abs.

Sharon chose an open table at the back of the room and scanned the bar in search of the night's entertainment.

"Do you need another?" a barmaid asked.

"Yeah," Sharon said, handing over a couple five-dollar bills. "Keep the change."

She downed her next drink, savoring the warm burn as the vodka slid down her throat and made its way through her body.

The band came on stage and started with a ZZ Top classic. An older man with a well-used face covered in gray stubble approached her. He wore a cowboy hat, boots, and a pair of faded Wranglers that accentuated his ass just right. She couldn't resist his proffered hand. They glided across the floor and, like any small-town cowboy, he sure could two-step. When the second song ended, he guided her up to the bar.

"What are you drinking?" he asked.

"Vodka. Good vodka."

Sharon accepted one drink, then another. As they traded small talk, a door appeared in the mirror behind them. Only Sharon seemed to notice. The door opened, and a priest walked out and peered straight at her.

No. No. No. Not Father Abrams.

She gulped her drink and jumped off the stool. The man she had been dancing with grabbed her arm. "Sweetheart, where are you going so fast?"

She pulled her arm free. "Did I say you could touch me, asshole?"

Before the man could respond, the bartender placed a beer on the bar and glared at Sharon. "No trouble here. Have this beer on me."

Her dance partner accepted the beer, but not before he uttered "Bitch" in Sharon's direction.

Father Abrams leered at Sharon as she walked away from the bar.

Time to get serious. She finished her next drink with gusto and yelled at the barmaid. "A double shot."

***

During the band's next break, Sharon struggled to her feet, weaved around some patrons, and bumped into others as she headed to the bathroom. In that mirror, Father Abrams sat in a confessional. She giggled. Nobody would confess their sins tonight, and the only prayers would be to the porcelain god.

The empty bathroom reeked of urine and the smell of artificial pine. Sharon sat down in one of the stalls and peed. The graffiti written on the wall made her giggle again. She lit a cigarette and puffed on it until the nicotine high kicked in.

While she washed her hands in a stained sink, a woman old enough to be her mother and smelling like she hadn't showered in a month, staggered in, dropped to her knees in one of the stalls, and vomited.

Sharon turned off the water.

Why have you forsaken God? Father Abrams judged her from the cracked and yellowed mirror.

"Why are you tormenting me?"

"Sorry, I drank way too much," the woman said as she left the stall. She wiped her mouth with the back of her hand. "Burritos don't taste any better the second time."

Sharon waited until the woman stumbled out of the bathroom before she stared back into the mirror. Father Abrams held out his hand, beckoning her.

I can save your soul.

Sharon's fingers grazed the glass then recoiled as if bitten. The surface of the mirror rippled like the waters of the pond. The bathroom filled with the fetid, cloying odors of death. If she pressed her hands against the mirror, she would be pulled inside with no way of escape. Just another secret that returned home against its will. Her life might be a mess, but she didn't want to die that way.

Sharon threw the bathroom door open and pushed her way through the crowd. She found her table and ordered another shot. Father Abrams reappeared in the mirror above the bar, his hands folded in his lap, an impenitent smile splayed across his face.

Repent your sins.

Sharon needed to rid her mind of his intrusion. She scanned the bar for somebody who might be able to take her mind off her troubles.

Flee fornication.

"That's it." Sharon grabbed an unattended beer bottle from a nearby table. Marching toward the bar, she threw the bottle at the image of the priest. Shards of glass and beer flew everywhere. She lost her balance and stumbled into a couple waiting for their drinks.

"Hey," the man said, "what the hell?"

With her eyes glued to the shattered mirror, she pointed at the priest. "Leave me alone, you fucking bastard!"

"You better leave now," the bartender said, picking up the phone.

"Fuck off."

The brisk November night air did nothing to sober up Sharon. The need to get home overwhelmed her. Where was her car? She staggered in a full circle. Nothing appeared familiar. Where in the hell was she?

"Hey, ...hey...you," Sharon said to a couple who had just parked, "Where am I?"

The couple laughed.

Why was that so funny? Sharon glanced at the keys dangling between her fingers. "Yes, yes, I need to find my car. The keys are right here."

"Keys open doors." She dropped them on the ground and backed away as if they would attack. "No...no more doors, no more remembering."

She wobbled over to a car she thought was hers, but the door would not open. She needed her keys. Dumping her purse out, she dropped to her knees and ran her fingers through the gravel. Not there.

Father Abrams appeared in the side mirror. After all these years, he had finally found her, and he would not let her disappear again.

"Leave me the FUCK alone," Sharon screamed into the mirror.

Car after car, she banged on the windows and pulled on the door handles. After each failure, she screamed to the heavens in frustration. "Have you not tormented me enough?"

Father Abrams smirked, eyebrows raised.

The next car didn't open either. She slumped to the ground. "I'm not going back. You can't make me."

Everywhere Sharon looked, Father Abrams glared at her. Why couldn't she find her car? She stumbled to the back parking lot. In the darkness, she could hide. Father Abrams wouldn't be able to see her. "Shh..., if we're quiet, he won't be able to hear."

The toe of her high-heeled shoe caught on a piece of cement in the gravel. She landed in a drunken heap. "God damn it!"

She stood, wobbled, and fell again. Kicking off a broken shoe, she crawled until she found a fist-sized chunk of concrete, then smashed the two outside mirrors of the nearest car. "Take that, you son-of-a-bitch."

As she tried to hit her next target, someone grabbed her wrist. The momentum spun her to the ground.

"That's enough," the young man said. His boyish face hovered over her. "We need to leave. The police will be here soon."

The keening wail of an emergency vehicle grew louder. The young man pulled Sharon to her feet and placed both hands on her shoulders to steady her.

"I'm Adam, an associate of Tom's," the man said. "He had a family obligation and apologizes for not being here himself."

"Don't you fucking touch me," Sharon said, slapping at his hands.

The sirens drew closer.

"Stand still.

"I don't need your help." She brushed the dust off. "I'm fine."

A flicker of a smile disappeared as the emergency lights came into view. The man grabbed Sharon's forearm and dragged her to his car. He unceremoniously pushed her inside. Getting behind the wheel, he wasted little time leaving the bar. He turned onto First Avenue and headed east toward Minnesota.

Somewhere between the Nestor and the intersection of Broadway and First, Sharon's demeanor took a one-hundred-eighty-degree turn. No longer an angry drunk, she slid closer to the young man who drove. She twisted one of his brown curls around her finger and placed her other hand on his thigh. "You don't have to take me home, do you?"

The young man took Sharon's hand off his leg and dropped it back in her lap. "I had plans tonight. Thank you very much."

She took a quick breath, wondering what it would take to woo this young man. Before she could say something cold and wounding—her standard practice when rebuffed—the young man beat her to the punch.

"Just sit there and shut up. You're almost home."

Sharon leaned against the passenger window and stared outside as they crossed the bridge into Moorhead. By the time they turned down her street, she'd fallen asleep.

The young man carried Sharon to her house, leaned her against the door, knocked, and left.

# Chapter 32

T he story burned inside. The words wanted to escape, to come alive on the page. Until Isabelle's troubled mind emptied, sleep would be out of the question. She took a deep breath and picked up her favorite pen.

One of the King's men had killed her best friend. Princess Belle needed to know why her father ordered the killing. She stole into a part of the castle her father forbade her from entering and grabbed a door handle. Her fingers swelled and turned black. Large, angry blisters blossomed on the back of her hands, and fire raced through her veins. She hurried towards the gate and the market outside, to get the Crone's help. She might be the only person who knew more about poisons and their antidotes than the King's man. Besides, Princess Belle might learn something to use as leverage against her father. The Crone's tongue could be loosened for the right amount of silver.

Mingling with the crowd, Princess Belle left the castle without being noticed. The Crone's ramshackle hut sat at the far end of the market. Princess Belle weaved through the villagers, her damaged arm pressed to her side, hidden beneath a cloak. At the entrance to the Crone's hut, she pulled the cord hanging by the door. A deep coppery clang echoed inside.

"What do you want?" the Crone barked as she opened the door.

A barrage of smells escaped from inside. Metallic, sulfur, sweet, and pungent mixed with something dead and decaying. Belle held out her arm. "I need your help."

The Crone squinted, her brows knit in consternation. "If it isn't the whore's whelp. Come in, come in."

Princess Belle's eyes watered from the smells in the room. A little light-headed, she sat down on a nearby stool. The Crone pulled up another seat next to a bubbling black cauldron dominating the space. Rivulets of sweat poured off the Princess.

The Crone grabbed Princess Belle's arm. "Eh...dragon venom... looks like the girl has been playing where her father doesn't want her to—again."

Isabelle dropped her pen and rubbed the moisture from her blurred vision. Tears or weariness? Thoughts of Carson drove her to her feet.

"Relax, Isabelle," she told herself.

Hands on her head, she took two ragged breaths then circled her room. On the second go-around, she stopped at her window and peered outside, hoping Carson would be leaning against the streetlight, his sweet music wafting into her room. Or More tears wetted her cheeks. He would never be there again.

A shadow filled the living room window of Carson's apartment. Opal watched from behind the curtains. Isabelle leaned against the cold pane of glass and whispered, "Opal, I didn't kill Carson."

Bob's car rolled down the block, its lights harsh in the twilight. The vehicle stopped in the middle of the street, paused, then pulled to the curb underneath Carson's streetlight. The driver blinked his headlights twice. After a few seconds, the car settled comfortably at the corner.

Isabelle balled her hands into fists and waited for the driver to exit.

Opal came charging outside, her open housecoat flapping behind her, and great puffs of breath escaped as she ran across the snow-covered yard.

She stopped in the middle of the street, an accusing finger pointed at the car, then jabbed another one of her sausage-sized fingers at Isabelle's house.

Isabelle rushed to the front door and flung it open, but the street was empty.

The outside wrapped around her like an icy blanket. The cold cement burned her bare feet. She hugged herself tightly and shuffled in place.

Where had they gone?

She rubbed her arms and stepped back inside. In her room, she pulled on a sweatshirt and settled at her desk.

Poised to write, her hand paused in mid-air. The realization of something strange happening in her neighborhood sat hard on her shoulders. The weight of possibilities filled her mind with improbable thoughts. Was she to blame for this too?

Bleary-eyed and exhausted, she sat in the uncomfortable silence of her room. Could her imagination be to blame? In the chaos of her mind, she listened for the voice, any voice, telling her everything would be alright, that she was not crazy.

She shook her head and placed pen to paper. Inside these pages was the only place she felt safe at the moment.

The Crone muttered and shuffled over to the cupboard. She smelled the contents of each drawer, dipped in a finger, and sampled each ingredient. Every time the Crone found one to be suitable, a giggle or snort burst forth. A pinch would go into her pestle, then she'd move to the next drawer, dancing around the large cabinet in glee.

"What's that?" Princess Belle asked when the Crone pulled an oddly shaped plant from one of the drawers.

The Crone looked up, surprised by Princess Belle's interest. "Plumeless thistle. The roots are used in a drink that helps combat the poison in your arm."

The Crone picked up a large wooden spoon and mixed the contents of the pot boiling on the fire. After each rotation, her fingers glowed. The faster the Crone stirred, the brighter the light pulsed and danced upon the walls. A glint of gold drew Princess Isabelle's attention. She pointed to the ring the Crone wore and inquired.

"It's not mine," the Crone said. "I'm safekeeping it for a friend of ours."

"Ours? A friend… of ours?"

The Crone cleared her throat and spit. The ring wouldn't come off without a fight. Rubbing the glob of phlegm into her hand, she twisted and pulled until the ring slipped from her finger.

She whispered into the Princess' ear, "I think our friend will need this," and placed the ring into her hand. "You should close your eyes and rest."

Isabelle paused her pencil and put her head on her desk.

Bang. Bang. Bang.

Isabelle's head shot up from the desk.

Bang. Bang. Bang.

She jumped to her feet, her heart racing.

After the next round of bangs, she pinpointed the origin. She turned on the outside light and peered out the window. One of the shutters hung loose. With each gust of wind, the shutter would bounce against the siding. She grabbed the hammer and a couple of nails from the kitchen. At least for tonight, she could keep it quiet. She opened the front door a crack and peeked outside.

"Mom? What are you doing out here?"

The frame of the house seemed to be the only thing keeping her mother upright. Vomit coated the front of her jacket, and littered the steps. Isabelle caught her before her head hit the threshold. The jingle of metal drew Isabelle's attention. She plucked a set of antique keys and a tarnished coin from the snowy ground. The coin resembled the one Sarah had brought to school.

Caw. Caw.

Two large agitated blackbirds hopped along the sidewalk. The bigger one glared at Isabelle with the same expression as the one in the park. Feeling exposed, she dragged her mother inside to the living room floor and closed the door. The ammonia smell of sweat and urine wafted off her mother in waves.

Sharon attempted to sit up, but when Isabelle reached down to help, her mother slapped her hands away. Isabelle had to find a way to get her cleaned up before putting her to bed.

"Shiny," her mother said.

"Where did you get the coin?"

Instead of offering an explanation, her mother gagged. Isabelle grabbed her, and half dragged, half carried her to the bathroom. Isabelle held her mother's hair while she vomited.

"Oh, Mother. Why do you keep doing this to us?"

Isabelle used a towel from the closet to cradle her mother's head in her lap. She smoothed her hair and with a gentle touch, wiped out streaks of vomit. Pulling her mother to her feet, she helped her into the bedroom. All tucked in bed, her mother looked old. The wrinkles around her eyes were more pronounced. A touch of gray dotted her hairline.

Isabelle's childhood seemed long ago. Only sixteen years old, but she'd been taking care of herself for so long already. Where had her mother gone?

"Mom, what are you running from?"

Her mother rolled over and giggled. "Shh! I have a bad secret. I can't tell anyone."

Isabelle placed a cool damp cloth on her mother's forehead.

"Fucking... leave me alone."

"You can't continue to drink like this."

"I'm an adult. My decisions. Drinking keeps the bad things blurry."

Isabelle picked up the discarded washcloth and turned to leave.

"I keep hiding, and he keeps finding me."

"Who keeps finding you?"

Her mother looked at Isabelle with vacant eyes. "It doesn't matter if I'm sober or drunk, it's all the same." She tried to sit up but fell back into the bed. "I prefer this."

"You might, but this isn't how I want to live."

"It's my life."

"It's not always about you."

# Chapter 33

Heather drove home in silence, wondering what had just happened. Her head ached from the possibilities of Adam's revelations. As she waited for the underground parking garage door to open, she pounded on the steering wheel. "Why? Why? Why?"

Darkness enveloped the car, and the stillness of the space crept inside her. She shivered; a nervous sweat covered her forehead. As she headed deeper into the garage, her headlights danced on the concrete walls. Shadows moved in and out between the parked cars. Icy fingers of uneasiness slid up her spine.

She found her parking spot and exited the car.

The silence surged around her.

She didn't lock the door until she scanned the garage to make sure it was safe. Arriving at the stairway, she found a puddle of murky water pooled in front of the door, just like the one at school. The same pond stench beckoned.

The lights in the stairwell flickered. She listened for movement, then hurried to the first floor, her heart racing. The sound of running feet and giggling children greeted her. The lights flickered off as she neared the next landing. After a few seconds, the emergency lights kicked on. With her hand pressed against the wall, she followed the wet footsteps in the dim glow to her second-floor apartment. Almost home.

The children laughed and mocked her. "Come find us," they whispered. "If you dare."

Their voices faded into silence. Wet footprints continued down the hall, glistening in the weak light and puddling in front of her apartment. While turning the key, her hand brushed against mud and moisture dripping from the door. Vile images flashed in her mind. "Oh, God, not again."

Just like in her dream the other night, invisible hands groped her. When a scream clutched at her chest, she stepped back, and the door swung open.

Her hand wavered in front of her face. Little black worms slithered in between her fingers, nipping at her flesh, sending bolts of pain shooting through her arms. She slapped her hands against her pants, causing the creatures to pop like blood-filled ticks. She leaned against the door while the scream ripped its way out.

She pushed away from the wall. Someone was inside her apartment.

"Hello?" she said, before entering her dimly lit apartment.

Her senses flooded with the memory of a particular smell: the fragrance of July when the water was low and the mud along the shore was deep, the odor of rotten fish mixed with the decay of vegetable matter.

She waded through the smell of the pond and gasped. Her dead father sat on the couch.

This couldn't be real. She had sat in the front pew holding her younger sister Avery's hand as they each dropped a clump of dirt on their parents' caskets. She had visited their graves.

Another man, his face obscured in shadows but his clerical collar glowing in the dark, sat beside Heather's father.

"Good evening Heather," he said.

"What are you doing in my house?"

"We are here because you refused to heed the warnings."

"What warnings?"

"To stay away from Isabelle and quit meddling in her life."

"Meddling? I don't understand." Heather's nerves grew taut with apprehension. This was the second time in the last two hours somebody had warned her about Isabelle. "What's so special about her?"

The man chuckled. "For being Teddy's daughter and Bernice's granddaughter, you know so little. She's the key. She can open all of the doors and let the monsters in."

"Are you real?"

"Nightmares are very, very real," the man said. He checked his watch and smiled. "Midnight is fast approaching. The payment has been made. Someone has bought your soul."

Had her mind come undone?

The lights in the room blinked off.

***

She woke up with a start. Rolling to her side, she groaned, a crescendo of pain flooding her head. An empty wine bottle, a single glass, and two coins littered her nightstand. How had she gotten in bed, and why was her phone in her hand? Had she called someone? The answers fluttered out of reach. She closed her eyes and went back to sleep.

***

Heather...Heather....

Yes, Dad.

Can you come to the living room? I need to speak to you.

She bounded down the stairs, her pigtails bobbing. She had been packing for a big dance competition, but she now settled on the couch next to her father in his recliner. He removed his pipe clenched between his teeth, tapped it twice to remove the ashes, and placed it on the table beside him.

"Everybody chooses their own friends. Sometimes you choose and sometimes...well, sometimes others choose you. Not because they like you, but because they want something from you."

"They wouldn't be true friends, would they?"

"No, they wouldn't. Sometimes you don't know the truth until it's too late."

"Dad, I don't understand."

"I have a group of friends who know the details of my life, but I wished they didn't. Because of this, I have made decisions I'm not proud of. You don't need many friends, just a couple of true friends."

He pulled a pouch of tobacco from his table drawer, took a pinch, packed it down in his pipe, and lit it. Heather didn't approve of her father's habit, but she loved the aroma of a freshly lit pipe. The smoke swirled around his head like a halo.

"What I'm trying to tell you is to choose your friends wisely."

"Dad, are you alright?"

"Just getting sentimental. Good luck this weekend."

Heather hopped off the couch and gave him a big hug. He held her a beat too long and called after her as she left the room. "I'm sorry."

***

This time Heather woke with her father's last words echoing inside her head. All the pain resurfaced. Sorry for what? Missing her dance competition? Killing Mom and taking his own life?

Heather's dry tongue filled her entire mouth. She brought back a glass of water from the bathroom and upon detecting a foul odor, wrinkled her nose. The garbage would need to be taken out in the morning. 11:30 pm. Sleep beckoned.

She tossed and turned, tired of the nightmares, tired of the images of her parents' violent deaths holding her hostage. Thoughts of Adam usually pulled her out of the vast gulf of despair she wrapped around herself—but not tonight. She tried to bring the evening into focus. What had happened?

She shrugged. Who was she kidding? Hope and longing tumbled away like a tower built with children's blocks. She was scared of being alone. Since her parents' death, she was afraid of not finding someone to love.

Now wide awake, her overburdened mind raced from one tribulation to another. What did the man look like? She could no longer picture his face. Had he been here? Why was Isabelle the key? And the key to what? 11:55 pm. She drifted off again, recalling something the man had said about midnight.

She woke again, her mind fogged over with sleep. Noises drifted into her room.

"Adam?"

A sudden rush of joy and elation. For a moment, she believed he came to apologize, but the optimism was extinguished by the weight of the silence.

The floor outside her room creaked.

"Hello?" She pulled back the covers and placed one foot on the floor. "Is somebody there?"

Giggling and the sound of running feet in the hallway had her sit upright.

"Ring around the Rosie," voices sang outside her door.

"Son of a bitch," Heather said, springing out of bed. She ran and yanked open the front door. A fresh puddle of muck sat outside.

The smell punched her in the face like a fist. Before she could scream, a hand clasped over her mouth. She bit the soft flesh. Instead of blood, embalming fluid and decayed tissue filled her mouth as she stared at the watch given as a birthday present.

No. No. No. It can't be.

Vomit spewed forth and leaked from between her dead father's fingers. His other hand pulled her head back by her hair. The rope scratched her skin as it was placed around her neck. She kicked but lost her balance. The noose tightened.

Heather grabbed the rope with both her hands. She pulled and yanked until blackness crept in at the edges of her consciousness. Her ears rang as she worked her fingers underneath the rope.

"You don't have to do this."

The rope was yanked violently, the coarse fibers biting into her flesh. Her feet flew out from underneath her, and she crashed to the floor.

Sweat beaded and slid down her face. Was that fire she smelled? She kicked and thrashed as she was dragged across her apartment. The tension on the rope momentarily gave way when her dead father pulled open the patio door. She struggled to breathe, the inside of her throat swollen and raw. Cold air rushed to greet her.

Her father picked her up and, for a moment, their eyes locked.

"Dad, stop. I'm Heather, your daughter. I don't want to die."

Heather searched for understanding, but an evil man leered back. He tossed her like a rag doll over the railing. Time slowed as she tumbled head over heels toward the ground. She thought first of her grandmother and how she was going to cope with another death. She thought of her sister Avery and hoped she would find what she longed for. Most of all, Heather couldn't wait to wrap her arms around her mother.

Her father had lied. He wasn't sorry for what he had done.

The speed of descent slowed as a pair of hands from above tried to grasp the rope, but it was too late to stop the momentum. It was too late to save her.

# Chapter 34

"Sharon... Sharon."

The vodka ran thick in her blood. Sharon rolled over, pissed that somebody disturbed her sleep. "Will you leave me the fuck alone?"

"Wakey, wakey.

Sharon's heavy eyelids refused to open.

"Goddammit." Sharon slurred the words. "I said leave me alone."

Blinking several times, unable to clear her blurred vision, she scanned the room. Where was the fucker who woke her? The curtains fluttered as if somebody had walked by. A dull yellowish glow seeped into the room. In the darkest corner, something more ominous than a shadow lurked. Or could this just be Isabelle?

"Isabelle! Get your ass back to bed!"

No answer. Maybe Sharon was wrong.

Sharon closed her eyes to keep the room from spinning. When she opened them, the figure had materialized, unmoving. A whisper of terror ran through her, and she grabbed the bottle of vodka from the bedside table. Most of the night a blur, she couldn't remember where the bottle had come from; she was just happy it was there. Drinking would stop her from thinking or feeling.

With a steady hand, she poured two fingers of liquid into a glass, hoping this would calm the pounding in her head and release the vise-like grip on her temples. She focused on the corner of the room, but no matter how hard she squinted, she couldn't see who sat there.

She staggered to her feet, one hand out for balance, and placed the drink on the nightstand. The glass, too close to the edge, teetered and fell to the floor.

"Fuck! Look what you made me do."

She lost her balance reaching for the bottle. Face and floor met with a thud. All attempts to push herself to her knees failed. Her ass stuck up in the air like a target. Like a stool with one short leg, she was not having much luck staying upright.

"Jesus Christ! Are you just going to sit there?"

His laughter echoed again through the room.

"Do you think this is fucking funny?"

The shadow in the corner swirled and shifted, fading in and out of the darkness. Elongating and stretching towards the ceiling, the disfigured shape moved towards Sharon. The outline of a person came into focus. A priest dressed in black, his face weathered and old, stood looking at her with disdain. She recognized the face of Father Abrams.

He peered down the pointy end of his nose. His hands, brittle with mottled skin, were folded together chest high, his head bowed in prayer. "Look how the mighty have fallen. Is this how we taught you to live your life, so far from God's grace?" he said, his voice soft yet condescending.

Sharon peered up at the priest and angrily spat back. "You taught me what? My future happiness was solely based on the sufferings in this life. I have suffered plenty."

"Are you ready to open your heart once again to God's love, to bathe in His everlasting glory? I can save your soul."

"Why are you tormenting me?"

He smiled. "Sometimes the children pay for the sins of their mothers."

"You knew my parents?"

"A little. There's not much to tell. Both your parents were dregs of society." The priest's smile did not reach his eyes. "Why have you forsaken God? Why do you continue to walk down the path of fornication and sin?"

"Isn't that what you taught me?"

The walls she had spent a lifetime building around herself momentarily disappeared as tears rolled unfettered down her cheeks. "When I was a naive child, you told us during one of your sermons that if we said one hundred Hail Marys on special religious days, God would answer our prayers. For a full year, I prayed on every holiday. I asked for parents. God never answered. Why?"

The priest was reflected in the mirror, not sitting in the corner like she had assumed. Why were all the sheets piled in the corner, instead of covering the mirrors? Her anxiety made her cringe.

At the convent, Father Abrams had been a sexual voyeur. Tonight was no different. His eyes traveled up her long shapely legs to her crotch then glued themselves to the silken panties that hugged her in the most seductive ways. She had worn them in hopes of enticing Tom. Now she second-guessed her decision.

Thoughts of the pleasures Tom could have delivered coursed through her. The urge to touch herself was overwhelming, her hand slid up her thigh to the frilly edge of her panties.

"I remember," Sharon said. "You like to watch, but did you forget, I like to be watched too."

The cell-like rooms of the convent, brim with memories, sorrow, and lost dreams, filled her mind. Like an onion, years peeled away until she stood staring out through the glass at the pond.

***

Lightning lit up the sky at the end of that warm and humid day. The heat in her room hovered above sweltering. All the girls wore wool nightgowns, even in the heat of the summer. Sharon's body had gone through a metamorphosis over the past year. Her body, once long and bony, had filled out in all the right places; a woman's body.

Unable to sleep, she stood at her window. Bolts of lightning reflected off the black waters of the pond, filling the forest with its luminescence. Eerie shadows danced among the branches, hiding behind ancient trunks. When wind rattled her windows asking for admittance, she obliged.

The wool sleeping gown irritated her sensitive nipples. Slipping it over her head, the gale ravaged her sweaty body as she stood naked at her window. Goosebumps covered her flesh.

All the novices' doors in the convent had small circular glass panes, set high in the doors, which allowed the nuns to spy and punish when needed. Father Abrams stood panting outside her door but never entered. The priest with the dark eyes, who Father Abrams brought on rounds at night, always visited her room last. They'd had this secret since she was a little girl. She was no longer a little girl. Would he still want to keep a secret?

Father Abrams' excitement built. "You were always his favorite."

Closing her eyes tight, she wished both men away. Buried memories, always haunting her, always wanting out.

"This can be our little secret," he had said before guiding her small hand to his penis.

How many boys and girls had he used that line on?

***

"God Dammit." No more memories. She needed to get drunk.

She picked the empty glass off the floor and threw it. The mirror splintered. Father Abrams disappeared in the cascading shards of glass scattered across the floor.

"You fucking hypocrite," Sharon screamed. "It wasn't my soul you wanted!"

She took a long swig from the bottle. The vodka lit her insides on fire. As the alcohol settled, her few lucid thoughts turned to sex and Tom. She could really use both right now. Maybe another swallow would be enough to make her pass out, to eradicate the images of the priest.

Her stomach heaving and now bathed in a clammy sweat, Sharon crawled across the floor, hoping to make it to the bathroom before she puked. Her mouth filled with a metallic taste, she swallowed, trying to force the rancid bile back down.

The priest with the dark eyes appeared in a large piece of the mirror leaning against the edge of the dresser, Sharon's younger hands under his robe.

"No!"

A nearby shard of glass, one that would fit in her hand, tempted her. End the pain and suffering now.

Her fingers wavered inches from the weapon. The nuns taught her the greatest sin wasn't Judas's betrayal of Jesus but his suicide. Did she believe the same? She held the sharp shard of glass against the soft skin of her wrist. Wouldn't this be quicker than killing herself with alcohol?

"What about your daughter?" Father Abrams asked.

Sharon pressed harder. Blood seeped from underneath the shard.

She couldn't do it. Her beliefs were too ingrained.

She punched her fist through the priest's face, letting the blood ooze between her fingers. Covering herself with an old blanket, she passed out.

# Chapter 35

Isabelle stormed into her room, closing the door behind her.

"Bitch."

She threw herself onto the bed and let the rage run its course. Not only was her mother killing herself with alcohol, but she was ruining Isabelle's life.

After changing into a pair of shorts and an old t-shirt, she sat down and turned to the next page in her composition book splayed open on her desk. A colored pencil drawing of a woman tied to a burning post caught her attention.

When did she draw that?

Red, orange, and yellow flames licked at the body. Whiffs of smoke circled the woman's head like a halo. Isabelle traced the outline of the fire with her finger. The warm paper gave off a faint but distinct odor of smoke.

"Help me," the woman mouthed.

The corners of the paper blistered and turned black.

"Oh, shit." Isabelle shut the journal and tossed it on the floor. She stomped on it until the flames dissipated. A swirl of smoke and ash rose from the charred remains. Her feet turned an angry red and stained black in places but no blisters.

An eerie awareness prodded her senses. Something dark was out there, stalking, getting closer. Pain spiked and shot into her temples. Colored dots danced in front of her eyes. "No...No...," she said, shutting her eyes to blot out the images.

Isabelle stood in a hallway.

Children's voices echoed in the distance. "... and she fell dead," they chanted.

Their words brought shivers, a cold rattling up Isabelle's spine.

A door opened. Her teacher, Heather, stood framed in the entryway, her face troubled. She looked side-to-side, but the hallway was empty. Isabelle could have told her that. The darkness that Isabelle knew Heather feared was in the apartment with her. The shadow of death crept closer.

Isabelle rushed to the door. The creature met her head-on and threw her down the hallway as if she weighed nothing at all. Slumped against the wall, Isabelle yelled, "Heather! Watch out!"

Someone behind Heather clamped a hand over her mouth and dragged her inside.

The door closed.

Isabelle's eyes flew open. She grabbed the smoldering journal off the floor and opened it. Two words were written in the corner, 'Death' and 'Midnight.' There was no way she could walk to Heather's in fifteen minutes. Her only option was to take the car. She crept into her mother's bedroom and searched her mother's purse for the keys. How had she gotten home?

Bang... Bang... Bang....

"Dammit," Isabelle uttered. The broken shutter would have to wait. Ms. Dahl was in deep trouble.

She turned to her mother, who was passed out in her bed. "Where's your car?"

Her mother muttered gibberish.

Isabelle rushed to the living room, pulled the curtains aside. Her mother's car was parked in the driveway.

"Good evening, Isabelle."

Isabelle spun around, her pulse racing. Tom sat in the corner, jingling the keys to her mother's car. "Are you looking for these?"

"Give them to me," Isabelle said through gritted teeth.

"Where do you think you're going? Out for a midnight drive?"

"None of your business."

"You won't make it in time."

Too angry to respond, Isabelle glared at him.

"She has to die."

"Why?" She took a couple of aggressive steps forward. "Give me the keys. Now."

"I would prefer sex instead of you playing the hero."

"Not a chance."

Lust danced in Tom's eyes. He grabbed his crotch. "Do you want to touch it like your mother does? I would hate to waste this."

"Hasn't your niece Sarah been doing a good enough job satisfying you lately?" She took another step in his direction. "I will have to have a talk with her at lunch on Monday. Set her straight."

"The retribution of the damned is upon us. You will be judged. The world will be judged and found wanting. Darkness will once again fall upon the earth. Hope and innocence will be lost. Whose side will you be on?" He grabbed Isabelle's left wrist. Her right hand shot out, slamming into Tom's eye and knocking him back a step. With her left fist, she punched him, connecting with his cheek, causing a welt to bloom. She raised her leg and stomped on his hand. The keys fell to the floor near his feet. She lunged quickly and scooped them up. Tom caught a handful of her shorts, pulled her close, and slipped his hand under her t-shirt.

"You little bitch, hold still," Tom said. "If you don't submit, The Dark Ones will eat your soul."

Isabelle slammed her heel down on his foot and swung her elbow at the same time. Both connected. He staggered backward, a trickle of blood leaking from his nose. "The right side."

She headed for the door, her muscles quivering, her body flushed. How dare Tom touch her breast? As she jumped from the front steps, her body became translucent. Instead of a sidewalk beneath her, a small stream flowed. For a split second, she traveled somewhere else. Her body became whole again when she landed on the grass. She ran and locked herself in her mother's car. Did Tom see her disappear?

He stood in the open front doorway, wiping the blood from his nose. His wrathful grimace softened into a smirk.

Isabelle's heart thundered in her ears as she sat behind the wheel. She had taken Driver's Ed her freshman year, so she had a basic understanding of how this worked, but she had never driven alone. She turned the key, and the car started. So far, so good.

"You're too late," Tom said

Isabelle flinched.

He spoke not from the steps, but from next to the car. His smile unnerved her.

She threw the car into reverse and stepped on the gas a little too hard. Tires squealed as the car fishtailed into the grass. Her neighbor's mailbox became a casualty of her overcorrection. By the time she entered the street, she had the vehicle under control. Now in Drive, she sped off.

On her right, a police cruiser approached the intersection at Eighth Avenue. She wiped her palms on her pants and tried not to stare into the mirror. When the light turned green, Isabelle eased into the intersection. Bob's dark-colored car sat in the parking lot across the street. She gasped as pain burst behind her eyes, her vision blurred, and the car slowed.

An image of her teacher being dragged across the room, a noose around her neck, popped up outside the windshield. The dark automobile flashes its lights and interrupts her vision. Time was running out.

The police cruiser turned the corner and followed half a block behind her. She needed to hurry.

11:58 pm.

She had two more blocks before she reached the one-way. She stepped on the gas.

With the police car no longer behind her, Isabelle increased her speed to thirty-five then forty. The image of flames danced on the windshield. She pushed the car to forty-five. Going too fast when the light turned red, she slammed on the brakes, slid through the intersection, jumped the curb, and skidded onto the sidewalk.

The clock read 12:01 am.

Isabelle jumped out of the car. Running to the street-level door, she could already smell the smoke.

Caw…Caw…Caw…

Two large black birds that harassed her all evening were perched on the streetlight closest to the bridge, their beady eyes tracking her movement. As Isabelle reached the door, they took flight and headed straight for her. She swung her arms, avoiding beaks and talons, and opened the door. She took the steps two at a time to the second floor. The sound of laughing children and running feet filled the halls. There was something creepy about their laughter.

Isabelle followed the children's footsteps.

The laughter faded. A single girl's voice sang, "She falls dead."

A girl in a calico dress and bonnet stepped out of the shadows at the end of the hall. "Are you one of them?"

"One of whom?"

"You're a witch, aren't you?"

Isabelle wasn't sure of anything anymore. "I don't know."

The girl's eyes glinted cold and dark. Her skin glowed pale in the hallway light. A cheerless giggle escaped from her smiling lips. "Don't fear the reaper. Tonight, he isn't here for you."

Death slid its icy fingers down Isabelle's spine.

"I warn you, he will kill all of you."

A knot formed in Isabelle's chest, and her heart thumped one painful beat after another.

The girl slipped back into the shadows.

As Isabelle approached the door, footsteps echoed to her right. She spun around and caught a glimpse of a shadow as it disappeared around the corner.

In the distance, a chorus of voices chanted, "We all fall dead. We all fall dead. All fall dead!"

Isabelle could not wait any longer. She grabbed the doorknob, and a searing pain shot up her arm. The fire was likely in full bloom behind the door. She grasped the handle with the bottom of her shirt, and the door swung open with a whoosh. The intense heat crisped the ends of her hair. She spied a fire alarm down the hallway. Pulling it, she screamed, "Fire!"

Behind the flames inside the apartment, shadows moved. Isabelle took a deep breath and plunged into the inferno just as Heather crawled onto the balcony railing. A rope dangled from her neck.

Isabelle rushed to the balcony doors. The creature from her dream blocked her path.

Isabelle charged. Her hands touched the creature's cold flesh. A high-pitched, angry roar, like a thousand flies caught in a mason jar, detonated inside her head. Her brain filled with the ancient wailings of the seven demons: Grief, Terror, Shame, Rage, Loneliness, Desperation, and Despair. Despair currently inhabited the creature's body.

The creature disappeared into a roughly drawn door, its stench trailing behind, sticking to Isabelle's skin and clothes.

Ms. Dahl stood atop the railing, her legs wobbling. She took one deep breath then flung herself off the ledge.

"Noooooooo." Isabelle raced to the falling rope. Pain erupted when the coarse strands bit into her blistered palms. She couldn't hang on. For a split second, they locked eyes. Once the rope snapped, Isabelle looked away, sorrow and pity ripping open her insides.

# Chapter 36

"Avery, stop the car," Bernice yelled.

Avery shifted into park and raced towards the apartment just as Heather flew over the top of the railing.

Avery screamed, but Bernice stood in stunned silence. Her biggest fears had come to fruition.

A young girl, standing on the balcony with Heather, held the end of the rope attached to Heather's neck. Bernice couldn't see the girl's features clearly, but something about her struck Bernice as vaguely familiar.

"What's your name, girl?" Bernice said, pushing the words into the girl's head.

The girl on the balcony turned, her eyes now fixed on Bernice. "Isabelle," she answered.

Heather's lifeless body swung in the wind. Great billows of smoke cascaded from the patio doors behind the girl. As the bystanders gathered in the streets, the sirens of the emergency vehicles drew closer. None of that mattered.

"You should probably get out of there," Bernice said.

"Who are you?" Isabelle asked.

A sad smile formed. "I'm your grandmother."

***

Isabelle left the burning apartment as fast as she could, but the implications of the old woman's words consumed her thoughts. She made her way to the street and some much-needed fresh air. Her lungs burned, and her heart ached.

Someone yelled, "That's her. That's the girl from the balcony."

Isabelle needed to escape unnoticed. But it was too late for that. Sarah's father, the Sheriff, stood on the sidewalk in front of her mother's car.

Someone grabbed both of Isabelle's arms from behind. Cold hard steel slammed down on her wrists as the cuffs snapped shut.

"Gee, look at who we have here," the Sheriff said. "Second crime scene this week. Is that your mother's car?"

Isabelle shrugged.

"Do you have a license?"

She stared at her feet.

"Take her to County Lock-up, the adult side. I'll call her mother."

***

'Nobody's going to die,' her grandmother had said.

Avery knew she had lied once the apartment came into view and Heather stumbled out onto the balcony. They had arrived too late.

Heather climbed onto the railing and wavered. Just before she fell, a girl rushed through the patio doors. She grabbed for the rope, but it slipped through her fingers.

Everything slowed.

Each second of Heather's fall became a single frame, a picture etched into memory, multiple arrows piercing Avery's heart.

Her sister jerked to a stop and swung freely at the end of the noose. As the girl stood on the balcony and stared into the crowd Avery tracked her gaze. A flicker of a smile rose at the edges of her grandmother's mouth then fell. Heather's body hung limp.

Avery's chest tightened, and her throat constricted as the girl disappeared into the apartment.

"Kyrie Eleison. Lord, have mercy," someone said.

Who had whispered? Avery scanned the crowd gathered in front of the building. Instinct drove her forward. She bumped and shoved people out of her way. An elderly man slipped in between the shadows and she caught a glimpse of his priest's collar as he disappeared into a vehicle.

A drooling, disheveled man, dressed in tatters, who looked like they belonged in an asylum leaned against the same dark car. Another man with a scar etched deeply into his face stood on one corner, obsessively checking his watch. On the other side of the street, an obese woman leaned against a light pole, a cigarette dangling from her lips. None of them seemed concerned about the fire or her dead sister.

Avery jostled her way toward the building. The crowd appeared to be waiting for something or somebody. She knew these people. All of them had visited her parents' house in Pine Bluff right before her parents' accident and their death. They were her father's friends, and they did nothing but watch Heather die. Like it was just another witch burning.

Red eyes glowed inside the car. Whispered words fluttered against her neck. "Come, my children."

Shadows slid along the ground, weaving between people's feet, disappearing into the car. Avery took a step, desperate to see who else or what else was in the vehicle.

"That little bitch on the balcony killed my son," the fat woman from across the street yelled.

A flush rose to Avery's cheeks, and a fire ignited inside.

The girl killed my sister.

Red and blue emergency lights flashed against the bricks. Multiple tendrils of smoke drifted above as Avery broke through the crowd.

A fireman stopped her. "You can't go in there."

"But... my... sister...." She turned toward her grandmother standing in the middle of the road and yelled, "Grandma."

The girl from the balcony, who could have passed for her sister, appeared at the door then scurried away from the building. Warning bells sounded inside Avery. The girl was a witch. Avery needed answers.

"That's the girl from the balcony," Avery yelled.

A cop grabbed the girl from behind, snapped handcuffs on her wrists, and whisked her away.

All the pain from the day congealed into a single ball of agony in the pit of Avery's stomach as the squad car drove off. The girl from the roof was a witch, part of their family, and another one of her grandmother's secrets.

Anger seethed from Avery's pores. Life wasn't fair. Why couldn't it have been her? The night she signed her name in her family's Book of Shadows, she overheard the conversation. She was not the one, her ancestor said. She hadn't realized what those words meant until now.

More cops arrived and pushed the crowd back to make room for the ladder truck. Two firemen scurried up and while one held Heather's lifeless body, the other cut the rope. They rushed her to the waiting stretcher.

"Wait, wait, that's my sister," a tearful Avery pleaded with one of the cops as the ambulance drove away. "Where are they taking her?"

"Meritcare, the ER on Broadway. Do you know how to get there?"

"Yes."

Avery pushed her way back to the car. Her grandmother sat on the curb, crying. A lump formed in Avery's throat, but her anger had dried up all the tears. She helped her grandmother into the car, did a U-turn on the bridge, and headed towards the hospital.

They arrived just as the doors to the ambulance bay closed. Avery parked on the ramp right next to the stairs then helped her grandmother out of the car and down the steps. Halfway to the entrance, she could no longer hold back her anger. "I thought nobody else would die. Anything else you'd like to tell me?"

Her grandmother let go of her arm, planted her feet, and faced Avery. "Do you think this is what I wanted?"

The ache Avery felt for all the people she lost had never faded. With the death of her sister, her grief only festered and intensified. "Are you going to tell me about the girl on the balcony?"

Bernice's shoulders drooped as if whatever had been holding her upright had suddenly let go. Her face turned ashen. "We all have our secrets and our own crosses to bear," she said, then headed for the emergency room entrance.

Avery stomped after her. The automatic doors whooshed open, and they were greeted with a cacophony of noises. A moaning middle-aged man sat with a bloody towel wrapped around his hand. A young woman rocked a crying child while another gripped her hip demanding her attention. A young Fargo police officer babysat a drunken man in a wheelchair who screamed obscenities at anyone who looked his way.

Avery approached the desk. A haggard-looking nurse handed her a clipboard, but Avery shook her head. "My sister just came in from Moorhead."

The nurse picked up her phone and spoke to somebody briefly, then turned back to Avery. "Somebody will be right out."

Avery paced in front of the doors that separated the lobby from the treatment area.

A few minutes later, a male RN pushed through the doors. "Are you here for…?" He reviewed the chart. "Heather Dahl?"

Avery nodded and put her arm around her grandmother. They followed the nurse into one of the treatment rooms.

"Please sit. A doctor will be with you soon."

Avery sat, stood, paced, and sat again, her nerves raw and heart palpitating. Every time someone passed their room, she leaped to her feet.

After fifteen long minutes, a doctor entered and sat across from them. His face was devoid of emotion, but his eyes spoke volumes. "There was little we could have done for her. I'm sorry."

Avery stopped listening. Her mind skipped like an old record, replaying the same thought: Not my sister. Not my sister. Not my sister.

They followed the doctor down a short, sterile hallway to a door with a rectangular window. A slit between the curtains revealed a body covered by a white sheet. Was that Heather?

"I'll give you a few minutes," the doctor said. "A Moorhead officer is in the lobby. He would like to have a few words with you before you leave."

Avery nodded, but could she really do this?

Avery held tight to her grandmother's hand, and they entered together. A nurse pulled the sheet from Heather's face.

Something squeezed Avery's heart so tightly it came close to bursting. A ball of ice grew in the pit of her stomach. She cradled Heather's hand and pressed her lips to her sister's cold fingers. Her heart broke in the silence.

No more late-night talks about boys. No more crying over Saturday morning chick flicks. Who would she talk to about her upcoming date with Jacob? She squeezed her eyes shut. Whole sections of her body seemed to be missing, torn away by grief.

Avery kissed Heather on the forehead.

The nurse pulled the sheet back over Heather's face. "I'm sorry for your loss."

A Moorhead Police officer waited for them in the hallway. "We're very sorry for your loss," he said.

The grief and sorrow, a crescendo of rage, had become too much for Avery. Her nostrils flared, her muscles and veins strained against her skin. She ran through the automatic doors, across the parking lot to the corner, and collapsed to the ground.

On her hands and knees, she begged God for help, for a way to unload some of her anger before she exploded. If only she could run forever.

Her hands clenched into fists, she took a deep breath and screamed into the night sky.

None of the million stars even blinked, but she felt a little better. Still, she wondered, with so many people missing from her life, would she ever feel whole again?

One night after her parents' deaths, her grandmother told her that after a person dies, they become a star, watching over those they love. Was one of those stars her sister?

"Oh, Heather, so much is going on. I really need my big sister now."

The icy block inside her grew. A gentle touch from her grandmother pulled her out of her reverie.

"The sheriff would like to ask us some questions in the morning. There's a Howard Johnsons a few blocks away. He thought we could get a room."

The car ride over to the hotel was strained at best. Ever since the failed spell, an ever-increasing gulf of misunderstanding separated them. Her grandmother didn't say anything until after they had checked in and gone to their room.

"I know you blame me for the death of your sister."

"Yes, I blame you."

Her grandmother's shoulders sagged, her eyes filled with a glazed look of defeat.

Avery walked into the bathroom and, for good measure, slammed the door. She turned on the shower, sat on the toilet, and undressed slowly, her mood alternating between tears and anger. "Why, why, why? Mom, Dad, and now Heather. All dead. Am I next?"

The bathroom filled with steam. Avery let the hot water cascade over her head, but the shower did nothing to thaw the chunk of ice in her stomach. Thoughts of Heather and the girl on the balcony tormented her. There were too many secrets in her family.

Her grandmother had fallen asleep by the time Avery came out of the bathroom. Though fatigue oozed from every pore, she did not think sleep would come quickly. She slipped under the covers and stared at the dark splotch on the ceiling.

Chapter 36

Avery stared at the spot on the ceiling until her eyes ached. Barely able to think, recall, or even breathe, she squeezed her eyes shut and rolled over. Every time sleep approached, another scab ripped off and she bled more. The night moved on, exhaustion overcame the memories, but the nightmares persisted.

She opened her eyes, unsure of where she was. The door opened, and her mother entered, holding a large mug of hot chocolate with clouds of floating marshmallows. How did her mother know when she had trouble falling asleep? Avery cradled it in her hands, inhaling the aroma of home.

Her mother sat on the edge of the bed and smiled. Avery took a big sip. Marshmallow and chocolate dripped off her lip. They both laughed. Avery slipped back under the covers and her mother tucked the blankets under her chin. The scent of lilac shampoo made Avery ache with regret.

Her mother smoothed her hair with gentle strokes. "Don't be mad at your grandmother. We all have secrets we can't share, even with those we love."

"Why did Heather die?"

"That's a tough one to answer. I should get your father. He knows." She headed toward the door.

"Momma, don't leave, I'm scared. I don't want to be alone."

"You'll never be alone, my dearest Avery. I'll always be with you."

"Do you have secrets Papa doesn't know?"

"Yes."

"Can you tell me?"

"They wouldn't be secrets anymore."

"I miss you."

"I miss you too. We'll be together again soon. I promise."

"Momma, I don't want to die."

"I know, but your dad says...."

"What does Dad say?"

Her mother shook her head.

"Momma?"

"Shh. Don't tell your father that I know his secrets."

"Don't tell me what?" her father said as he strolled into the room.

Her mother gave him a hug and a peck on the cheek. "Oh, nothing, dear," she said and left the room.

Avery's father faced her. Something was wrong with his head. It wasn't the same shape as she remembered. His lips curled into a smile as if fury lurked just below the surface. She caught a glimpse of a dark presence in his eyes.

"What didn't your mother want to tell me?"

"We were talking about secrets."

"Our family seems to have a lot of secrets," her father said. "I know yours."

"I didn't keep anything from you." Avery pulled the sheets tighter under her chin.

"Are you sure?" Her father reached into the top drawer of her dresser and lifted a book into the air. "What the fuck is this?"

She shifted uneasily under the covers.

He moved toward her, his right leg dragging. He stopped at the edge of her bed and thrust the book into her face. "Let's see." His eyes lit up as he thumbed through the pages. "Did you sign your name in this book?"

"Papa, you're scaring me."

"Answer my goddamn question." He slammed the book shut. "I'm waiting."

The smell of the pond filled the room. Her father was dressed in his burial clothes. His suit jacket, caked in mud, reeked of decay. He had left muddy footprints all over the floor.

The reality confused and repulsed her, but she had to answer. "Yes, I signed it."

He threw the book. Pond scum splattered the walls and dripped from the ceiling. "That makes you a fucking witch just like your whore of a grandmother."

"Grandma is not a whore."

"Did she tell you about the girl on the balcony?"

"No."

"Did she tell you who she fucked?"

"Papa, stop it.

His eyes burned with anger. He tossed the dresser aside. He drew the outline of a door with his finger and when it swung open, cold air and snow swooped into the room. A group of children with ashen faces appeared and they stared at her. A girl with gleaming green eyes stepped forward, holding a severed head.

"Avery, listen to me." Her father's eyes burned with malice. "Heather helped the little witch, and you signed the book. I take care of my problems."

Avery bolted upright, her chest heaving. She gulped mouthfuls of air. A scream stuck in her throat. "Help me."

Her grandmother appeared at her side, concern etched across her features. "I'm right here."

Avery snuggled against her grandmother until her breathing returned to normal. "What time is it?"

"Time for us to get going."

Hoping some time alone to gather her thoughts would put a stop to the nightmares, Avery grabbed the clothes she'd worn the day before and walked to the bathroom. She wanted a clean washcloth, but the shelf was empty. No hand or bath towels, either. When she pulled back the shower curtain to retrieve the one she had already used, the smell hit her. The tub was littered with towels caked in mud.

"Grandma?"

Her grandmother's pale face had collapsed into a complex set of wrinkles, making her look like she had aged overnight. A bible laid open on the desk next to her.

Avery held out one of the towels. "Where did this mud come from?"

"We had company last night."

The remnants of a hastily cleaned mess remained above the bed. Something dank and vicious dripped from the ceiling.

Her grandmother addressed the question Avery hadn't asked. "He didn't stay long."

Unable to take anymore, Avery collapsed onto the bed, curled into a ball, and closed her eyes. The icy numbness spread outward. She seemed to be floating in and out of a dream. Hunting her, taunting her, taking up residence, the things lurking in the shadows of her mind left her always afraid. When she opened her eyes, she hoped she would be in her bed at home. She could then pick up the phone and call her sister. She needed to tell her how much she loved her.

"Avery? Are you ready?"

Avery uncurled her legs and sat up in bed. She took a couple of deep breaths. "Let me run a brush through my hair, then I'll be ready to go."

They checked out of their hotel and drove to the Moorhead Police Station. At the entrance, her grandmother gave the officer the business card the sheriff had given them. "We're relatives of Heather Dahl. Sheriff Erickson wanted us to stop by on our way out of town. Is he available to see us?"

The woman made a quick call to check the sheriff's availability before she offered an answer. "Why don't you have a seat? The sheriff will be with you shortly. Can I get either of you something to drink?"

They answered in unison. "Coffee, please."

The policewoman brought them steaming mugs of black coffee and a handful of creamers and sugars. "I warn you, the coffee's strong."

Five minutes later, neither one had taken more than a sip.

The sheriff strode over and helped Avery's grandmother to her feet. "Please follow me."

They were ushered into a room. "I'm so sorry for your loss. Is there anything we can do for you?"

Avery's grandmother didn't waste time. "When will you be releasing the body?"

Sheriff Erickson ran his hand through his hair. "It was sent to St. Paul for an autopsy."

"Did the girl on the balcony kill my sister?" Avery blurted.

Her grandmother glared at her.

The sheriff sighed. "We're in the middle of an investigation. I can't release that information at this time."

Anger bubbled up from Avery's core. She gripped her coffee so hard her knuckles turned white. She walked to the two-way window. "You won't or you can't?"

"Let me ask you a question." He looked at each of them in turn. "Why did you drive to Moorhead during a winter storm, and arrive just as Heather died? I don't believe in coincidences."

Avery set her mug on the table and stretched her fingers. "I need to use the restroom. Is that alright with you?"

"Yes, go ahead. Your grandmother  and I can have a private conversation."

Avery left the room just as the door to the conference room across the hall opened. The girl from the balcony, dressed in orange, sat handcuffed to a table. They stared at each other.

Her grandmother had pinned all their dreams on this girl. Avery hoped she was good as promised. Her life depended on it.

# Chapter 38

J ingle. Jingle.

Jingle. Jingle.

The sound woke Sharon. She reached over her head and swatted at the noise. "What the fuck?"

She rolled over carefully, fearful of disturbing the full-blown roar in her head. When would she learn? Tom stood above her, unsmiling. She managed a half-smile and asked, "Are you real?"

He nodded.

"I've been thinking about you," she said, sliding her hand up his leg.

He brushed her hand away. "You need to come with me."

"What's wrong?" She batted her eyes.

Tom laughed. "You're a piece of work. Look at yourself. You have blood all over and you're covered in vomit. A dirty bar rag would smell better.

She tried to pull herself up. Tom grabbed her arm before she fell to the floor.

"Jesus Christ! That hurts." Sharon couldn't pry his fingers from her arm.

"You need to take a shower and sober up—quickly."

"Goddamnit, slow down."

He ignored her whining and marched her straight into the bathroom.

"Are you sure you don't want some of this?" Sharon asked, unhooking her bra. "There's room in this shower for both of us."

"That's enough. You're drunk, shut up."

The tone of his voice put her on edge. She wasn't some dog he could reprimand.

"The fuck I am. I thought you were man enough to handle my needs."

He turned on the water. "Get in. I'm not here to play games."

Sharon slipped off the frilly panties. "Doesn't this body turn you on? These are the breasts of a real woman. Would it excite you if I shaved? I know you like them young."

Tom spun her around. "Enough of this shit. I promised the sheriff I would get you sober and to the county jail. He needs to ask Isabelle some questions. And you need to be there."

"What?"

Sharon's uneasy stomach birthed large butterflies.

"One of her teachers is dead."

"So, what does this have to do with Isabelle?"

"Isabelle was at the crime scene. The Sheriff wants to ask her what she knows about Miss Dahl's death and the death of your neighbor's son Carson."

"Are they going to charge her with anything?"

"Probably driving without a license." He pushed her into the shower. "Is your car insured?"

"What the fuck?" Sharon stuck her wet head out from behind the shower curtain. "She took my car?"

When Tom didn't answer she closed her eyes and placed both hands on the wall. The sensation of nausea, no more than a twinge, announced its claim on her. After a few moments of controlled breathing, her stomach and the shower stopped spinning. The reality of the moment gradually took hold. The more she thought about the current situation, the more pissed off and scared she became. How could she keep Isabelle from being a fuck-up like her?

Dressed now, but with a towel wrapped around her wet head, she stumbled down the hall into the kitchen. Tom placed a fresh cup of coffee on the table. She wobbled to a chair and sat. After taking a sip, she lit a cigarette and inhaled deeply. "Are you planning to be there for questioning?"

"I thought you might ask, so I drew up the papers. You need to sign these before I can."

He pointed out the places where her signature was needed. The words all blurred together, but against her better judgment, she signed every single document anyway. "How much is this going to cost?"

Tom shrugged. "Let's wait and see how the interview goes."

"Isabelle is a little weird, but she's a smart kid. She doesn't have the stomach to kill anyone." She pointed to the bruise on his face. "What happened to you?"

"Nothing."

He tucked the signed documents into his briefcase. They both put on their jackets and headed out into the brisk morning. She'd just have to let her hair air dry. Above the horizon, a blood-red sun rose. She shielded her eyes and collapsed onto the seat. Holy shit, Isabelle is in jail. Sharon had never been officially charged, but she had spent plenty of nights in detox, too drunk to take care of herself.

Sheriff Erikson waited for them in front of the conference room, a cold, hard-pinched expression on his face. He reached out his hand as they approached. "Tom, thanks for your help." He inspected Sharon with silent scrutiny. "Sharon."

She turned away. In an interrogation room to her right, Isabelle sat calmly at a table.

"Can I have a few minutes with Isabelle and her mother before the interview starts?" Tom asked.

Sheriff Erikson nodded.

Isabelle was dressed in an orange jumpsuit, her hands bandaged. She sipped on a can of ginger ale. Sharon didn't waste any time. "What the fuck did you do to my car?"

Her daughter glanced up but ignored her question. She smiled at Tom. "I see I left some bruising."

Sharon turned to him, pointing to the bruises on his face. "Isabelle did this?"

"Tom, you didn't tell her?" Isabelle stared at her mother, a blue flame of defiance dancing in her eyes. "While you were passed out, your boyfriend here came into our house and grabbed my boobs without asking."

Sharon stood nailed to the floor, looking first at her daughter, then at Tom.

Isabelle's smile disappeared. "Did Tom have you sign any papers?"

Uncertain if she was sober enough for this conversation, Sharon locked her gaze on Tom.

His expression wavered for an instant. "Yes."

Isabelle shrugged in defeat. Teary-eyed, she said, "I should've warned you, Mom."

Tom pulled up a chair next to Isabelle. She scooted farther away. "I knew my mother would bring you. Leave. I don't need your help."

"I'm all you got."

Isabelle's eyes, cold and hard, cast daggers at Tom. "Why did Ms Dahl have to die?" she asked. "You knew, didn't you?"

Sheriff Erikson and a female officer walked into the room before Tom could answer.

"This is Officer Amanda Black. She's from Juvenile and will be joining us." He pulled a tape recorder out of his jacket pocket. "Our conversation today will be recorded."

"Is she currently being charged with any crime?" Tom asked.

"Not at the moment." Officer Black told him.

"State your full name," Sheriff Erickson said.

"My name is Isabelle Marie Gunderson."

"Before we talk about Heather Dahl and the fire, I would like to ask you a few questions about your friendship with Carson."

Isabelle nodded. "We were friends."

"Carson's mother thinks you know more about his death than you're admitting. She thinks he died because he was your friend."

"That fat bitch," Sharon muttered.

Isabelle nodded.  Her mother had said what she was thinking.

Both Tom and the sheriff gave Sharon a stern look, a warning to keep quiet. Officer Black handed her a couple of tissues.

"I don't know why Opal blames me for Carson's death. He was like a brother to me," she said, blowing her nose.

Sheriff Erikson glanced at his notepad before he asked his next question. "How did you know it was Carson's body at the park?"

Isabelle bit her lip, and her gaze darted across the room. She took an audible breath before she answered. "I don't know. I had a feeling something terrible happened. John, Carson's foster dad was back in town, and something bad always happened when he was around."

"What do you mean something bad?" Officer Black asked.

"Did you see his back? Both of his foster parents found different ways to abuse him. They were not fit to take care of anyone."

"Did you ever tell anybody about the abuse?" Officer Black asked.

"We've only been living here since summer. Once I threatened to tell the counselors at school and he freaked. Said if John ever found out, he would kill both of us. Carson pleaded with me not to tell."

"And being a good friend, you kept your word," Officer Black added.

"When I saw you walking towards the crime scene, your eyes were darting all over the place." Sheriff Erikson said, "What were you searching for in the park?"

Sharon had never heard any of this before. She knew Opal was white trash, but she didn't know anything about John. She thought they were his biological parents. Isabelle had taken his death hard, much harder than she'd realized, and the last question the sheriff asked had knocked Isabelle off balance. For the first time, her daughter appeared scared.

"I wasn't looking for anything," Isabelle said, but her gaze went to the floor.

Isabelle had just lied. If she knew Isabelle had lied, then everybody in the room knew she had lied too.

The sheriff shifted in his chair, took a drink of water and eyed Isabelle. "This process goes smoothly when people tell the truth. Isabelle, would you like to try again?"

Tom grabbed Isabelle's arm, and whispered into her ear. She shook her head at him and said, "I had a dream Carson was killed in the park. The killer wrote something on the wall. I was curious to see what was written."

"Was the dream you had about Carson, the same type of dream you had when you broke into Ms. Dahl's dance studio?"

"Wait a goddamn minute." Sharon stood, hands on her hips. "I thought we were here to talk about Isabelle driving without a license."

"We will get to that topic soon," Sheriff Erikson said. "Please sit down so we can continue."

"Are you charging Isabelle with any crime?" She slammed her hand on the table for emphasis.

"Please calm down," Tom told her.

She turned her attention to Isabelle. "Did you break into the dance studio?"

"I don't know," Isabelle answered, fighting back tears.

"What do you mean, you don't know?" Sharon asked.

"I remember leaving the house and the next thing I knew I was dancing at the studio."

Sharon picked up her jacket. "Since you're not charging her, I think this discussion is over. We're leaving."

Tom stood, blocking Sharon's path of retreat. He grabbed her arm. "Don't do this. Let the sheriff finish his questions."

She pushed Tom out of the way and headed for the door. He caught her arm and swung her around. "Why don't you take a smoke break?" He turned to Sheriff Erickson. "Can we take a ten-minute recess? I need to talk to my client, in private, before we continue."

Sharon stormed out of the interview room before the sheriff gave permission. She needed to pee but what she craved was a cigarette. A sign indicated the bathroom was located on the lower level.

The interview was not what she had expected. In the interrogation room; she had heard aspects of Isabelle's life that were a mystery to her. Maybe she didn't know her daughter as well as she thought. It pissed her off when Tom placed his hand on Isabelle's shoulder and leaned close, his lips just inches from her ear. The hairs on the back of her neck rose just thinking about his breath caressing Isabelle's skin.

She found the bathroom downstairs, in the darkest corner, as far from the stairwell as possible. Her footsteps echoed in the distance as if they belonged to someone else. She looked over her shoulder, but there was no one there. This stretch of the hallway was a haunting but familiar place, like the ones she walked down as a youth.

The heavy industrial scent of cleaning products drifted out of the open restroom door. Sharon thumbed the switch, the light sputtered and flickered before staying on. She jumped a little at her reflection in the mirror but sighed with relief. The priest was nowhere to be seen.

There were two stalls in the bathroom and she chose the farthest one from the door. The "No Smoking" sign was posted, but she wasn't going to stand outside in this cold and smoke. She lit up, enjoying the rush of nicotine. Fucking daughter. She really put them in a bind this time. What was she going to do with her?

After a couple of more deep puffs, she felt better. If only Tom were here to scratch the itch she had between her legs. She doubted he would come home with her after this. He seemed more interested in Isabelle, which irritated her to no end. She would have to take care of her own needs later.

She flushed the cigarette and stood in front of the mirror. Still, no priests, no doors.

The door swung open. The sound bounced ominously off the walls and down the corridor. Outside the restroom, written on the yellowed tiles in large capital letters was the phrase MASTURBATION IS A SIN!

"Look at me when I'm talking to you."

Paranoia seeped into her veins, and a sense of dread washed over her. She peered up and down the hallway but no one was there. The door closed. The radiators hissed and popped. The harsh overhead lights glared just the way she remembered when she was....

"Are you afraid of me?" the nun said, tapping her ruler on the desk.

"No... No...." Sharon picked up her pace. The end of the hallway seemed as far as a football field away.

"There are scarier people here than me," the nun reminded her.

She wasn't going to remember this. She would lock those memories away, hide them someplace where nobody could find them. Her brisk walk turned into a fast jog. Then she started to run. The stairs at the end of the hallway weren't getting any closer.

"You know they watch you at night, when... when you touch yourself."

The city girls giggled somewhere behind her. They were always so cruel. She slid around the corner. Taking two steps at a time, she made it to the landing between floors and gripped the railing. This was something real, and she wasn't letting go.

Several minutes later, she entered the interview room. Between ragged breaths, she announced, "It's time for us to go."

Isabelle glanced at her mom and then at Tom. "No. I want to help find who killed Carson and Heather because no matter what Sheriff Erikson thinks, I did not kill anybody." She pulled the chair closer to the table and glared at the sheriff. "Ask your questions. Let's find the real killer."

# Chapter 39

"Isabelle?" Bernice said.

"Who are you and why are you in my head?" Isabelle asked.

"It doesn't matter."

"Are you the old woman from the bridge? The one who claims to be my grandmother?"

"Yes."

"What do you want?"

"Take care of your mother. She's in danger."

"Isabelle? Isabelle, are you listening to me?"

She turned toward Sharon. "What?"

"What the hell was that in there?" Sharon glanced around. "Are you fucking crazy? Do I need to take you to a shrink?"

"Are you kidding me?"

Her mother grabbed her arm. "Because of you, we'll have to move again."

"Because of me?" Isabelle laughed and ripped out of her grasp. "Are you still drunk?"

Sharon struck her squarely on the cheek. Heat spread across Isabelle's face, but she smiled and raised her arm in retaliation.

Tom came from behind and grabbed her wrist. "What the hell are the two of you doing?" He eyed them both.

"Yes, Sharon, answer your boyfriend." Isabelle glared defiantly at her mother. "Don't you ever fucking hit me again."

"You ungrateful little...."

Tom stepped between them. "Hey, everyone just calm down. I've got good news. The police don't have any real evidence. They're letting Isabelle go. I just got the release order."

Fuck them both. Fuck them all. Isabelle walked away.

Halfway down the block, a car approached, but Isabelle didn't look back. If it was Tom and her mother, she was not ready to deal with their bullshit. She needed to be alone with her grief. The car followed her to the end of the block. At the red light, she crossed the street, sprinted down the sidewalk, and cut through an alley. She eventually slowed to a walk and glanced around. No one had followed.

The cold air burned her lungs and frosted her lashes. Her mind returned to the conversation from earlier. The sheriff didn't believe anyone else was in Miss Dahl's apartment. She tried to describe the person, but how do you explain something not quite real? His theory did not include demons or dead fathers. The sheriff was too uptight to believe in the supernatural. He believed she had killed her teacher, or that she had committed suicide. Couldn't he or any of the other officers smell the unnatural stench of the demon in her apartment?

What about Carson? She told the sheriff all she knew, but he still thought she hadn't told the whole truth. Why wouldn't anyone believe her? Because her answers sounded crazy, that's why. Did that make her insane? Probably.

There were no cars in Isabelle's driveway. A good sign her mother probably wasn't there. She went to her room.

Sleep came quicker than she expected. If she had dreamed, she did not remember.

***

The house was silent when she tiptoed past her mother's door and out the front. A new day awaited.

The brisk morning air stung the inside of her nostrils. It was Saturday, and the first order of business was to find coffee, black and strong. There was a coffee shop not far from the library where she could get her morning fix. Some of her fellow students started their mornings off with a Mountain Dew or a Coke, but she couldn't stand that cloying sweetness first thing in the morning. It made her teeth hurt.

Keeping her head down and her hands in her pockets, she stayed on the side streets, zigzagging along Twelfth Avenue, never straying more than a block or two on either side. A house with several days' worth of newspapers sitting on the front step caught her attention. She grabbed the newest edition so she would have something to read while sipping her coffee and waiting for the library to open. Today, words and books would be her distraction, instead of thinking about what she called her 'craptastic' life.

There was a bounce to her step as she neared the coffee shop. She had a plan for today and wouldn't worry about tomorrow. The jingling bell announced her presence. Tom and a strikingly beautiful woman turned as she walked in.

Is that his wife? Oh shit!

Isabelle spun around. Her mind told her to run and scream, but she kept calm and decided to get her caffeine fix across the street at M&H.

Behind her, the door opened. "Isabelle. Wait," Tom yelled, but she just kept walking.

"Isabelle, stop."

The light turned red, forcing her to stop. "What do you want?"

"How's your mom this morning?"

Isabelle headed back toward the coffee shop.

"Where are you going?"

"Let's have a cup of coffee and a chat with your wife. She is your wife, isn't she?"

"I'm trying to help you and your mother."

"You're so full of shit. Does your pretty wife know you like to fuck young girls and drunk women?"

Did his eyes just change color?

"Your mom is right. You are insane," he said. Yanking her close to his chest, he whispered, "Listen, I'm only going to explain this once: Do not mess with The Family." He flashed her a deadly smile and released his grip.

"Find a knife and gut him like a fish!" someone whispered.

She laughed as she uncoiled a massive kick to his groin. "Explain that to your wife, you son of a bitch!"

He gasped and dropped to one knee.

A large shadow suddenly loomed over them and said, "Explain what?"

The air turned frigid, and everything fell quiet. The woman hovering over them stared, her dark eyes appraising Isabelle. She cocked her head, and a cold, lifeless smile spilled across her face. She was all too familiar. Her eyes, the way she cocked her head, and her expression reminded Isabelle of the crows that she'd seen on several occasions.

The woman chuckled. "Little witch, you should listen to my husband. You shouldn't mess with The Dark Family." The woman reached for Isabelle.

Without thinking, Isabelle grabbed the woman's arm. An icy chill spread throughout her body and instantly drove her to her knees. Black bile spewed from her mouth and covered the sidewalk with little white worms. She wasn't a raven like she thought. "You don't care what your husband does as long as he finds and delivers you prey." Isabelle rises to her feet. "Your kind sustains itself by devouring innocent souls."

Someone touched Isabelle's shoulder, and she yelped in surprise.

"My lady, I'm sorry for startling you. Has that wretched man hurt you?"

Isabelle stared at the man's hideous scar that stretched from ear to mouth. She had seen him before. He was the naked man John had punched and tossed into the street. She was dumbstruck.

The man whispered, "Come with me. The Queen needs you." He held onto Isabelle's arm and pointed a finger at Tom. "After the last disaster, we told the two of you to stay away."

Tom brushed himself off but kept an eye on the large dark-colored vehicle parked at the end of the block.

Isabelle pulled from the man's grasp. "Who are you?"

"It's important that you come with me."

"I'm not getting anywhere near that car or anyone else's car," Isabelle said and took off running.

As she ran, Isabelle thought about how Tom frightened the scar-faced man, but the woman scared them both. The unsettled thoughts of who she might be made her chest tighten. After a couple of blocks and no signs of anyone following, she circled back to the building that housed the library. In the foyer, she pushed her way into the bathroom and splashed water on her face. She stood in front of the mirror and wondered what the hell was going on. Every day seemed to get stranger. She needed answers to put her life back together. The only two people she trusted were dead, and those deaths might be her fault.

She waited until she could breathe easy, left the bathroom, and entered the only place that felt safe: the library.

The stillness of the room enveloped her. The serenity calmed her nerves. She found a table with a view of the doors and emptied her pockets. A wad of papers rolled to the edge of the desk. She separated the pages and smoothed them flat. These were the questions that plagued her sleep. On them, she had written: Mental illness, Pine Bluff, The demon in Miss Dahl's apartment, An old lady who claimed to be her grandmother, and finally, Tom. She added two more items to the list: first, Tom's wife—what type of creature could turn into a bird, and second, witchcraft? If she could cross a couple off the list, she would be happy.

Isabelle searched the card catalog for the books she needed. After writing down their location, she pulled them from the shelves and lugged them to the table.

Doubt clouded her thinking. Tom was a sleaze and wanted to have sex with her, but he had gotten her out of jail. She rode an emotional roller coaster. When she wrote or danced, she floated in the clouds. Lately, a devouring gulf of despair filled her with hopelessness. Were these feelings caused by the death of Carson and her teacher, or by her mother's drinking? What was going on inside her head scared the hell out of her.

The other topic high on her list was Pine Bluff. Her mother's irrational fear of a simple question made Isabelle wonder what scared her. She thought she knew her mother well, but there was always something more, a secret she hid.

Isabelle paged through her pile of books and pulled up a checklist: How To Tell If Someone Is Mentally Ill

An exciting place to start.

- Silent, Listless Behavior- This didn't apply to her. She hadn't lost interest in life. She just didn't care sometimes.

- Poor Work Performance- Other than the test she didn't remember taking, her grades at school were okay. She could do better.

- Paranoia- She left that one blank. Yes, she feared Sheriff Erikson's persecution of her for both Carson and Heather's deaths, but was his suspicion justified? He did find her at both crime scenes. One word stuck out, and it scared her: Schizophrenia. She would have to read up on that illness.

- Hallucinations- She put a big check mark for yes. She heard voices and saw things that could not be real.

- Anxiety Over Imagined Problems- This was another toss-up. Many things made Isabelle anxious and nervous. At times, fear was a problem. Did these feelings interfere with her daily life? Maybe.

- Physical Ailments- Besides the voices, her headaches were a significant concern. They came and went at will. She would have to check this one off too.

- Sudden Changes in Mood- Her mood changed often. But were they abrupt changes, extreme shifts in her attitude? She wasn't sure how to answer. It was a good possibility.

She had more than a single symptom. Was it a continuing pattern of unusual extreme behavior? At times, yes. Did she have a mental illness, a medical condition, or a brain tumor?

She finished writing her notes. The library was filled with noisy children who gathered for Storytime. A young man sat down in front of the kids on the floor, his boyish face beaming as he opened the first book. He was cute, with brown curly hair. How enjoyable would it be to twist curly hair like that around one of her fingers?

What the hell? Where did that thought come from? Did she know him? He looked familiar.

Time to get back to work. She flipped through the indexes of several books, searching for any references to "Pine Bluff, MN." A couple of entries but nothing of interest. While she contemplated which book she should pursue next, groans erupted from the group of children. She glanced up at the young man with the curly brown hair who was headed her way. She went back to her research, hoping that he'd pass by.

"Is your name Isabelle?"

"Little witch," someone whispered.

Isabelle ignored the voice and looked at the young man with the curly hair. "Yes."

"I was a friend of Heather's," he said, then shooed away two little girls who had followed him. "Miss Dahl's, that is. Can we talk?"

Isabelle glanced down at her book, which was turned to a section labeled: Boundary Waters Residential Treatment Center, Pine Bluff, Minnesota. She would review that later. Right now she had to get away; she didn't know why exactly, only that she must. She grabbed her notes and turned to leave.

"Where are you going?" he asked.

"I can't talk to you about Miss Dahl."

She pushed her way through the throng of children and escaped into the fresh air.

# Chapter 40

Sheriff Erickson slapped the table and the sound ricocheted in the room like a gunshot. He pushed his chair back with a screech, stomped to the door, hesitated, and pivoted. "Are you going to answer my question?" he asked her.

"Avery's hockey practice ran late. She wanted extra ice time because she was going to miss today's practice."

The sheriff turned a chair around and sat facing her. "Was Heather depressed?"

"No."

"Was she dating anyone?"

"I'm not sure."

"Here's one thing I'm sure of." He slid a folder across the table. "Heather called you like

clockwork every Friday night. What did the two of you talk about?"

Bernice smiled. "Life."

He stood and pulled a small notebook out of his front pocket. "We found traces of mud in your granddaughter's apartment."

Bernice glared at him.

The door opened, but he put an arm out to block Avery's entrance. "Could you give us a couple more minutes?"

Once Avery left, he returned his attention to Bernice. "How was Heather and Avery's relationship?"

"Like any sisters. What are you implying?"

"Just trying to get some answers."

"I want answers too. Who killed my granddaughter?"

"I'll know more once the autopsy is completed."

"Don't you need the family's consent?"

"Not when the medical examiner deems it necessary."

"Do you believe she was murdered?"

"I didn't say that."

"What are you saying then?"

A knock on the door interrupted the conversation. The woman from the front desk stuck her head in. "Sheriff, you have a call. Important."

"Okay."

A few minutes later, he returned and sat back down in front of Bernice. He opened his notebook and tapped a page with his finger. "The hotel informed us that they found muddy towels in the bathtub and mud smeared on the walls in your room. What happened?"

Bernice shrugged.

The door opened, and Avery peeked in.

"Have a seat."

Avery slumped down into the chair. Sheriff Erikson pushed a picture across the table. "Do either of you know this girl, Isabelle Gunderson?"

"No," Bernice said. "Why are you doing this? We have done nothing wrong."

He studied Avery for a moment then stood. "I think that's all. When the autopsy is finished, the body can be picked up in St. Paul."

"I'll have the funeral home pick her up." Bernice remembered something else she wanted to ask but changed her mind. Since Heather's apartment was a crime scene, she didn't think they would be allowed in.

It was close to noon by the time Bernice and Avery left the police station. The silence between them intensified, causing Bernice concern.

Avery's anger and fear had grown to unhealthy limits. Bernice scoured her brain, trying to find the right words to soothe Avery's anxiety, but found none. "Avery, you need to talk to me, please."

Avery stayed mute, her brow scrunched, her lips pursed. Bernice noticed there was no sign of hopes and dreams, only darkness and pain. Everyone had a dark unknown self filled with hidden feelings and evil desires. She could not let Avery dwell too long in that darkness, or it would destroy her soul. She had to find a way to put the light back in.

A few more miles down the road, Avery turned to her. "Alright, how could my dead father kill Heather?"

"Dark magic."

"Dark magic?"

"Yes, dark magic draws its power from the hate and anger inside the user. The more negative emotions the user stores, the stronger and more powerful the magic becomes."

"I understand someone used dark magic, but how did they do it?"

"Whoever reanimated your father's body, controlled him with a powerful spell. A demon could have been summoned, but that would have been dangerous."

"Why?"

"The necromancer would have to be close by."

"What would one look like?"

"The necromancer or the demon?"

"The Necromancer."

"The most powerful practitioners are often members of the Christian clergy."

Avery's eyes gleamed. "Like that priest?"

"What did you say?"

"There was a priest across the street from Heather's apartment."

Bernice stared at her in disbelief. "Can you describe him?"

"Very old and pale, almost gray. He appeared sick."

Terror slid through Bernice's veins. How could he be in Moorhead? He was on his deathbed, dying of cancer.

"Grandma, what's wrong?"

Bernice couldn't hold still her trembling hands.

"Oh my God, Grandma...You know who's responsible for Heather's death, don't you?"

She did. The name stuck in her throat. How could she have been so stupid?

"It's the Catholic priest, isn't it? Father Abram?"

"Maybe."

"How can I ever trust you again?" Avery wiped a tear from her cheek and grunted her pent-up frustration. "What other secrets are you hiding?"

# Chapter 41

Isabelle rode the city bus for hours, going no place in particular, thinking about the events of the last couple of weeks. Could she be suffering from mental illness? Was there a simple explanation for the voices, the hallucinations, and the blackouts? They would have to move again. Where this time?

She arrived home late in the afternoon, and her mother's car was parked in the driveway. Inside the house, everything was quiet. She had no desire to talk to her and went straight to her room.

The night seemed endless. Unable to sleep more than minutes at a time, Isabelle climbed out of bed and tiptoed to the living room. Her mother's car hadn't moved. The street lamp flickered, and so did the images in her mind.

She wandered into the kitchen looking for food. All she could find in the fridge was a couple of slices of leftover cardboard pizza and a spoonful or two of cottage cheese. She filled a glass with water and took her food back to her room.

A plastic bag with her personal effects, which she hadn't noticed earlier, sat on her desk. Did her mother bring it home? A cursory look and everything seemed to be there. She shook the last of the contents onto the surface of her desk. Something metallic clanged and bounced to the floor.

Down on her hands and knees, she ran her hands through the carpet. A simple black band of metal hid under the corner of the bed. She bounced the ring on her palm. The ring, more substantial than it looked, left smudges on her hand. Using a sock from her floor, she rubbed it clean and was left with an ancient gold ring that wasn't hers. She took a bite of cold pizza. Wasn't there something she had written about a ring? Didn't the crone say it belonged to a friend of theirs? Her fire-damaged notebook sat open on her desk. She read the part she had written before ending up in jail but couldn't remember writing some of it.

She read the passage aloud. "She grunted and pulled until the ring slipped off her finger. She then walked to where Princess Belle sat and whispered in her ear."

This couldn't be that ring, could it? Because if this was the ring she had written about …

"No," she said, shaking her head. "Impossible."

The police must have mixed up someone else's belongings with hers. Isabelle's eyes twitched, and the pain behind her eyes throbbed. The first signs of a headache brewed.

The rest of her supper was forgotten. With the onset of a headache, nausea soon followed. She dumped her uneaten dinner into the garbage, swallowed a few aspirins, and crawled back into bed.

Why couldn't she remember what the crone whispered?

That question echoed inside her head as sleep carried her away.

Unlike the previous night, she dreamed – but the dreams weren't her own. Death, blood, and burning bodies illuminating the night filled her with horror. Drenched in sweat, blankets wrapped around her legs, she woke with a scream. Gasping for air, she sat up. Two sets of beady eyes peered at her from her bedroom window.

Caw, caw.

Two large birds flew away into the night.

Isabelle waited for her heartbeat to slow. She untangled herself from her covers and pulled at her t-shirt that had bunched up high on her chest.

"Very nice," a male voice said from her doorway.

The knife she kept under her pillow was already in her hand when she faced him.

"Here is your chance. Castrate the bastard," someone said.

Tom held up his hands. "Whoa. Hold on a minute."

Isabelle jumped to her feet. "Haven't I warned you enough?"

He backed into the hallway "I just dropped off your mother. She's in her room."

"Drunk?" Isabelle stepped toward him.

"Yes. Your mother has problems."

"No shit, and you're one of them."

Tom feinted to his right and reached for her arm, but she danced away. With a flick of her wrist, she cut two buttons from his shirt. "Next time, who knows what I might cut off."

He flashed a wicked grin and kicked her feet from underneath her. She fell hard but was back up before he could take advantage.

"The sheriff thinks I'm a murderer. What's another one?"

"Isn't this fun?" Tom snickered, rolling up his sleeves. "Drop the knife before you hurt yourself."

The pressure built in her head. Pins and needles jabbed into her eye sockets. The darkness waited for a chance, a chink in her armor to exploit. It wanted in.

She pushed those thoughts away and lunged. A split second later, she was on her back, her own knife pressed against her throat.

"If you are not ready to kill someone, Princess Belle shouldn't play with knives." Tom stuck the knife in the wall above her, kissed her hard on the lips, and left.

Isabelle closed her eyes and let the darkness envelop her. What did it matter anymore?  Her best friend was dead. The only person who believed in her had been killed as well, and her mother had given up. Faces flashed like thunder and lightning, and voices boomed in her mind. The shadows advanced across the room. She wrapped herself in a shawl of self-pity--and waited. When the storm inside her ended, a day had passed and it was late Sunday afternoon. She spent the night finishing her homework.

Her mother was up and dressed for work when Isabelle walked into the kitchen. A glass of juice sat on the counter. Isabelle took a large swallow and coughed. The spiked orange juice burned the back of her throat. Perturbed that her mother started the day with vodka, she dumped the glass into the sink and glared at her mother

"Moving this time isn't because of my drinking," her mother stated. "We're moving because of you."

If Isabelle didn't walk away and bite her tongue, there would be hell to pay. No more. She did not want to fight with her mother, and she needed to catch the bus anyway. She slammed the door extra hard as she left.

***

The school hallways were buzzing with activity when Isabelle walked in, but most of the students stopped talking when she walked to her locker. Their whispers and taunts cut until her insides bled. Her mind overflowed with sadness. She locked eyes with Sarah and her friends, who were standing in front of their lockers. Sarah smiled and the look made Isabelle's skin crawl.

Isabelle found a Most Wanted poster taped to the door of her locker. Pictures of Carson and Miss Dahl stared back at her. The caption,

Killer of Women and Children, was boldly emblazoned across the front. Isabelle tore it off and threw it aside to get to the lock.

Tears blurred her vision. The combination escaped her. She tried, failed, and tried again. Her body trembling, she leaned her head against the door. After a few seconds, she straightened and walked over to Sarah, dropping her fingerless gloves to the floor. She cocked her arm and punched Sarah right in the face.

Sarah staggered backward, blood trickling from her nose. Isabelle pounced, grabbed the flesh of Sarah's biceps, and slammed her into the lockers, lifting her off her feet.

"Do you think this was funny?" Isabelle asked, their faces pressed together. She shoved the crumpled-up Wanted poster into Sarah's face. "Carson and Heather were my friends."

"You can't do this to me," Sarah sputtered. "Do you—"

"I know exactly who you are. Do you want all of your friends to know too?"

"Are you sure?" Sarah smiled, the flesh on her face wavering. A hideous creature with gaunt cheeks and dripping fangs lived beneath Sarah's skin, and it stared at Isabelle with coal-black eyes. Nightshade and arsenic wafted off Sarah's body; her breath reeked of the graveyard. Isabelle could taste the poison running through her veins. She was a hunter of children.

"Didn't I warn you," Sarah whispered. "Go ahead, tell everyone."

Isabelle let go.

Sarah landed on her feet. A black magic marker fell to the floor.

Oh...God. Trish and Carson. Sarah had drawn the doors.

Isabelle glanced around. Anger and fear rocked her body. Tears sprang to her eyes. The other students stood in silence, their eyes opened wide and their mouths agape.

The bell rang. Most of the students shuffled off to their respective homerooms, but Sarah's friends encircled their leader, arms raised. Their agitated voices rang clear. Sarah smiled with an air of triumph and strutted into her classroom.

"Beware the eyes that shimmer like emeralds."

Isabelle stood rooted. "Freya?"

All the doors slammed shut except for one. A teacher, the Queen's handmaiden, stood in the doorway at the end of the hall.

"They will draw you in and cloud their true purpose."

Not wanting to face her classmates, Isabelle's flight instinct was at full alert. She weighed her options and thought it best to leave. Someplace other than home, but she could not stay here. Before she could take a step, one of Sarah's memories buckled her knees.

"Your Grandmother killed my father and my brothers," Sarah whispered.

A man with the dark eyes pressed his lips to Sarah's, his tongue sought entrance, and she opened her mouth to receive. A black mist slid in. The demon 'Rage' had found a new home.

Someone grasped Isabelle's shoulder. A firm voice said, "Don't do it." The voice belonged to the young man who read to the kids at the library, the man who had wanted to talk to her about Miss Dahl.

"I can see that you want to run. What Sarah and her friends did was pretty shitty. Stand up to them. I'll have your back if there's any trouble."

"Why are you nice to me?"

"Because I want to know what happened to Carson and Heather just as badly as you do." He smiled, holding out his hand. "My name's Adam, but at school, you should call me Mr. Harris."

He walked Isabelle to her homeroom, spoke briefly to her teacher, patted her on the shoulder, and left.

The day seemed to drag. History class was strange without Miss Dahl. A few students talked to Isabelle, but like most days, they left her alone.

On Mondays, she usually caught a ride with Heather and danced at 4:30 pm. With her teacher dead, she did not know what was going to happen to the studio. She called once to see if the studio was open, but no one answered. Her only choice to find out was to walk to the studio.

Staring at the snow-covered sidewalk, she stuffed her hands into her coat pockets and trudged forward. She had just turned north onto Thirty-Fourth Street when a car pulled alongside.

The passenger window slid down and Adam called to her from inside. "Isabelle? Do you need a ride someplace?"

"I was going to see if the dance school was open."

"Get in."

Isabelle slid in and buckled her seatbelt. "Thanks."

"I didn't see you at Carson's funeral. I thought the two of you were close friends."

"Opal, Carson's mother, didn't want me there. She said they would call the police and have me escorted out of the church if I showed up."

"That's rough."

"Yeah..." A lump caught in her throat. She missed Carson. He was like a little brother, and she failed him. "Well...I..." She shrugged and stared out the window.

"I know it hurts." Adam headed over the railroad tracks. At the stoplight, he said, "Carson was a brilliant boy."

"He was." Isabelle paused, her chest heavy and tears beaded at the corner of her eyes. "Wasn't he working on a project with you?"

"Yes. Carson and a group of talented students worked together on a project for me." Adam pulled into the parking lot. "I know you and Carson talked a lot. What did he tell you about the project?"

"Nothing really. Thanks for the ride."

"Just to be on the safe side, I'll wait."

Isabelle smiled and walked to the front door. It was locked, and the lights were off. A note was taped to the door. She walked back to the car. "Classes are canceled this week."

"Why don't I give you a ride home?"

She accepted his offer, but the entire ride home she couldn't shake the feeling she'd get blamed for the studio closure. The girls blamed her for everything else. All those girls probably had money and parental support for their dancing. They could all afford to go somewhere else. No, it was only her dream that had ended. Her mother would never spend money on classes.

In her driveway, Adam turned to her and placed his hand on hers. "If you need someone to talk to...."

"Thanks for being so nice," she said, stepping out of the car.

The rest of the week was the same. School, no dance, homework, and an empty home. She didn't see much of her mother, but every morning a Post-It note would be stuck on the fridge, identifying another city where Sharon had applied for a job. They were moving, and her mother made it clear—it was all Isabelle's fault.

# Chapter 42

For Isabelle, the following week was much the same—school and home. Thursday morning, the Post-It note her mother left on the fridge said she had found a job on the West Coast, they would be moving next week, and be prepared to pack all weekend. Isabelle hoped her ambivalent feelings wouldn't get in the way of packing.

The day went surprisingly fast. After school, she stopped at the gas station across the street from the high school and grabbed a can of pop for the walk home. Adam, standing at the pumps while he filled his tank, smiled and waved her over.

"Do you need a ride home?" he asked. "I found some of Carson's stuff in the lab and thought I would drop it off at his mom's."

"I'm not sure if Opal is home. I haven't seen her for at least a week."

"Doesn't matter. Can I still give you a ride home?"

Isabelle nodded.

The family car sat in her driveway. If Sharon looked out the window and saw that a man drove Isabelle home, her mother would think the worst. Her daughter must be having sex.

Isabelle opened the front door. "Mom?" To her relief, nobody was home.

Adam walked across the street to Opal's house, a small box clutched in his arms. He entered the building and a short time later returned with the same box in his arms. He shrugged at Isabelle still standing in her doorway and waved goodbye.

Empty boxes cluttered the living room. There was no use in delaying the inevitable, she pulled a sweater off a hanger and tossed it onto the growing pile on her bed. Each one held a memory, a reminder of the fights and the harsh words her mother spoke. Sharon bought her love with gifts.

Isabelle found her six boxes of composition books hidden behind her sweaters and stacked at the back of the closet. She crawled over to them and caressed the cardboard. Because of all their moving, the boxes hadn't collected dust this time.

She lifted the cover off the first box and pulled out one of the books. With her back pressed against the wall—the outline of the door she had drawn still visible—she ran her fingers over the words and pictures.

Ah, to be a little girl again, innocent and clueless to the cruelties of life, when her mother was the queen, her father the king, and she was their princess.

"You're needed here. Come quick," Freyja said. "The queen is in trouble."

Pain stabbed deep into Isabelle's chest. She winced and blinked away the tears. A face appeared in her mind: the teacher from the hallway, a person she recognized. She yanked more books from the box. Colors exploded inside her skull. Nausea gurgled. She contracted into a ball and cradled her head until the spasms of pain receded. With gritted teeth, she said, "No headache, no darkness. Not this time." She would not give in without a fight.

She willed herself up to her knees. Sweat beaded on her forehead and dripped into her eyes. She placed the chosen book on the desk. A chorus of muffled voices filled her room. Somebody had to be in the house, playing games with her mind.

Using the back of the chair for leverage, she pulled herself to her feet and stumbled down the hall to the quiet living room. A knock at the window caused her blood to run cold. Her mirror image stared back from the outside. The image whispered, "Mother."

Isabelle was poised to chase the girl down and confront her. She needed answers, but her legs wouldn't move. Her common sense had no desire to mess with the creature outside. The green-eyed girl smirked and disappeared. Isabelle's heart thrummed for several minutes.

The crowd of voices became boisterous again as she approached her room. The sounds emanated from the composition book on her desk. The roar washed over her.

Isabelle sat on the edge of her chair. Her fingers toyed with the page, pictures drawn in crayon so long ago. She hid between these pages when the fighting between her parents had been at its worst. She found the face of the Queen's handmaiden Freyja that she illustrated when she was seven or eight, the woman who spoke to her in the hallway at school and whispered to her earlier. One problem solved, but how could Freyja have leaped from the pages of her composition books to her reality?

Turning back to the page with the picture of her mother, Isabelle traced the drawing with her fingertip and flinched. As she rubbed away the pain, a wave of grayness, a dark premonition, passed over her. She flipped through the rest of the pictures. There were others here; people from her current life, not just Freyja. The man with the scar and their landlord Bob were both captured within the pages of the notebook. Was Adam one of the King's black cloaks? She was sure there were more. Her everyday life seemed to be interwoven with her imagination. Had she overstepped the boundaries of reality?

The phone rang. Isabelle made her way down the hall and answered. Silence filled the other end.

"Who's there?" she asked. "This isn't funny."

After several seconds, a muted voice, maybe her mother's, uttered a sound.

"Mom?"

"Hello...Issy..." Sharon slurred her words. "Dear... can you...come... pi-ck me... u-u-pp... please?"

"Where are you?"

"I... I... d-d-do-n't kn-n-now."

A clank and a thud came from the other end.

"Mom, are you still there? Is everything alright?"

Only the ceaseless hum of a dead phone filled her ear. A few seconds later, there was a click. She slammed the phone down in frustration. Her mother was beyond drunk this time, and the tone of her voice scared her. She grabbed her jacket, the car keys, and ran outside.

Even though Isabelle was nervous about driving, the growing ball of fear outweighed her jitters. She needed to find her mother.

Isabelle climbed into the car and, after two tries, backed out of the driveway without hitting anything. A headache tugged at the edges of her brain. She needed to stay calm. Where should she look first?

She drove down Broadway and hit most of the side streets. She checked all the bars, even the sleazy ones. People stared, but she ignored them. At Rick's Bar, one bouncer gave her trouble. When she asked about her mother, his smirk sickened her. He wanted to know his reward, wink, wink. Her self-control vanished.

"Get bent."

He laughed. "A spitfire. Just like your mother."

"Fuck off. I'm nothing like my mother."

Unsuccessful and not sure where else to search, she headed home. It was well past midnight when she walked through the door. The flashing light from the answering machine caught her attention. She pressed the Play button.

"Help," her mother whispered.

Isabelle sprinted back to the car. The cruel voices started again. "You know she's dead, don't you? Picked a psycho, raped, and murdered. You'd be better off without her."

Isabelle couldn't get the sounds out of her head. Her mind enveloped in a thick fog, everything moved in slow motion.

"Enough!" Shaking her head to clear the cobwebs, she concentrated on her driving.

Why does my mom have to be so stupid? Does she even remember she has a daughter to take care of?

Once downtown, she no longer needed the car. She pulled into the nearest empty parking space and Sarah suddenly appeared in her mind's eye. "You know she's dead, don't you?"

Pinpricks of light danced before her eyes. If the pain did not subside soon, her head would cleave in two. Outside, shadows stalked the car. The street lights flickered and went out.

The crone whispered, "Beware the King, he knows."

Isabelle opened the car door, and her body faded into nothingness.

***

Belle stormed into her mother's bedroom. One of the Queen's girls jumped out of the way.

"Where's the Queen?" Princess Belle demanded.

The young girl stared long and hard at her feet before she answered. "One of the King's men took her away."

"Which one?"

"One of the black cloaks," the young girl said, cowering. "Please don't hurt me. I know nothing."

The princess rushed out the door and peered down on the courtyard below. No sign of her mother, she pushed her way down the back stairway. Where would the Black Cloak take her?

A cold draft brushed the back of her calves. One of the tapestries on the wall wiggled. She pushed the fabric aside and found a door ajar. She unsheathed her short sword and eased the door open. A set of stairs led down, deeper into the castle. She stepped to the edge and peered into the darkness. The steps were steep, damp, and crumbling. The thump of boots many floors below echoed against the stone walls.

Belle toed each step, checking for solid footing, moving as fast as she dared until she reached the bottom. Her breath came in huge gulps. She pushed open the door and found a dark, narrow stretch of wall. She picked up her pace and followed the footsteps down the alley.

A murky shadow flowed from the depths of the alley. Before she could bring up her sword, the dark figure struck. The side of the blade hit her temple. Her knees buckled. Her attacker stepped out of the shadows as she slumped to the ground. The last thing Belle remembered were the tiny brown curls, the kind you twisted around your finger, under the dark hood of her attacker.

# Chapter 43

I sabelle opened her eyes. The darkness pressed in all around her. Beside her, the outline of a door appeared, the edges bright against the black sky. The giggles of demented children sent shivers through her.

"You're too late. You're too late. Your mother is already dead," the children chanted.

The slap of running feet on pavement caught her attention. The magic-marker-drawn door opened and for an instant, a bright light made her look away. When she glanced back, child-size shadows swept through, and the door closed.

The knot on the back of her head throbbed. She rolled over and stared at the knife in her hand, not comprehending the gravity of her situation. Blood dripped off the blade and onto the sleeve of her jacket. Something dark leaned against a dumpster.

Oh, God, what have I done?

She took a tentative step forward. Deep in the shadows of the alley, tires squealed. As a car sped past, she jumped out of the way. The vehicle's headlights brought into focus what she hadn't previously seen.

"No!"

Isabelle dropped the knife and rushed to her mother's side. Multiple stab wounds stained her front. As Isabelle pressed her hands against Sharon's chest, blood leaked between her fingers. A check for a pulse revealed a faint beat.

A door opened, and a man stuck his head out. "What's going on out here?"

"Please help me," Isabelle whispered.

"Stay right there. I'm calling the police."

The police? She couldn't be here when the police arrived, but she didn't want to leave either.

"God, please save my mom." She leaned in closer, tears streaming down her face, and squeezed her mother's hand. "Mom...Mom, hold on. Help is on the way, but I need to leave before the police get here."

She ran down the alley and determined she was blocks from the hospital. Her only choice was to get there and wait for her mother to arrive. Would anyone believe she hadn't stabbed her?

An ambulance and police car roared into the alley. Isabelle hurried toward the hospital, arriving at the emergency room before the ambulance. On her way down the long hallway to the waiting room, she thought about all the people who came there daily. Many of them never left alive. She hoped–no, needed–her mother not to be one of them. At times Sharon was a bad mother, but Isabelle wasn't ready to be on her own.

She collapsed into a chair, her bloody hand slipping on the armrest, and realized that everyone in the room was staring at her. She pushed herself upright and closed her eyes to the sorrow all around her.

Someone tapped her on the shoulder. "Miss, are you all right?"

The question seemed ridiculous to Isabelle. "Ah, no...no, I'm not."

"Are you hurt?" The nurse asked. "Do you need to see a doctor?"

Isabelle's exhaustion made every sentence a chore. "Not my blood. It's my mother's. Is the ambulance here yet?"

The people in her head laughed. "On her way to hell."

"I don't know. I'll check. What's your mother's name?"

"Sharon." Isabelle grabbed the nurse's hand. "Please take me to her."

Two Fargo policemen walked in and stopped at the intake desk. Isabelle, trying not to call attention to herself, quietly hung her bloody jacket on a coat rack, then sneaked into the bathroom while the policemen talked to the nurse in charge. She needed to get her mother's blood off her hands.

Entering the bathroom before anyone else, Isabelle frantically scrubbed at the congealed blood that stuck to her hands and hid under her nails. The soapy, bloodstained water gurgled as it flowed into the drain. A red residue ringed the sink. Satisfied that she'd removed most of the evidence, she leaned against the wall until she gained control of her emotions.

Back in the waiting room, she immediately noticed that one of the policemen held her bloody jacket as the other spoke into his radio. She'd been found. Shadowing a couple of nurses into the emergency department seemed her only option at this point.

Most of the rooms were full, but after some searching she found her mother. She stepped inside and closed the door.

A pale and fragile-looking Sharon lay on the gurney. Isabelle brushed her fingers along her mother's cold cheeks but got no reaction.

"Who are you? You shouldn't be in here."

Isabelle startled at the intrusion. She hadn't heard the doctor come in. "I'm her daughter," Isabella said, wiping her nose with her arm. "Please, help her."

"We're doing the best we can. Your mother's wounds are very serious."

A chorus of voices chimed in. "She's been a naughty girl! Both of you have been bad."

Isabelle grabbed the doctor's sleeve. "Don't let my mother die."

He gestured to a nurse outside the door. "She will take you somewhere comfortable to wait. Your mother is going to surgery soon."

The nurse brought Isabelle to one of the surgical family waiting rooms and pointed to a chair where Isabelle should sit. Isabelle closed her eyes, but they popped open seconds later.

Mom might not make it through surgery...and she has to make it.

The stress over the last few weeks eroded what little was left in her energy reserves. Depression pushed its way past her defenses. Her head slumped against the armrest, and she fell asleep.

"Everyone invents a story about themselves, always, all the time," someone said to her in a dream. "That story makes you who you are. We build ourselves from that story. Isabelle, what will your story be?"

Before she could answer, a nurse woke her. "Your mother is out of surgery. I'll take you to her room."

In a daze, she followed. A doctor spoke to her, but most of his words floated in and out of her mind. Only two of the things he said stuck: The next few hours would be critical. Prayers were needed.

She ignored the grim faces of the doctor and the nurse standing next to her mother's bed. The steady rhythm of the machines that kept her mother alive lulled her into a restless slumber.

Beep... Beep... Beep....

A nurse shook her. "Is your mother religious?"

Isabelle nodded.

"Catholic or Protestant?"

Isabelle tried to sit up. "Protestant."

"A Protestant whore," a man shouted.

Her eyes closed.

"Isabelle?"

Isabelle jumped to her feet. "Mom?"

Her mother grabbed her hand. "Can you hear them?"

"Hear who?"

"The babies. Can you make them stop crying?"

"Mom, should I go get your doctor?"

"Isabelle, beware."

"What are you saying?"

"Beware of Pine Bluff. Beware of your father." Her mother's grip relaxed, and her fingers slipped from Isabelle's hand.

"Mom!"

Her mother's body tensed, then a sigh escaped her lips. "Shh...it's alright. Mama's coming," she said and smiled.

The room filled with the scent of roses. The shrill alarm of the heart monitor pierced the silence of the space.

"Mom! No!"

A blue light flashed outside the room. A priest sat waiting in the corner. He rose and stepped towards the bed.

"No!"

Her fury stopped the pastor in his tracks. The door to the hallway slammed shut. She stabbed a finger at the priest. "Don't touch her. Don't get any closer. Just. Sit. Down."

Some invisible force pressed the priest back onto the chair. He grabbed his crucifix from inside of his robe, but it was jerked from his hands. Doctors and nurses pounded at the door.

"You did this. Your church is responsible for my mother's death. When she needed you the most, you weren't there. Everything the church teaches is bullshit." Isabelle gazed at her mother for the last time. Her worst fears had been realized. Her mother was dead, and she was alone.

She pushed her way out the door, scattering the hospital personnel. She ran when the children started laughing. The people in the hallway moved to the side as Isabelle sprinted down the corridor.

God damn it, where are the payphones?

Isabelle took the first stairway, flew down the steps, and at the end of the hallway, she finally found one. She dialed her father's number.

"Can I talk to my dad?" Isabelle asked his new wife when she answered.

"Just a minute."

The silence stretched on forever. "Hurry. Please, hurry."

"Isabelle?"

"Mom's dead." Isabelle started to cry again.

"Oh, Isabelle, I'm sorry."

"Dad, can you come and ...."

"He's not your father."

The truth hit her like a slap in the face. Isabelle dropped the phone, darted back up the stairs, and headed to the nearest exit. The voice was right. She had known it all along. He was not her father.

She skidded around a corner and came face-to-face with Tom.

"Isabelle, is your mom all right?"

For a second, Isabelle glowed with power. She roared and thrust Tom aside.

The Emergency Room exit sign loomed ahead, freedom only steps away. Bursting through the doors, she crashed into the waiting arms of Sheriff Erikson.

# Chapter 44

The gavel silenced the courtroom. Tom pulled Isabelle to her feet. She gazed at the handful of people attending the hearing while he explained to her the different outcomes of today's proceedings, but she wasn't listening. The authorities believed she had killed her mother, and they were going to lock her away until she wasn't crazy anymore.

The judge paged through the papers in front of him then cleared his throat. "Isabelle Gunderson, you will not be transferred to Adult Court today. You have been found incompetent to stand trial. The charges have been suspended until you are deemed competent. You're being transferred to the Boundary Waters Adolescent Treatment Center until you no longer pose a threat to yourself or to society. Do you understand?"

What did it matter? For the past several days, doctors had poked and prodded both her mind and body. She nodded and answered only the questions she wanted to answer. While in her room, she either slept or stared at the beige walls. The drugs they gave her kept the voices away–and most coherent thoughts too. She was lost in a haze of nothingness, every day the same. The Sheriff and Tom visited, but all they did was ask questions about why and how. She had no answers for either of them.

Tom leaned close and whispered, "Isabelle, answer the judge."

"Sure," she said. Tom squeezed her arm. She corrected herself. "Yes, your Honor."

The judge banged the gavel. "Court is adjourned."

A short time later, Isabelle was staring at the walls of her jail cell. Tomorrow, she would be headed to the one place that scared her mother, the one place Sharon warned her about, but exactly where Tom wanted her to go.

Isabelle picked another piece of the flaking pale green paint off the wall and added it to the growing pile. The meds that were supposed to make her sleepy failed. Soon, the faces would appear, like the night before, and the night before that—silent screams of terror etched forever in the foundation and walls of this place. Like her, terror was trapped inside with no way of escaping, no way of finding their way home.

The next morning Sheriff Erickson and Tom arrived before the sun had crested the horizon. They pushed her into the backseat of the police cruiser and closed the doors. The lights of Moorhead disappeared behind them. What would happen next? No answer came. The road hummed in her ears, and the drugs rocked her to sleep.

"Isabelle?"

Isabelle woke. The sign read: Pine Bluff fifteen miles. She looked at the sheriff and Tom in the front seat. Neither could have spoken to her. They were locked in a heated conversation about college hockey. Then who had spoken?

"Isabelle?"

Isabelle winced. Something moved inside her head. It didn't hurt, but it felt wrong. An intrusion, like a million ants crawling in the nooks and crevasses of her brain.

"Are you in my head?" She waited for an answer. "If you are, get out."

She recognized the voice. It was the same person, the one who'd claimed to be her grandmother outside of Miss Dahl's apartment. She spoke again. "I'm sorry about your mother."

"I said get out."

"I know you think something is wrong with your mind, but you aren't insane. You're my granddaughter. Our family comes from a long line of witches. Someday you're going to be a powerful witch."

She slammed the door in her mind and refocused in an attempt to block out the voice.

Tom leaned over the seat. "Is everything alright back there?"

Isabelle ignored him.

Outside, the trees no longer dotted the landscape; instead, they filled it. The car slowed and turned onto a gravel road. The tires spun and spit rocks rearward. Between the snow-covered branches of birch and pine, bits and pieces of a frozen pond became visible. The sheriff took a sharp curve in the road too fast and for a split second, the car lost traction and slid towards the edge of an embankment. Below them, the pond waited.

The space behind Isabelle's eyes tingled. One of Heather's memories broke free—it showed a car flying off the road and plunging into the water. A shiver rocked her to her core. If they got too close, the black ice would open and swallow them whole. It had done so before. Somehow she knew that this was the corner where Heather's parents died.

Isabelle braced for impact. At the last moment, the car righted itself, and the sheriff steered back onto the road.

"Oh shit," he said. "That was close. Where in the hell was the sign?"

Isabelle didn't comment. Her gaze was glued to the pond. Shadows weaved between trees and bushes, keeping pace with the car. It was more than her imagination could take. She told herself it wasn't real. The girl with the emerald eyes was out there. They reached the top of the bluff, her new home silhouetted against a backdrop of blue sky.

The police car pulled in front of the Boundary Waters Adolescent Treatment Center. Isabelle gazed at the structure she didn't want to enter. Like a giant creature, wings sprouted from a large stone central building. Above two massive wooden doors, two windows blazed with light. From within, dangerous strangers watched. This place ate children and spit out monsters.

Two goons, dressed in white, emerged from the building and strode down the sidewalk. Isabelle pressed herself against the door. The largest goon peered into the backseat and smiled. "Isabelle, welcome to The Center."

She squirmed away from his outstretched hand.

His smile disappeared. "We can do this the easy way, or we can do this the hard way. Your choice."

The door behind Isabelle opened, and the other goon grabbed her arm. She thrust her body forward and kicked her legs. "No, I don't want to go."

Her defiance was short-lived. They had her in their meaty hands within seconds, gripping her shoulders and forcing her down the walk. There was no chance of escape.

"Tom, please," she begged. "Take me away from this place."

He chuckled. "Where you're going, God's eyes don't watch."

# Chapter 45

Isabelle grabbed the little white cup from the nurse's hand. She dumped the pills into her mouth, took a swallow of water, and managed to get them down on the first try. It has not always been easy, but practice makes perfect. The tablets kept the voices in her head at bay, but they couldn't quiet those who roamed the halls at night.

She did not like The Center. The old building scared her, especially after lights out. It creaked, moaned, and sighed, like a living being. Pain and suffering oozed from its foundations. The teenagers who lived behind its walls were crazy and violent. The Center housed the worst of the worst. No wonder most of the staff looked like weightlifters and probably ate steroids like candy.

Darkness closed over this part of northern Minnesota like an ebony lid. The full moon slid from behind the clouds, its beams bouncing off the freshly fallen snow and filled her room with an iridescent glow. Trees hugged the shore of the nearby pond. Pillows of snow dotted the landscape. The pond radiated serenity.

The top of her head began tingling, a sign that the pills were starting to work. She'd found it was best not to resist. She crawled under the covers and waited to be dragged into slumberland. Closing her eyes, she listened to the voices in the hall. They were more like the sighs of the wind rather than spoken words.

Some nights she stood at her door and watched. Outlines of figures, splashes of color, and faces hidden by hands, wandered in and out of the shadows. Lost souls with blank stares walked the halls at night. She kept this to herself. The nurses and doctors didn't need any more ammunition to prove she was insane.

A key jiggled in the lock. Isabelle sat up. She wasn't expecting visitors tonight, and the nurses usually left her alone until morning. The door swung open, and a gust of air opened it further. Her room filled with the fragrance of a memory. A picture of her mother, the Queen, filled her mind with a longing that brought tears to her eyes. This was how her mother had smelled–like roses–before the drinking, before the smoking, and before the running away took over their lives.

"Mom?" Isabelle whispered.

A swirl of air pushed papers off the desk. Dust motes sprang to life and twinkled in the moonlight. The end of her bed sank, the springs creaked. She crawled out from underneath the covers and sat on her haunches, ready to run. A faded image of her mother came into focus.

"Mom," Isabelle said, reaching out a hand. "Is that you?"

"Belle. My princess."

She threw herself into her mother's arms. "I miss you."

Her mother pulled her close, her hair caressing Isabelle's cheek. Neither time nor death could disguise the feel or scent of her mother. How could have she been so stupid and acted so irresponsibly? Her mother was trying to protect her all this time. She still needed her mom, and always would.

Tears streamed down Isabelle's face. "Oh, Mom, I love you."

Her mother's delicate fingers brushed the hair out of Isabelle's eyes. "Shhh..., go back to sleep. You'll need your rest. He's coming for you."

"Who's coming for me?"

Her mother rose from the bed. She stopped at the door, clasping the handle, and smiled one last time.

"Am I crazy? Is anything real?"

"Belle, everything is real. We sent you to this realm to hide you from the Guardians, but they found you too soon."

"Mom, please don't leave."

"I have to. Your sister needs me."

"Sister?"

Her mother left through the opened door and closed it behind her. Isabelle wanted to run after and embrace her. "Mom, I'm sorry. I forgive you." She rattled the door to no avail. "Please come back." Chasing after her mother wasn't an option.

Isabelle crawled back into bed and fought the pills for as long as she could. Her eyelids grew heavy, her vision flickered, and sleep pulled her under. The memory was ripped away.

Minutes later, she bolted upright. He was getting closer, a beast of dark appetites, a stealer of souls.

She was neither asleep nor awake, a part of her still lost in a dream, but a scream crawled up the back of her throat. She pulled at her hair. "Help me, please. Someone, help me."

Isabelle scrambled out of bed and jumped onto her desk. Her heart pounded wildly against her ribcage. Somewhere in the shadows, her true father, the King of the Dark Ones, waited.

"Mom, be careful."

All around the pond, children rose like specters and joined her mother and sister, the Queens, on the snow-covered ice. Her sister, the girl with the emerald eyes, grabbed their mother's hand and smiled at Belle. They burst up into the air, sprouted wings, and two large black ravens disappeared into the falling snow.

Isabelle struck the window frame with her fists. "Mom...Mom...." She fell to her knees, gripping the bars. "I hear them. I hear the babies." She shook the bars harder. "Oh, God, make them stop. Make them stop crying."

# Letter to our Readers

Dear Readers,

Thanks for purchasing this book. We hope you enjoyed, *Sins of the Mother* by Chris Stenson. You can learn more about Chris on his website. https://www.chrisstensonauthor.com/

Please leave a review wherever you purchased this title. It will help other readers find us.

You can find our other Anthologies; *Tales from the Frozen North, Welcome to Effham Falls – Tales from a Small Town, Tales from the Water's Edge, Return to Effham Falls – Tales of Lost Souls, & Where Monsters Hide – Tales of the Uncanny* on our website. https://www.moorheadfriendswritinggroup.com